WHEN HEATED ANGER BECOMES HEATED DESIRE

"You're a fiery little Rebel, Jess . . ."

"Miss Windsor to you, Captain Steele!"

" . . . but you seem to be under a great deal of strain today. Has someone been bothering you?"

"Yes—*you!*"

"Such a quick tongue you have! But what is causing you to act so nervous?" Alex saw the brief flicker in her eyes. What was the little minx up to now? Reaching out, he jerked her to him. "What have you done, you little fool?"

"Let . . . me . . . go!" she managed to say. Wrenching away, she stared up at him with blazing eyes. "You damned Yankee! Don't you ever put your hands on me again! There's not enough water in the world to wash your touch away—"

Suddenly, Alex jerked her close again. "If you've got to wash anyway, Jess, let me give you something else to wash away."

Before she could avoid it, his mouth came down on hers. His lips were warm and hard, pressing against her mouth in a hot, consuming kiss; and Jessamy felt the slow kindling of a fire deep within her. . . .

ONCE A REBEL

MICKI BROWN

ST. MARTIN'S PAPERBACKS

ONCE A REBEL

Copyright © 1992 by Micki Brown.

Cover illustration by Kevin Johnson.

All rights reserved. No part of this book may be used or reproduced in any manner whatsoever without written permission except in the case of brief quotations embodied in critical articles or reviews. For information address St. Martin's Press, 175 Fifth Avenue, New York, N.Y. 10010.

ISBN: 0-312-92102-0

Printed in the United States of America

St. Martin's Paperbacks edition/January 1992

10 9 8 7 6 5 4 3 2 1

IN LOVING MEMORY OF BRENDA FRANCES TRAYLOR, my friend since the fourth grade. I shall always miss your sweet Southern charm and grace, Brenda. You may be gone, but will never be forgotten . . .

ONCE A REBEL

Chapter 1

April, 1856

ALEXANDER STEELE STRETCHED LAZILY, shifting position on the hard, uncomfortable seat of the carriage. After the long trip aboard the train from Lexington, Kentucky, to Bolivar, Tennessee, he now had to endure a long ride to their final destination, a destination he was not eager to reach. He slid his mother a quizzical glance, and she gave him back a smile.

"You know that these visits are required, Alex." Her tone held a hint of reproof, and he shrugged shoulders already broad for a young man of eighteen.

"Family duty calls are not my preference, Mother."

"They're not always mine, either. But William Windsor is your stepfather's brother, and I must admit I've always rather enjoyed the Windsors' generous hospitality."

"*You* don't have to endure their passel of brats like I do," Alex replied with a grim twist of his mouth. "The Windsor boys are little more than irresponsible hellions, and the daughter—I do believe she instigates more mischief than they can, if that's to be believed."

Charity Steele Windsor hid a smile behind her gloved hand, and coughed softly. "Alex, that will do. Jessamy is a well-bred young lady, if a bit—well, *energetic*—and I know that she will mature into an impeccably mannered young lady."

"I believe we must have different definitions of the word *lady*. Applied to Jessamy, it takes on a different meaning entirely," Alex muttered with a doubtful shake of his head. "I warn you— if she plays one more trick on me, I'll take her over my knee and give her the well-deserved spanking she's never had!"

"Alex!" Charity sounded horrified, but then saw the glint of amusement in her only son's eye, and relaxed. "You shouldn't tease your mother, Alexander Steele!"

His voice held a note of sincerity as he said, "I'm not sure I'm teasing. These yearly visits grow quickly tiresome when confronted with the wild Windsor brood. Remember that I warned you of my limits, Mother."

"I'll remember, as long as you remember that your father was a gentleman and so are you."

Alex's dark eyes softened, and his mouth thinned into a straight line at the memory of his father. Shifting his long legs into a more comfortable position, he looked out of the carriage and across rolling green hills, watching the countryside slowly pass in a glory of springtime.

"Yes," he said after several moments had passed, "my father was a first-rate gentleman.

But even he would not tolerate the abuse those brats deal out so liberally."

Charity laughed. "You know, Alex, I do believe you are right! But Joshua Steele was never known for his patience or even temper. Besides, they may have grown up in the year since we've visited."

"I doubt it."

When he grinned, Alex achingly reminded his mother of his late father. He had Joshua Steele's strong face and square jaw, the same devilish glint in his dark eyes, the same dark hair and—unfortunately—the same air of reckless energy. Joshua's recklessness had led to his death ten years before, leaving behind a young widow and heartbroken son. Thankfully, Alex had inherited his mother's caution to temper the bold recklessness of his father. She hoped.

"We're almost there, Alex," she said into the silence that lay comfortably between them. "Now mind your manners, and do try to ignore any small irritations. It's only for a month, and then you're going off to West Point and never have to return. Abigail Windsor is a dear, dear lady, and she has always been fond of you. Please do not make her think less—"

"Mother." Alex's tone was amused. "Do you really think I would embarrass you? I am old enough to be able to restrain any homicidal tendencies the Windsor brats may nurture."

Charity had the grace to look slightly chagrined. "I suppose you're right. It's just that I *do* know how trying those children can be at times, and I would hate for Abby to alter her high opinion of you if you were to allow your wretched temper to get the best of you."

"My temper is not wretched, thank you, and I believe that I can ignore those miserable brats if I put my mind to it." Alex sat back in the cushions as the coachman turned the new carriage up the long, curving drive leading to Clover Hill, the Windsor home. "I'm just glad this will be my last visit," he added in a mutter that was not intended to reach his mother's ears.

She leaned forward to lay a hand on his arm, her fingers curling around the swiftly maturing muscles. "You've grown up so fast, Alex, and once you've gone to West Point, you will cease being my child. Oh, you'll always be my son, but you will be a man, and things will never be the same. I intend to enjoy this last holiday with you."

Smiling, Alex would never have admitted that he felt the last shreds of his boyhood fading away without a bit of regret. After all, he was eighteen, and ready for the world and its challenges. If anything, he was impatient to be on his way, but understood his mother's reluctance to let him go. He laid his broad hand atop hers.

"You've always got Huntley, Mother, and he will take care of you while I'm gone."

Charity smiled. "Yes, Huntley is a good man and has been an excellent husband. I've wanted for nothing, and neither have you. I was very fortunate to have found him."

"No, he was fortunate to have found you," Alex corrected with firm gentleness, and Charity laughed, her soft blue eyes lighting. Only the smallest hint of gray touched her light brown hair, and her face was as smooth as a young girl's.

"You're right, of course!" she replied with an

impish tilt of her head. "Now, let's brave Huntley's family with a courageous heart."

"It'll take more armor than that to emerge un-
scathed," Alex murmured, eyeing the gracious,
white-columned house with a mixture of impatience and resignation as the carriage rolled to a
halt in front.

Alex wasn't the only one displeased by his arrival. Jessamy Windsor, poised on the delicate
threshold between childhood and womanhood,
stared with dismay out her upstairs window.
She didn't even see the brilliant display of carefully nurtured flowers in their neat beds lining
the drive, nor did she notice the fat buds of clover nodding in broad lawns sweeping down to
the road. All she saw was the family carriage
and the arriving guests.

"Oh, bother!" she said aloud, startling her
cousin, who came up behind her to peer over
her shoulder.

"What is it, Jess?" Maribelle asked, drawling
out the word *Jess* until Jessamy was tempted to
shake her. Then, without waiting for a reply,
she said in an interested tone, "Oh. It's Cousin
Alex from Kentucky."

"He's not really our cousin," Jessamy murmured, watching from behind fluttering curtains as Alex leaped agilely down from the
carriage and reached up to help his mother. "I
think he's half Indian and half wolf."

Maribelle stared with wide eyes. "Why do you
say that? I thought you liked him."

Whirling, Jessamy glared at Maribelle with
thick-lashed eyes that swiftly darkened from a
stormy blue to a smoky gray. "Like Alex? I de-
test him! He's always so . . . so condescending

to us! As if he's better than us because his father was from a fine family in Virginia, while we're just backwoods Tennesseans with no breeding." She curled her arms around her body, her full mouth tightening into a line of displeasure.

"I'm from Baltimore, remember?" Maribelle said. "We only come here for the summers because Mama can't stand being away from Aunt Abby so long. I reckon it is nicer here than in the city, but I always miss Papa, so . . ." She paused, frowning. "Besides I've never heard Alex say that, or even hint that," Maribelle ventured, but Jessamy wasn't listening. She was pacing the bedroom floor with a brooding frown.

"Well, he isn't any better than we are! My father may have been born into poverty, but he's certainly managed to work hard and make something of himself, while Joshua Steele was a hothead who managed to get himself killed in a duel! And I just might tell Alex that too if he acts high and mighty again!"

Maribelle gave a horrified gasp, her pale blue eyes growing even wider. "Oh, Jess, you wouldn't!"

"Oh, wouldn't I? Just wait and see," Jessamy said with such determination that Maribelle moaned in dismay.

"But . . . but I don't think he acts high and mighty," Maribelle said unhappily. "He's just quiet, not uppish."

"That's your opinion." Jessamy chewed on her bottom lip for a moment, then turned back to the window again. "He's grown a lot taller than he was," she commented after a moment. "And Mama says he's going to West Point in a few months. I can't imagine why the academy is allowing him in, when they wouldn't take Nick."

Maribelle looked down at the floor for a moment. Late afternoon sunlight glimmered on her brown hair and still babyish features as she quietly studied her toes in their soft kid slippers. Then she looked up at her taller, more slender cousin with a frown. "Maybe it's because Nick's bad temper has gotten him thrown out of every university he's attended," she suggested in a timid voice, and Jessamy just looked at her.

"That could be true," she said thoughtfully, and Maribelle heaved a sigh of relief. Though scrupulously honest about herself, Jessamy wasn't always tolerant of any criticism of her brothers, especially Nick. He was her favorite, her idol, and she adored him. The twins, James and Charles, she tolerated, and the youngest Windsor, Bryce, was still too young to be considered an actual sibling. At seven, Bryce was still in the nursery under the close eye of his mother and the tyranny of Celine, the Windsor nanny.

"Well," Jessamy said calmly, "Alex probably won't last long at West Point. Not if he's got a temper like his father, anyway."

"Or Nick," Maribelle said, then realized that she had pushed it a bit too far.

"Nick may be a little bad-tempered, but at least he's good-hearted, and not at all hateful like *some* people I could name!" Jessamy snapped.

Maribelle's narrow chin shook, and her mouth quivered pitifully. Jessamy was immediately penitent. "Oh Belle, I didn't mean to be cross with you. I'm sorry. Don't cry, please don't cry. I can't stand it when you get all weepy."

Looking up with drowning eyes, Maribelle sniffed. "Oh, I shouldn't have said anything about Nick. I know how you are about him. And maybe you're right about Alex."

"Oh, I know I'm right about Alex. But maybe we can think of a way to make him human before he leaves for West Point," Jessamy said with a sudden flare of mischief that made Maribelle shudder. "It'd be good for his soul to learn that he's subject to normal emotion, don't you think?"

"Jess," Maribelle said uneasily, "I don't think you should tease Alex. He's never been very gracious about it."

"Then don't you think it's time he learned how?" Jessamy gave a determined nod of her small head, and the blond hair that never seemed to quite stay in its neat braid dangled in front of her eyes. She gave it an impatient push to one side, and a smile tugged at the corners of her mouth as she said slowly, "Yes, I think we should give Cousin Alex something to remember! Come on, Belle, let's go talk to the boys."

It was with a soft shriek of apprehension that Maribelle allowed herself to be pulled along with her cousin, and she could not escape the feeling of impending doom that dogged her heels.

Chapter 2

FOR THE NEXT TWO DAYS, Jessamy Windsor appeared to be the most demure, well-mannered fifteen-year-old girl in all of Hardeman County, Tennessee. She smiled politely at her cousin from Kentucky, and even spoke civilly to him, stunning her father and making her brothers choke on stifled laughter. She would think of the grandest masquerade she had ever invented, and it would certainly make stuffy old Alex abandon his iron control at last!

At least, that was the plan, vague as it was.

Jessamy wanted to catch Alex off guard, make him think she had forgotten all her old ways, then administer a coup de grace that would make him fairly boil with anger! He would leave Clover Hill knowing he had been bested, that his cool self-control had been shaken for once.

And somewhere underneath her firm resolve to prick him, there was a curiosity gnawing at her soul, a curiosity about Alex's limits. He'd fascinated her since the first time Aunt Charity, Uncle Huntley's new wife, had brought her tall, quiet son to Clover Hill. She had felt him out warily at first but had gotten no results, and no one—not Jessamy or any of her brothers—had ever been able to get beneath Alex's tightly held control to see the real person. He was unfailingly—maddeningly—polite, even when provoked to his very limits. It had tortured Jessamy no end, and she had often found herself thinking about him even after he'd gone back to Kentucky.

Once, just once, she had tentatively offered the olive branch of peace, but Alex had merely gazed at her with a detached stare that had made her snatch it back quite rudely, and she had never offered it again. She had thought it obvious that he didn't like the Windsors, so the Windsors were determined not to like him, either.

"I still don't think it's a good idea," Maribelle was heard to say one lazy afternoon when they lay beneath the gauzy folds of mosquito netting to wait out the heat of the day. Garbed in only pantalettes and chemises, their stockings rolled down and shoes off, they lay atop cotton sheets while shadows cooled the bedroom.

"Why not?" Jessamy was almost asleep, her heavy lashes weighting down sleepy lids, but she opened them slightly to stare up at her cousin. Poor Maribelle. She was still plain as mud, but so tender-hearted she cried at the death of a sparrow. "Don't you want to see if Alex is human?"

"Not really. What does it matter? I mean, why should he have to react if he doesn't want to?"

Maribelle glanced away from Jessamy's penetrating, suddenly wide-awake stare.

"Why, Maribelle Mullen, I do believe that you actually *like* Alex Steele!"

"No! I don't! I mean, not really, except that I . . . I know how he feels, that's all. Well, I do," she added in a strangely sullen tone. "Sometimes people don't like to have pranks played on them, Jess. I know it used to annoy me no end until ya'll finally quit."

"Did it?" Jessamy looked interested. "Did you want to shout at us, or play a prank back?"

Nodding, Maribelle said, "Yes, only mostly, I just wanted you all to stop."

"I see." Jessamy lay back on the fat feather pillow and arranged her pale blond hair in a thick coil atop her head as she gazed thoughtfully up at the canopy of mosquito netting. "Well, perhaps we shouldn't, but it's always so funny when he just glares at us," she conceded. "And to tell the truth, Belle, sometimes I don't know why I feel compelled to tease him! It's odd, isn't it? I mean, I think about him all winter, and how I'm going to devise the perfect prank to make him furiously angry, so angry he'll have to laugh, and then summer comes, and it never quite works out that way."

"Maybe he doesn't want to laugh."

Jessamy didn't answer for a moment, just fiddled with a silky curl of her hair, one leg propped on her bent knee, and her mouth pursed thoughtfully. "No, maybe he doesn't. But then I wonder why."

"Well, his papa was killed in a duel, you know, and I heard Mama tell my father that Alex was there. It was all supposed to be very terrible, and a great scandal, and then Aunt Charity moved away from Virginia and went back home to Kentucky, where she met and married Uncle Huntley."

Jessamy's tone was slightly impatient. "Oh, I know all of that! But that was years ago. Why is he still so sad?"

"Wouldn't you be sad if it was your father?"

Jessamy thought of her portly, gruff father, and could almost smell his favorite tobacco and see the way his eyes crinkled at the corners when he smiled. She'd always admired William Windsor, especially since she'd practically cut her baby teeth on stories of how he and his three brothers had come from England and each made their own fortunes in America.

"And my greatest fortune is my Abigail and my children!" he always ended his stories, which made Jessamy feel very loved and very secure.

"Yes, of course I would be sad," she said to Maribelle with a stubborn tilt of her chin. "But I wouldn't let it ruin the rest of my life."

"I hardly think that not caring for practical jokes played on one could be considered 'ruining' the rest of a life," Maribelle pointed out in a dry tone, and Jessamy giggled.

"You could be right. But there's not enough laughter sometimes when you're all grown-up, have you ever noticed that, Belle? I mean, Mama hardly ever laughs out loud, till her sides ache, like we do sometimes. She may smile, or even make a soft noise in the back of her throat, but that is all."

"Papa and Uncle William laugh aloud."

Sitting up, Jessamy drew up her knees and

hugged them to her chest, and her blue-gray eyes sparkled with amusement. "Yes, I've seen them! And it's usually after they've been in their cups, too!"

"I remember they laughed that time you and Nick tied sheets in the hickory grove to make Old Billy think there were ghosts out there, and he came running back with his face almost white!" Maribelle laughed softly. "I heard my papa say that darkies are always scared of the supermatural and—"

"Supernatural," Jessamy corrected. "Not matural."

"Well, whatever it is. Anyway, Papa said that Old Billy was too frightened to talk, and could only gabble like a goose!"

"I guess that was kinda mean of us, but Old Billy had been trying to scare us with spooky tales, so we decided to scare him back. I didn't mean to scare him so badly."

"He still won't go back in that grove, will he?"

Regretfully, Jessamy shook her head. "No. And Celine says until he does, Nick and I have to gather the hickory nuts he was sent to get."

"Well, by the next time the nuts are on the ground, he should be over it."

A silence fell, and they could hear the muted noises from outside, the distant sounds of men working in the fields and servants going about their chores. It was a safe, familiar sound, one Jessamy woke to each day and fell asleep by each night. It was as familiar as summer relatives, and it had been this way since she could remember. She supposed that it would never change.

She stretched comfortably, and let her mind

drift back to the earlier problem of a prank to play on her cousin. It would have to be a good one, an inventive prank that would take him by surprise. Since Alex had grown taller and even more remote, he would not be taken in by a clumsy attempt. No, it would have to be a good one, for he would be wary of them.

No more burrs under the saddle of his pony, or buckets of water drenching him from a tree limb. No, it would have to be a skillful, sophisticated prank, and one that would make him finally admit he had been bested, one that would make him laugh.

"I will think of the best yet," she murmured sleepily as the heat of the afternoon and the soft southern breezes lulled her into slumber. "Alex Steele will know he's been bested!"

"Oh, Jess, I think this is crazy!" Maribelle's eyes were wider than normal, appearing like gigantic lamps in the dim shadows of the gazebo. "Are you sure about this?"

"Of course I'm sure!" Jessamy's voice sounded much more confident than she felt, but she was determined not to allow her plan to alter. It had taken her a week to think of it, and then another week to plan it all out. Nick, that fiend, had flatly refused to assist her at all in it, saying she didn't know what she was doing, so she had enlisted the aid of her twin brothers as well as her cousin Maribelle. Only now that she was about to set it all in motion did she have doubts.

It seemed so perfect, a truly diabolical, ingenious plan, that she could foresee absolutely no

hint of disaster in it. She still couldn't understand Nick's frowning refusal to help.

"You're too young and innocent to know what
you're thinking of," he'd said flatly, rudely, startling her. Nick had never talked to her quite like
that before, and she'd stomped her feet angrily
at him.

"Nicholas Windsor, either say you want to
help, or say you don't, but don't mouth stupid
platitudes at me!" she'd stormed.

Sighing, he'd shaken his dark head and spoken more gently, but still had refused. "Jess,
there are certain ways you don't tease a man,
and that's one of them."

"I would hardly call Alexander Steele a man
yet," she had said coldly, turning away from her
older brother. "And for that matter, what would
you know about being a man?"

Nick had shouted after her, "Don't say I didn't
warn you!"

Well, she wouldn't, and Nick would get none
of the satisfaction of a well-planned prank, either.

"Are you certain you know what to do?" Jessamy asked Maribelle again.

Exasperated, Maribelle heaved a sigh. "I've
heard it a hundred times! Yes, I know what I'm
supposed to do!"

"Good. Now, if James and Charles can just
keep their minds on what to do, we have Alex
where we want him."

"I hope so." Maribelle sounded doubtful, and
Jessamy glared at her in the dim light of the
gazebo.

"It will work! Look at how dark it is in here
already, and it's not even dusk yet. And I'm

wearing the same sickly sweet perfume she wears, though how I'm going to stand it until I can wash it off, I don't know. Alex won't know the difference until it's too late."

"Maybe Nick was right," Maribelle said slowly. "Maybe we shouldn't try to trick him like this. He'll be powerful angry when he finds out it's you and not Becky Anderson."

"He'll probably be grateful! I've watched that cow-eyed heifer hang on his arm at every tea and church picnic we've attended for the past two weeks, until I'm certain he has to be as sick of the sight of her as I am!"

"I don't think so. I mean, I did see them kissing out behind the rosebushes, you know. That doesn't sound like he's sick of her to me."

"Well, after tonight, he won't be able to look at her without remembering the joke I played on him," Jessamy said in a matter-of-fact tone. "Now, you just do your part and get him out here. You're the only one he'd trust to deliver a message. He'd know something was up if I were to tell him, and he'd be suspicious of James or Charles, too. Have they already gone to fetch Becky?"

Maribelle gave a miserable nod. "Yes."

"And you're going to make sure Mama and Papa don't miss me for a while?"

Another miserable nod. "Yes, but if they ask me outright, I can't lie for you."

"I don't expect you to. I do have *some* honor, you know! All I need is a quarter hour of freedom."

"Why do I have the feeling that something bad is going to happen?" Maribelle moaned softly.

"Because you're a nervous goose, that's why. Now, give me those rags, and go give Alex the message. And make sure that James and Charles keep Becky well occupied."

As Maribelle left the gazebo at the far end of the garden, it grew very quiet. Jessamy felt another pang of doubt, and firmly thrust it aside. Of course the prank would work. What could happen, except that Alex would not be fooled? She allowed herself a moment of satisfaction at the sheer simple genius of her plan. It had come to her at the Leatherses' family tea, where she had seen Becky Anderson gaze up at Alex with wide cow eyes, simpering and cooing so disgustingly that Jessamy had felt nauseous. Then, when Maribelle had told her that she had seen them kissing, it had brought into focus the Perfect Plan.

What better way to fool Alex than make him think Becky was waiting for him in the dark gazebo? And then, after she had lured him into whispering honeyed words—she just hoped she didn't giggle and spoil it—she would reveal her identity. Oh, he might be a little angry at first, but he would have to admit it was a good joke on him, and very well planned. After all, she'd gone to a lot of trouble to ensure that Becky Anderson was attending the barbecue and dancing after, and that Alex would be certain to know it. It all hinged on exact timing, with the twins keeping Becky away from Alex without his realizing it, and then Maribelle bringing him a note, supposedly from Becky, asking that he meet her in the gazebo at the end of the garden. After waiting a suitable length of time, Maribelle was to arrive at just the right moment, "surprising" them and thoroughly embarrassing Alex. Then he would discover that his alluring temptress was none other than his laughing cousin. . . .

Yes, Jessamy thought with a smile of satisfaction, it had all the earmarks of genius!

"Now, if I can just stuff enough rags in my bodice so he'll think I'm Becky," she muttered with a frown as she wadded the strips of cotton and tucked them into her gown. "Why does she have to be so . . . so *bosomy*? Reminds me of a sow sometimes."

With the rags in place, Jessamy adjusted the wide brim of the straw hat she wore, tilting it to hide her face. Even with the shadows, she didn't quite trust Alex not to immediately recognize that she wasn't Becky. The fuller silhouette and the disguising hat should keep his suspicion at bay for a short time, at least long enough for her to coax a few impassioned words from him.

"Wouldn't it be funny if he were to kneel and beg a kiss from me?" she wondered. Then she had the startling, daring thought that she might just allow him a single, chaste peck, just to find out how it felt. She'd never been kissed before—never wanted to be kissed—but now it seemed faintly interesting.

Nervously smoothing her long, full skirts, she heard the starched rustling of her taffeta petticoats beneath the overlay of cotton skirt. It sounded too loud in the shadowy silence.

"Goose!" she muttered aloud, sucking in a deep breath to steady her quivering nerves. It was only Alex, and what could he do to her even if he grew angry?

It wasn't until she heard the solid tread of his

boots on the pebbled walkway that she thought of at least ten or twelve different calamities that could befall her at his hands. But that didn't matter now. She wasn't a coward, and she would see this through and have the last laugh.

"Becky?"

Alex paused in the doorway to the latticed gazebo, one hand propped against the frame, a foot on the top step. His deep voice penetrated the soft gloom, and Jessamy could see his solid frame outlined against the dusky light. He seemed even taller than before, his shoulders broader, and his size daunting. She swallowed hard, then made her voice as soft and husky as possible, imitating Becky Anderson's throaty voice.

"Alex? Is that you?"

He stepped up into the gazebo, and stood just inside. "Who else did you send a note to?" He sounded faintly mocking, and he leaned lazily against the doorframe, peering into the dark shadows on the far side of the tiny garden house. "What's so important that I have to meet you in private?"

Not daring to push her luck too far, Jessamy affected a husky, inviting laugh, hoping he would take the hint. He did. Alex levered his long frame away from the door and took several steps forward. Jessamy wished that she could see his expression, but with the light behind him, his features were in shadow. She tried to breathe past the constricted muscles in her throat, and finally managed a shaky breath.

"Do I have to have a reason?" she murmured in what she hoped was a sultry tone. She kept her head slightly tilted so that the hat brim

shaded her face. When would he react as Maribelle had said he did with Becky? When would
Alex press his suit, so that she might bring this
joke to an end?

Alex laughed softly, and somehow, the sound
was jarring. He took another two steps toward
her, his long legs bringing him to the bench
where she sat. Instead of bending to one knee as
she'd hoped, Alex sat beside her—close beside
her. Jessamy could almost feel his warm breath
across shoulders bared by the peasant sleeves of
her new party dress, and wished suddenly that
she'd worn something more conventional. Oh
well. Too late to worry about that now. She
edged slightly away, half turning on the bench
and keeping her face averted.

"Now, Becky, did you call me out here to tease
me?" he asked. One hand reached out to touch
her bare shoulder, and Jessamy shivered. "Ah, I
see that you didn't. Is it so hard for you to say it
aloud?" he murmured, his fingertips grazing
along the curve of her jaw. His thumb and forefinger gripped her chin softly, and turned her
face toward him. Jessamy tried to pull away,
gamely meeting this new and unexpected challenge. He held her fast.

"Alex . . . Alex, you must know why I asked
you to meet me," she tried at last, forcing the
words out in a kind of breathless rush. Why did
just the pressure of his warm fingers on her
make her feel so flushed and funny? She did not
understand it at all. It wasn't exactly unpleasant, but it wasn't very pleasant, either. It was
more frightening and confusing than anything.

"Yes, I think I do," Alex was saying, his words
coming to her as if through a long hallway. He

was leaning forward, too far forward, his other arm sliding behind her back to turn her toward him. Jessamy drew back, her body stiffening.

At any moment, he might lift the brim of her hat and recognize her, and he hadn't yet said anything compromising! And where was Maribelle? She should have arrived by now! The joke was about to turn on her, and she *must* act quickly or lose control!

"Alex, Alex, don't you . . . isn't there anything you want to say to me?"

"I'll say it with actions instead of words," he replied in a lazy voice, his hand making small circles on the nape of her neck, rendering her almost immobile with apprehension and a strange lethargy. His face lowered, and he lifted the brim of her hat at the same time as he drew her close against him, almost onto his lap. His strong arms circled her quivering body and held her tightly.

Jessamy could feel his warm breath whisper across her cheek, could sense that he was going to kiss her, and she waited in agonized silence, at a loss for once as to how to react or reply. She hadn't considered that he might actually kiss her without asking permission, but it was obvious that was what he intended to do. Should she allow it? Should she try to carry off the joke no matter what happened?

Jessamy held onto the ribbons of her hat in desperation, defying Alex's efforts to remove it until he finally brushed away her hands. She bit her lip in consternation. What would Becky do? The wretched girl had already allowed him the liberty of kissing her at the Leatherses' tea party, so acting prudish would be a dead give-away now. But she was not Becky, and when Alex realized that—should she scream? Should she demand an apology? Should she be outraged? Or did all that come after he had actually kissed her? Not having had any previous experience, she hesitated, and that was disastrous.

Alex pressed his mouth down over her half-open lips, and she could feel his sudden start, but didn't know why. It did not occur to her that he had not expected to find her mouth open, nor tasting so sweet. Inexplicably, he held her even more tightly, his mouth moving over hers until the world grew darker and faintly hazy. Her head swam, and there was a peculiar churning in the pit of her stomach, almost, she thought, as if she had eaten too many spring apples. When would it end? When would the warm, blurry feeling that oozed through her sluggish body go away? And oddly enough, she realized that she didn't really want it to go away.

Lifting her arms without conscious thought, Jessamy let her head fall back as she put her hands behind Alex's neck. That was when he tore himself away, cursing harshly and bringing her crashing back to reality.

"Dammit! What do you think you're doing?"

Blinking rapidly to clear her fogged senses, Jessamy let her arms fall to her sides, surging to her feet to face him. It was an instinctive reaction, and she saw that Alex was standing, too.

"Being kissed, it looks like!" Jessamy retorted as strongly as she could. She allowed a smug smile to play at the corners of her mouth. "Isn't that why you came here?"

Alex's hand flashed out to grab her by the

arm, and he jerked her close to him. His other hand yanked away her hat, and she could see the angry glints in his eyes.

"I have to admit I've been expecting another one of your foolish pranks for the past two weeks, but this is not quite what I imagined!" Alex glared at her. "It's been like waiting for the other shoe to fall, but—"

"The other shoe?" Jessamy blinked in confusion. "What do you mean?"

"You know," he said impatiently, "letting one shoe fall to the floor, and listening for the other to fall, but—"

"But it doesn't!" She clapped her hands together. "Now I understand!"

"I wish to hell I did!"

"It's quite simple really," Jessamy began, taking a wary step backward as Alex continued to glare at her. She hadn't expected that he would react so strongly, or take it so badly. It was fascinating to see him angry after all those years of no reaction at all. Did he know that two white lines formed on each side of his mouth when he ground his teeth together like that? Or that his nostrils flared like an angry bull's? Maybe he did, which was why he rarely allowed himself to become angry. It made sense, but now was hardly the time to point that out to him. Especially since he was interrupting her, his voice clipped and sharp.

"I should have known you were up to something when I saw you in here, but I had no idea you really intended to be so loose!"

She recoiled in surprise. "You knew it was me?"

"Of course I did! Did you really think you

could fool a *goat* with that ridiculous disguise? That field hand's hat, and those—those!" With the last word, he snatched at a tiny corner of material peeking from the top of her bodice, and Jessamy's bosom was immediately deflated as the wads of cotton fluttered through the air. She had the grace to flush, but kept her chin held high.

"Oh, so you knew it was me, did you?"

"Of course I did!"

"Then why," she said with a note of triumph, "did you kiss me?"

"To teach you a lesson."

"And what lesson was that, pray tell?"

"Not to play with fire, young lady."

Jessamy's voice was scornful. "And you think I've been warned about fires now? Do you think you're so dangerous that I will never be tempted to play another joke?"

"How old are you, Jessamy Windsor? Thirteen?"

Affronted, she stiffened. "Fifteen! In a few weeks, anyway," she amended.

"Fifteen." Alex shook his head. His fingers dug into her shoulders, and her eyes lifted in alarm as he drew her to him in a smooth motion. "You're old enough for your first real kiss then, aren't you?"

Before she could give more than a shocked wheeze, Alex had brought his mouth down over hers again, his lips moving against hers with forceful pressure. This time, instead of the hazy feeling, Jessamy felt a sudden jolt, as if touching a hot stove. It seared through her body in shock waves, leaving her trembling, weak, and angry. She tried to jerk away but he held her fast, and she was much too conscious of the hard pressure of his lean thighs pressing against her. It was almost as if she weren't wearing a single petticoat, and a heated flush spread over her like wildfire.

When Alex finally released her, setting her back from him and gazing down at her with narrowed eyes, Jessamy fought for the self-control that had somehow escaped her. She was shaking all over, and he put out a hand to steady her. She slapped it away.

"Leave me alone!"

Alex's mouth curled in a mocking smile. "Isn't that what you wanted?"

Without stopping to think of the consequences, Jessamy reacted with a swinging hand, her fingers curled into a tight fist. But her blow barely grazed Alex's jaw. His iron-hard hand caught her wrist in a numbing vise before she could jerk it away, and his eyes glittered furiously.

"Look, you brainless little hoyden, don't think for a single instant that I will tolerate your stupid pranks any longer! I've endured them for the past eight years, and I'm sick of being the butt of your practical jokes! If I did what I threatened to do, I'd turn you over my knee and tan your backside."

"You wouldn't!" Jessamy tried to pull away, her eyes widening with horror at the determined rage in his face.

"Oh, don't think I'm not tempted, because I am. But then I'd have to fight your hotheaded brothers, and I'm not eager to embarrass my mother. You, however, seem to have no qualms about that sort of thing."

As he released her wrist, flinging her arm
from him, Jessamy rubbed the bruised flesh in
thoughtful silence. Then, her voice slightly sullen, she said, "Nick told me not to do this, but I
wouldn't listen, so he probably wouldn't mind if
you behaved badly to me."

"He has more sense than I thought."

Silence fell, and in the swiftly gathering
shadows, Jessamy had a sudden thought. "Why
haven't you ever minded our pranks before?"

"I told you—I have."

"But you never said anything."

"Would you have stopped?"

"Maybe."

Alex laughed shortly. "I don't think so. It
would have just encouraged you."

"You may be right," she admitted slowly.
Then her eyes gleamed mischievously as she
looked up at him in the swift-fading light. "So—
are you *very* angry?"

"I should be."

"But are you?"

Alex's eyes narrowed slightly as he gazed
down at his young cousin. Jessamy had always
been reckless and undisciplined, and when he'd
seen her waiting for him in the gazebo with a
wide hat and wider bosom, he'd almost turned
and left. But curiosity had lured him inside—
that and amusement at her latest prank. He'd
always been able to tell the difference between
Jessamy's pranks and those of her brothers.
Hers had been more creative than theirs, and
therefore more maddening.

"Yes, and no," he finally replied when she
shifted from one foot to another in impatience.
A small smile lifted one corner of his mouth.

"I'm angry because you tried to trick me, but not angry because you failed."

Her voice was indignant. "I did not fail! You didn't know it was me in here, or you would never have come. Of course," she admitted with a surge of honesty, "you didn't fall to one knee and pour out your heart as I'd hoped, but one can't have everything."

Alex grinned. "Try to remember that in the future, Jess. I have a feeling that most of the young men in Hardeman County will be grateful if you do."

"I shall break all their hearts," Jessamy announced with a return of good spirits. "At least, that's what Celine says, and she's Creole, you know, and knows all about love and broken hearts."

One dark brow lifted as Alex gazed at Jessamy's heart-shaped face for a long moment. "Those sorts of notions are what comes of having French nursemaids instead of a proper one, like the nursemaid who raised me. She was stout and black as coal, and didn't have fanciful ideas, just good common sense."

"You sound like Mama, but you know my papa. He refuses to consider anyone but a French nanny. He says his children are going to be brought up as he was never brought up."

"I believe he has accomplished that aim quite effectively," Alex said in a wry voice. He glanced from Jessamy's face to the gazebo door. "If we don't return to the barbecue and dancing, someone will be searching for us, and then how will you explain our being alone together?"

An impish smile curved her lips as she snatched up the straw hat and replaced it atop her head. "I won't have to! Papa will be asking *you* the questions, not me!"

Alex half turned as Jessamy skipped past him and out the gazebo door, his mouth opened to speak, but the words died unuttered on his lips. He smiled as she flew down the pebbled walkway, her footsteps as light as a child's. In spite of the fact that she fought it so hard, she was growing up, and he'd felt it in her kiss, in the soft velvet of her mouth under his. He'd felt almost ashamed for kissing a girl just fifteen, three years younger than he was and still immature, but it had been an irresistible urge he could not deny. And it wasn't so terrible a thing, for girls younger than Jessamy got married every day.

The bewildering truth was that he had felt a powerful spark of attraction to her—to Jessamy Windsor, who had bedeviled him for eight years! He couldn't understand it. Why her? It certainly wasn't her looks, for she was still too awkward and coltish to be considered a beauty, though there was certainly promise in her lush eyes and ripe mouth. And her hair, hair the color of corn silk, thick and tawny and luxurious, but usually uncombed and hanging in wild tangles in her eyes, would be beautiful if combed and bedecked with diamond clips.

Alex shook his head, and shoved his hands deep in the pockets of his trousers. "I should have stuck with my original plan, and tanned her backside," he muttered softly as he stepped out of the gazebo. "It would have been a sight less disturbing."

And less intriguing, his willful mind whispered.

Chapter 3

June, 1858

CLOVER HILL PERCHED ATOP a grassy knoll overlooking the county road that wound lazily through fields and pasture. It wasn't a spectacular house like some of those in the county, but a comfortable house that suited its owner. The two-story structure had been built only twenty-one years before, and nestled close to the ancient cedar trees that shaded it. It was built of whitewashed brick, as were most houses in the area, and the roof was made of dark slate. A long hall called a dogtrot bisected the house in the middle, with double doors at the front and back, and four white columns supported the front of a second-floor gallery that wound completely around the building. Behind the house were the kitchens—two of them—and they were connected to the main building only by a covered walkway. That lessened the ever-present danger of fire destroying the main house.

Dotting the grounds behind the main house were the slave quarters—neat, whitewashed cabins with private garden plots and small scatterings of fowl in the yards. There were only three houses, for Clover Hill did not have as many slaves as a huge plantation. William Windsor was fond of saying that it was "more of a working farm, comfortable, but not too comfortable."

Stretching beyond the slave quarters were the storehouses and the smokehouse, and the stone house where milk, butter, and cheese were kept. The stables had been built to one side of the tended lawns, and on a warm summer night Jessamy could sometimes hear the contented nickers of the blooded horses she loved.

The front lawns swept down to the county road in a bright green carpet of clover and bermuda grass, and the long drive was lined with towering cedars interspersed with a profusion of rosebushes. In the spring and summer, vivid blossoms embroidered the drive up to the house with color and a heady fragrance.

An uninitiated visitor, put off by the unpretentious name of Clover Hill, received a pleasant surprise when rounding the curve in the road and turning into the drive that led to the house. It immediately became apparent how the plantation had derived its name, for bursts of red and white clover buzzed with bees in the summertime and lured the epicurean appetites of the livestock. Usually a small black boy perched under a stately oak on the lawn, a long switch in one hand to drive away any animal so careless as to stray onto the grass. It was a never-ending task and one of the first responsibilities tendered a young male slave, for it was not physically demanding, just required hours of tedium in the heat.

Cool breezes blew under the shade of the porch that stretched along the front of the house, making it a favorite spot for those inclined to while away lazy days. On this day, the porch was decorated with female occupants in bright, sleeveless gowns, as colorful as spring flowers.

Summer was waxing strong and hot, and Jessamy felt strangely unsettled as she paced the porch.

"What's the matter?" Maribelle asked, languidly fluttering a paper fan back and forth to stir the air. "You have been so restless lately, it's like trying to talk to a river. Always moving around, never staying in one place for longer than a minute—are you feeling well?"

"I feel fine!" Jessamy snapped, then sighed at the hurt expression on her cousin's face. "Oh, Belle, I didn't mean to snap at you like that. It's just that . . . that I guess I do feel rather out of sorts."

"Is it because of Cody Baines?" Maribelle asked with a sly grin. "I saw him trying to kiss you at the Leatherses' barbecue last week."

"He'd kiss a fence post," Jessamy shot back, but a small smile tugged at the corners of her mouth, and she slid a careful glance around her. No one was within sight of the shady porch where they sat. She leaned forward, and her eyes glittered with bright sapphire lights as she said in a soft voice, "Cody doesn't kiss badly, either!"

"Jessamy Ann Windsor!" Maribelle's eyes

grew huge, and the fan stopped fluttering. "Why, you fast thing!"

Jessamy leaned back against the porch post, and her smile grew wider. "Fast? I'm seventeen years old, unmarried and not even engaged, and you call me fast? Slow is more like it, turtle-slow and a wallflower."

Maribelle's paper fan resumed its waving, and she rocked slowly in the cane rocker. A rhythmic creaking noise was the only reply for a moment, then Maribelle said, "If I didn't know firsthand that you dance almost every single dance at every barbecue or party, I might be tempted to believe that you're a wallflower. But you do dance, so I don't believe you."

"Believe what you like," Jessamy said carelessly. She leaned against the tall white porch column, and pressed her cheek against the cool wood. She looked across the lawns toward the road in front of the house. Dust boiled up in fine, gauzy clouds, and she said softly, "Company."

Maribelle was immediately interested. She rose from the rocker and came to stand beside Jessamy, peering curiously over the lawns. "Oh," she said in a disappointed voice, "it's only the Leathers."

"You should have known it would be. It's Thursday, isn't it?" Jessamy made a wry face. "They come every Thursday in time for tea, just like an eight-day clock. I declare, I don't know how Mama stays polite when those gabby sisters gossip for two hours and stuff their mouths with Delilah's best pastries the whole time! It's a wonder they aren't all as big as houses instead of so tiny."

Maribelle shrugged. "Oh, sometimes they're quite funny. And if you listen to them, you can hear things about every person in Hardeman County."

"You can hear things about every person from Cloverport to Memphis, if you can bear listening long enough," Jessamy grumbled, but her eyes had sharpened with interest. After a moment, she said, "I bet they know everything about everyone, don't you think, Belle?"

"They probably do." Maribelle gave her cousin a shrewd glance. "They probably hear about folks who are all the way up in West Point, too."

Jessamy gave a rueful smile. "Well, I just wonder if Alex has been thrown out of the academy yet. I mean, he may have gotten admitted, but that doesn't mean they'll let him stay!"

"Didn't Nick say that Alex was one of the top cadets? I am just sure I heard him say that Alex had the second highest grades in his class, and that when he graduates he can take his pick of commissions."

"Nick doesn't always know what he's talking about," Jessamy said, dismissing her brother, "and he never knows all the right gossip to tell anyway."

"Such as whether Alex is engaged to anyone?" Maribelle teased, and received an angry glare for her daring.

"I don't know what you're talking about!"

"You do, too. You've talked about Alex Steele ever since you played that mean joke on him two summers ago. I'd still like to know just what happened in the gazebo when he found out you weren't Becky Anderson," Maribelle said.

Affecting a careless shrug, Jessamy said, "Oh, I already told you. He knew it was me all along."

"Somehow, I think you're not telling me the entire truth, Jess."

"You know I don't lie!"

"Yes, but a half-truth is the same as a lie. My mama told me that."

"Well, I don't want to contradict Aunt Pretense, but I cannot agree." Jessamy stepped away from her cousin, not quite able to look at her. Was she that transparent? And how had she gotten this silly crush on a man she hadn't seen in two years anyway? Maybe it was because he had kissed her, and she'd discovered that it was very pleasant, indeed. No other young man she'd allowed to kiss her since then had stirred the same emotions in her, and while it was frustrating, it was also exciting. She wished Alex would come back and kiss her again, so she could decide if it was as nice as she remembered. Maybe it wasn't, and then she could forget him. After all, he could be quite exasperating when he chose to be, and he'd probably grown up to be an insufferable man.

"Here come the Leatherses," Jessamy said hurriedly when it looked as if Maribelle would continue the discussion. "Mama will expect us to join them."

Sitting beside Dorothy Leathers, the oldest of the Leathers sisters and the most animated, Jessamy began to wish she had not been quite so willing to join them for tea. She'd been sitting on the brocade settee for over an hour, and didn't know any more about Alex now than she had when she'd sat down. Twice, she had steered the conversation in that direction, and twice she had been interrupted. Now she gathered her determination and broke into Dorothy Leathers's long dissertation on the evils of drink with a loud clearing of her throat. They all turned to look at her.

"Didn't I hear that Alex Steele—you know, Papa's nephew by marriage—was sent down from West Point for imbibing too freely?"

Virginia Leathers spoke up eagerly. "Oh no! That was Teddy Tyree! His mother was just absolutely *devastated,* and his father was livid with rage, I hear."

"Oh, that's right," Jessamy said, unable to glance in her cousin's direction. She could feel Maribelle's appalled gaze resting on her, and knew that her mother would give her a good dressing-down later for encouraging gossip. But she was too determined to stop now, though she did wish for an instant she was young and impulsive enough to get away with asking outright instead of having to resort to this ridiculous roundabout questioning. "Then it must have been Cousin Alex who was sent down for failing to make the grade—"

"Oh no," Ann Leathers, the youngest of the three, said quickly. "Mr. Steele ranks the highest in his class, I hear. You must mean that incident about . . . about the young lady."

Jessamy sat forward on the edge of the settee, her teacup clattering on its saucer. "Ah yes, I believe that was it! Cousin Alex was very unwise in his decisions, if I am remembering correctly."

"Unwise?" Dorothy Leathers lifted a brow, and her mouth pursed in disapproval. "I would say that was an understatement, wouldn't you, Virginia?"

Abigail Windsor, aghast at the gossipy turn of the conversation, picked up the teapot, a family heirloom with huge flowers painted delicately on the sides, and asked, "More tea, anyone?"

The Leatherses ignored her, totally absorbed in this new topic, and Jessamy refused to glance at her mother. She knew what she would see in her face.

". . . understatement is quite right, Dorothy," Virginia Leathers was saying as Jessamy dragged her eyes from one to the other. "The poor girl is absolutely ruined! But then, his mother's family is from Kentucky, you know, and everyone knows how wild those Kentuckians can be at times."

Clearing her throat, Abigail Windsor said firmly, "I am quite closely connected with many Kentucky families, and have the highest regard for each and every one of them, Alexander included." Lifting a silver platter, she pushed it forward and said sweetly, "These honey cakes are truly divine. Delilah would never understand if they weren't all eaten, so do take several." Leveling a long glance on her chagrined daughter, Abigail added, "And Jessamy, if you would be so kind as to check on Bryce, I would appreciate it."

Smarting under her mother's unspoken rebuke, Jessamy nodded silently and left the parlor, closing the doors behind her as she stepped into the open hallway. A soft breeze filled the high interior, passing from the opened front doors to the rear, and she paused to peer into the gilt mirror hanging on the wall. Her cheeks were still hot with agitation.

A young lady! Ruined! Because of Alex?

"The wretch," Jessamy muttered, and gazed at her reflection without really seeing it. What terrible thing had he done? Had the girl done? Oh, she wished she could ask more, but her mother would be dreadfully disappointed and angry if she tried. Sighing, Jessamy turned away from the mirror and went up the staircase. She mounted the stairs slowly, as a young lady of breeding was supposed to do, instead of tearing up them as she once would have done.

Celine looked up in surprise when Jessamy entered the old nursery, her coffee-colored eyes fastening on her face. "What have you done to displease your mama?" Celine asked when Jessamy explained that she had come to check on Bryce.

Making a slight face, Jessamy sighed heavily again, and dropped into a chair by the window. "Encouraged gossip."

"Ah, the Leathers sisters?"

Jessamy nodded and smiled. "How did you know?"

"Because they like to talk, those women. They like to know all and tell all."

Leaning forward, Jessamy stared at the Creole servant for a long moment, at her familiar unlined face and huge dark eyes that held wells of knowledge. As a child, Jessamy had thought Celine possessed all the answers to the mysteries of mankind in her wise old eyes. It was a feeling that lingered still.

"Celine—were you ever in love?"

A delicate brow arched high. "In love? *Oui.* As a girl, I was always in love."

"Then why didn't you ever marry?"

An eloquent Gallic shrug dismissed the question, and Celine said instead, "You are thinking of falling in love, *n'est-ce pas?*"

"Is that something one plans? I always thought it just happened, sometimes when you didn't want or expect it."

Celine moved from the armoire, where she had been placing clothes, to the window seat where Bryce had left a jumble of toys. She slid Jessamy an oblique glance, and a small smile tugged at her lips.

"*Oui,* it often happens that way. And sometimes, it is just a warm feeling one has about an old and valued friend, a feeling that grows into more."

Jessamy frowned. She didn't feel that way at all about Alex. He was more an old enemy than an old friend. She looked down at her skirts, and toyed with a strand of pale hair that fell into her eyes, not seeing the soft smile Celine gave her.

"Well," Jessamy said, looking up after a moment, "I do not feel either way, so I guess it must be indigestion."

Celine laughed, her teeth flashing brightly in her dark face. "Perhaps it is, or perhaps it is just uncertainty."

"Yes, but still, it would be nice to know whichever it is, don't you think?"

"Not always," Celine replied. "Not always."

Chapter 4

May, 1861

"GUESS WHO'S COMING to Clover Hill?" Nick Windsor asked his sister in a sly whisper, and she gave an indifferent shrug of one shoulder.

"Oh, another one of your friends, I suppose? I confess that I'm quite weary of moonlight declarations, so I hope whoever it is, is already married or engaged!"

Nick grinned. "Are you sure?"

"Of course I'm sure!" Jessamy gave an impatient flick of her long skirts, and drummed her fingertips on the ledge of the porch railing. She stared out over the green lawns with a studied expression, knowing Nick would tell her and that she could continue to pretend indifference. But to her dismay, he gave an eloquent shrug and turned to go into the house, and she had to toss aside her nonchalance and say, "But you're so pigheaded, you'll tell me anyway, so you might as well go ahead."

Laughing, his dark eyes glittering with amusement, Nick brushed an imaginary speck of lint from his new gray uniform sleeve. He looked so handsome in his lieutenant's garb, with his hat at a rakish tilt and a sword dangling at his side, that for a moment, Jessamy felt a surge of pride instead of the usual choking fear at the thought of war.

Not for her the talk about secession, about states' rights. No, this talk of war, of slavery and abuse and human rights—it hung over everyone's head like a double-edged sword. There were slaves at Clover Hill, yes, but they were not mistreated. They were family members who had been with the Windsors for an entire generation. She could not imagine life without Celine, who wasn't a slave but a servant, or without Dempsey, who had been William's first purchase twenty-three years before. Dempsey was family, not chattel, as was Old Billy, who kept the stables and loved the horses as if they were his very own. He considered the horses his private property, and they were well cared for, including Jessamy's new Barbary mare, a birthday gift from her father in April.

Of course, Jessamy was not foolish enough to think that every Southerner thought of their slaves as the Windsor family did. She'd heard the horror stories often enough, and knew some of them to actually be true. Rage always filled William Windsor when he saw human beings cowering before other human beings, and though he had, indeed, purchased his slaves, he referred to them as his "people," not his property. They all had letters of freedom in his safe should he die. To be freed now would be dangerous for them, and Windsor knew it. It would only leave them vulnerable to capture and impressment into slavery for someone else.

No, it wasn't a perfect system—far from it. But slavery had existed since the days of the Old Testament, when the Egyptians had enslaved the Jews after a series of battles. Wars had been fought since time began it seemed, just like now.

War. It would destroy them all if they didn't whip those Yankees quickly, and she feared for her father and hotheaded brothers. They had all joined; the minute they'd heard Fort Sumter had been fired on, they had whooped and hollered and shouted about sending the Yankees howling back north in a few days. William Windsor had been more sedate about it, his face unusually grave, but he had accepted a commission in the Confederate Army without hesitation.

Jessamy's throat closed, and she studied Nick's face for a long moment, trying to quell the fears that rose in her.

"Well, what is it you're dying to tell me?" Jessamy prompted when Nick didn't speak. "You're as full of it as a fox in the henhouse!"

"We have an illustrious guest on his way, a guest who hails from the same academy as one of our great leaders, Robert E. Lee."

A slight frown puckered her brow, and Jessamy could not still the quickening of her heart. "West Point? Do you mean that—"

"Our brash Kentucky cousin and his mother are coming for a visit. The first in four years, and I thought you might be interested."

Oh, she was. She definitely was. But there was no way she intended to allow Nick to know just how interested she was by that information. Jessamy gave an elaborate shrug.

"Pooh! Interested in Alex Steele? Now that I'm past the age of playing pranks, I could care less about seeing him again." She ran an idle hand over the smooth wood of the porch column and slanted Nick a glance from beneath the fan of her lashes. He was looking at her with an uplifted brow and an insufferable smile on his lips.

"I don't believe you for a minute, Jess." Nick grinned wickedly. "You're telling a big tale and you know it."

Bridling, Jessamy glared at her older brother, trying to intimidate him. It didn't work exactly as she hoped.

"All I ever cared about was teaching Alex to laugh."

"Philanthropy in one so young?" Nick teased, and she gave another shrug.

"Something like that."

"And why did you care if he laughed or not? He never had much to say when we were children, and I always thought him a rather grim fellow."

"Maybe because you never took the time to know him," Jessamy said, then had to laugh when Nick pointed out that she was contradicting herself. "You're right. But he always intrigued me, I guess because he was so quiet and solemn when we were always so loud and rowdy. It used to make me want to prick him into reaction, *some* kind of reaction, even if he got angry."

"And did you ever manage to do so?"

Ignoring the faint warm flush that stole over

her high cheekbones, Jessamy said as lightly as she could, "I don't think so. He always succeeded in avoiding me."

But there had been a time, she remembered, *when Alex did react, when he did grow angry with me. And he kissed me when I didn't even know why. . . .*

"Aunt Pretense and Maribelle are late arriving this year," Nick said then, switching to a safer subject when he saw the flush on his sister's cheeks. She reminded him of a cat at the moment, with her blue-gray eyes tilted at the corners, and her expression faintly smug.

"Well, with the war going on, the trains aren't that punctual, and it's hard for passengers when troops are using them for transportation," Jessamy said. Her throat ached at the thought of war, and she hoped that it would never reach Clover Hill. War here? In these peaceful green fields with budding clover and bright flowers? What would happen to them all if it did come?

"I heard Mother say that Baltimore was already feeling the bite of war," Nick was saying grimly. "Aunt Pretense and Maribelle may not be able to come this year. The Tennessee legislature authorized the governor to raise a force of fifty-five thousand men on the sixth of this month, and we were one of the last Southern states to do so. I imagine the next step will be Tennessee's secession from the Union."

Jessamy turned blindly toward her brother, her eyes filled with apprehension and her skirts rustling as softly as the wind through the willows. "Nick—oh, Nick, everything is going to change so!"

He smiled at her gently, and put a comforting

hand on her shoulder. "Only for a little while, Jess. Then we'll send those Yankees back home with their tails between their legs!"

Her eyes narrowed thoughtfully. "Do you really think we will, Nick?"

"Sure." He hesitated, then said in a gruff voice, "It may take a little longer than we'd like, but everyone knows that it only takes one Southernor to whip a yardful of Yankees!"

She smiled wryly. "You sound like Bryce!"

Nick grinned at her. "I guess I sound like most twelve-year-old boys right now. But honestly, I do think we'll win this war, Jess. We have to. If we lose . . ." He paused, then said in a strong voice, "We can't lose. It would ruin our entire way of life, and we can't let that happen."

Sighing, Jessamy tugged idly at a stray strand of hair in her eyes. "At least you're not a fire-eater or hothead like Cody Baines."

"Or James and Charles," Nick reminded softly, and she nodded. Their twin siblings had entered the spirit of war with gusto and relish, having their uniforms made at the first announcement of the firing on Fort Sumter. William and Nick had been more reluctant, hoping that war could still be somehow averted, but that had not happened. Loyalty to the South was never in question; it was their loyalty to the United States that caused them both concern and heartache.

"Well," Jessamy said after a moment, "now that war has been declared, I just hope we hurry up and win. I'll have no hard feelings toward the Yankees if they'd just realize that we have states' rights, and should be recognized."

"But they have no intention of recognizing

that, or of losing this war." Nick leaned back against the white column beside his sister. "It's going to be a long, hard fight."

"Not with soldiers like the Windsors and Alex Steele in the Rebel army!" Jessamy said with a laugh, and Nick smiled.

Alexander Steele stood in the front parlor and gripped his brandy snifter tightly in one hand. He had brought his mother to Clover Hill with the intention of leaving her under the care of Abigail Windsor while Huntley was away at war, but now he knew that was impossible. She would be torn apart by dissension.

"But Charity! Can't you make him see reason?" Pretense Mullen gaped at her sister-in-law, while her sister Abigail remained quietly thoughtful. Drawing her stout figure up into a knot of indignation and outrage, Pretense flashed a hot glance at the subject of their argument. Alex did his best to ignore her.

"Pretense," Charity said softly, "Alex is a grown man. He has a right to make his own decisions, his own choices. If I or my family do not agree, that is our choice. I do not believe any human being has a right to force another to do their will. After all, isn't that what this war is all about—the right to make our own choices?"

Pretense rounded on her sister. "Abby, this is your home—aren't you going to say something?"

Laying her needlework in her lap, Abigail let her gaze shift from her angry sister to her sister-in-law, then to Alex, standing tall and stiff by the window. She sighed. It was a most difficult decision.

"While I believe that Charity is correct when she says Alex has a right to make his own decisions," she said slowly, "I must think of my husband and sons, who are now, by right of their decisions, Alex's enemies. Under those circumstances, I feel that life would be very difficult here for anyone who has conflicting beliefs. But I am also a woman who believes strongly in family, and while I cannot agree with Alex, I will defend his right to choose his own way. I will not harbor grudges, only a sincere desire that he, along with William and my sons, survive this grave conflict with no ill effects."

When Pretense opened her mouth and sputtered an angry protest, Abigail interrupted firmly. "While Charity and Alex are guests in my home, I will not tolerate any abuse by other guests!" Pretense shut her mouth with a snap, and swept from the parlor without a backward glance.

Standing, Charity directed a sympathetic glance at Abigail. "I apologize for bringing conflict into your home, Abby. If Alex hadn't insisted upon my coming, I would have stayed in Kentucky."

"You are always welcome in my home, Charity. Your husband is William's brother, and you are family." Abigail did not look at Alex when she spoke, and her meaning was clear.

Alex smiled slightly. He, of course, was not family. And worse than that, he was now the enemy, a hated Yankee. He had chosen to join the "wrong" side, and his decision had been greeted with a mixture of horror and outrage.

Giving a half-bow from the waist, he set his brandy snifter on the small mahogany table by the window and said, "I respect your decision, Aunt Abigail, and I will remove my objectionable presence from your home immediately. I regret any inconvenience or suffering I may have caused you."

Abigail looked distressed. "You do understand, Alex, that I will never refuse you my hospitality when you come here as a family member. I cannot, however, accept you as an enemy of my home and family."

He stepped forward, bent and took one of her hands between his own large palms. "Aunt Abigail, you have always had and always will have, my utmost regard and respect. If fate decrees that we meet again, I only hope that it is as friends and not enemies."

Tears welled in Abigail's eyes, and she gave a mute nod, not quite trusting her voice. Her unlined face puckered with pain, and she swallowed as Alex released her hand and backed out of the now deadly quiet parlor. When he had gone and she could speak again, Abigail said, "Perhaps we should have Delilah serve tea now." Charity nodded silently.

Jessamy, however, did not greet the news with shocked silence as her mother had done. Nor did she eloquently entreat for an explanation as her aunt Pretense had done. No, she was, oddly enough, furiously angry and grief-stricken at the same time.

"I don't believe it," she said flatly when her brother James told her that Alex had joined the Union forces. "You are making that up!"

"I am not." James looked at her closely, his

blue eyes narrowed with indignation. "Why would I make up a tale like that about a relative, even if he isn't blood-related?"

"Because you're jealous of him and always have been."

"Dang it, Jess, why would you say that!" James's young face creased with anger. "Alex told me plainly, and if you don't believe me, you can ask him about it yourself!"

"I would, but Mama insists that Maribelle and I stay up in my room, and I don't know why." Jessamy looked down the long hallway toward the staircase. "I guess it's because of this . . . this misunderstanding."

"It's no misunderstanding. It's fact," James said bluntly. He took a step away from her bedroom door. "I've got to go now. There's a meeting in town, and I'm expected."

Jessamy took a step out into the hall, careful to keep an eye out for her mother or the watchful Celine. "Where's Nick?" she asked. "He'll tell me the truth."

James made a disgusted sound. "He's already gone to the meeting. I'm late, and you don't believe me anyway, so I don't know why I bothered to tell you."

"I don't believe it," Jessamy repeated slowly, softly, as her brother descended the stairs in a series of running leaps. "It can't be true, it just can't!"

She lay awake that night, unable to sleep, tossing and turning until Maribelle muttered a sleepy protest and she got up to sit on the window seat and stare out across the shadowed lawns. Alex a traitor to the South? No, it just could not be so! He wouldn't do that, would he?

She heard the staircase clock then, the mellow tones chiming the hour as they had done every year of her life since she could remember. One, two, three . . .

Jessamy straightened suddenly, her gaze caught by a flicker of movement on the dark lawns that stretched down to the county road. Her breath caught in her throat as she recognized Alex's tall frame. He was walking slowly down the driveway, his shoulders hunched forward as if he were deep in thought. It was the perfect opportunity.

Jessamy hurriedly wrapped a long cotton dressing gown around her body and ran down the stairs, barefooted and careless in her haste. Her footsteps were light across the pebbled driveway, and he heard her coming and half turned to wait.

A faint smile tugged at his mouth as he was reminded of the dusky evening Jessamy had waited for him in the gazebo, and how when she had left, her footsteps were just as light on the pebbled walkway as they were now. Only she wasn't that young, impetuous child anymore, but a young woman. Her body had matured, and her face had lost that round childishness, gaining a sharp beauty that must break at least a dozen hearts a week. Why hadn't she married, he wondered idly as she approached him, her gossamer gown floating about her ankles in the hazy light provided by a full moon. It couldn't be for lack of offers. Jessamy paused in front of him at last, her hair wild and untamed about her shoulders, golden and thick and tempting a man to reach out and touch it. He resisted by sticking his hands even deeper into his trouser pockets.

"Is it true?" She confronted Alex boldly, gazing up at him in the dim light. "Is it true that you're a traitor?"

Alex smiled slightly. "I don't think of it that way, but if you listen to your brothers or aunt, I suppose that I shall have to say yes."

"I don't believe it."

"Why not?"

"Because no one I know, not even you, would sink so low as to join the Yankee army!"

"Are there never any areas of gray in your view of life, Jess?" he asked mildly. "Is there only right and wrong, and no in-between?"

"Do you think you're right?"

"If I didn't, I would not do it."

She paused, searching his face, the angles and planes highlighted by the moon's silvery light, and her throat ached. He was so handsome, so familiar, and she wondered why she had never understood him. Maybe it was too hard to understand someone you only saw once a year, and it had been four years since she'd seen him anyway.

"Did you really ruin a girl in New York?" she heard herself ask next, then flushed at her boldness. She was chagrined when Alex only grinned down at her.

"Is that on an equal level with treason?" he mocked.

"That depends on your answer."

"Jess, Jess, never a predictable moment with you!" He couldn't help it. He had to touch her, to run his fingers over her smooth, soft rose-petal skin, and feel the wealth of her golden hair in his palm.

Jessamy shivered at his touch, at the brief brushing of his fingers over her cheek, and the warmth of his hand on her nape when he lifted her hair from her neck. Her fingers curled around his wrist, not in protest, but in a brief, convulsive acknowledgment of his touch, then she moved away.

"We're enemies," she stated softly, her words floating through night air rife with the scent of honeysuckle and clover. "We can never be friends again."

"Because you don't like my choice of armies?" Alex asked her. "That's not a good reason."

Her eyes flashed. "No, because you're a traitor! You can't really believe that the South is wrong, Alex, you just can't!"

"It's not that I believe the South is wrong, Jess, it's that I believe that the Union is right. We can't split our country in two, it would be foolish and self-destructive. Why, they can't win! The North has all the factories for making ammunition and supplies, while all the South has is courage and cotton. It has to end disastrously before long. Only, most Southerners are too hot-headed and impetuous to see beyond the ends of their noses—"

"Like my father and brothers, you mean?" Jessamy's eyes flashed dangerously, and Alex realized he'd gone too far. He sighed.

"Your father and brothers are loyal, and I admire that," he said carefully. "But I think their efforts will be futile in the end."

"Oh, and of course the great Alexander Steele

is right and his cause just!" Jessamy stomped her foot in anger, and the sheer fabric of her gown rippled around her long, slender legs, attracting Alex's attention. That angered her even more, and he noticed. A slow, searing smile curved his sensual mouth, and Jessamy's heart skipped a beat in spite of her fury.

"Right," he said softly, his voice husky and making her shiver down to her toes.

"I hate you, Alex Steele!" she spat helplessly, trying to hide the quiver of her nerves, the anticipation that curled through her body at his steady gaze of appreciation. "I shall never, never forgive you! And I shall never speak to you again! Never!"

"You're not a little girl anymore, you know. Never say never, Jess," Alex replied huskily, and before she could move, he had reached out to pull her to him, his lips moving urgently over her mouth in a searing kiss that stole her breath and made her heart hammer loudly in her chest. When he released her, abruptly, his dark eyes burning into her pale face, Jessamy whirled around and fled back up the pebbled driveway to the house. He could hear the slight echo of the door's closing, and nodded. "Never may come one day," he murmured to himself.

But Jessamy, who watched him ride away with his mother the following morning, knew that never was a finality, not a maybe. She could never dream about Alex again, never try to make him laugh or invent another joke to play on him. It was over now, the playful times when life had been much simpler. She would not think about him again. She would throw herself into the Cause, the Confederate Cause that involved everyone she knew.

And she did become involved, her time consumed with the making of bandages for the war, to her a horrible pastime.

"Think about it, Belle," she muttered to her cousin one day as they stood in the parlor rolling clean strips of linen. "These have a horrible purpose."

"It would be even more horrible if our boys needed them and didn't have them," Maribelle said with a calm logic that was maddening to Jessamy.

"I suppose so." Sighing heavily, she wiped a hand across her forehead and tossed the last rolled strip of linen into the box that would be shipped to the soldiers. "I'm through for the day."

Maribelle looked up at her, and pushed aside a lank wisp of hair that was damp with humidity. Even in early summer it was already hot and humid. The afternoon rains cooled things off just enough to bear it, and she looked past Jessamy to the open window.

"It's still early. We could wrap another half-box full if we kept on rolling."

"If I keep standing here, I'll go mad with boredom!" Impatient with the task and her disordered thoughts, Jessamy moved to the open window and let a cool breeze blow across her flushed face. "Let's go for a ride, Belle, do you want to? I haven't ridden Sultana in so long, and she must be as fresh as a new-laid egg. Come on," she coaxed, "I'll saddle the horses."

"I thought Aunt Abby said we shouldn't ride out anymore since the Yankees have been seen this far south."

"Oh, pooh! That was a ragtag band of men claiming to be Yankees until they found out they'd been captured by our men. Then they changed their tune quick enough. Besides, no Yankee will get this far south. Our boys won't let them," Jessamy said with firm conviction.

"But the border states have declared for the Union, I heard my brother Neal say," Maribelle replied slowly. "A Unionist government has been set up for Virginia in Wheeling, and Maryland is now a Union state. Which is why we're here with you, of course," Maribelle added sadly. "In Kentucky and Missouri, Union sentiments may be equal to Confederate sympathies, but their governors cannot seem to get their commonwealths into the Confederacy in spite of their refusal to obey President Lincoln's requests for militia."

Jessamy glared at her. "Aren't you the little voice of doom! You listen to your brother too much, and everyone knows that Neal has always been solemn and bookish, too solemn for his own good, I say!"

"At least he was accepted by a university!"

Somewhat surprised by her quiet cousin's unusual flash of temper, Jessamy said, "Why, yes, he was, but so were my brothers." She smiled suddenly. "Only none of them could manage to *remain* accepted!"

Smiling back, Maribelle said, "Well, everyone

knows that the twins and Nicholas are brave and will make good soldiers."

"And Neal is in the Home Guard," Jessamy offered as a peace gesture. Maribelle smiled gratefully.

The clock on the mantel ticked loudly as the young women rested in the cooling breezes coming through the window. They fanned themselves with paper fans and thought their own private thoughts. War was on everyone's mind these days, intruding into every facet of their lives.

"Any word yet?" Maribelle asked moments later, and Jessamy shook her head gravely.

"None. All we know is that the Ninth Tennessee is fighting at a little place in Virginia near Manassas, and that there's fearful casualties rumored."

"Aunt Abby is bearing up well, I think."

"Mother has always been strong. I wish I could be like her," Jessamy said softly. Didn't her mother ever have doubts and fears? She did, and at night, when she lay in her bed alone with the mosquito netting drifting around her in gauzy folds and the shadows lurking in the corners, she thought of her father and brothers. Were they all alive? No word had come, and the waiting was endless.

And sometimes, unbidden in the night, the memory of Alex Steele would haunt her, his dark eyes and sensual lips and the brief kiss that had burned into her mouth and never been forgotten.

Never. She'd thought it would be easy to forget the betrayal she'd suffered at his hands. After all, life would never be the same, would it? And she'd never see Alex again. He would never have the nerve to come back to Clover Hill, not after what he'd said and what she'd said. Never in a blue moon, would he return. . . .

Chapter 5

"ANY NEWS?" Jessamy asked Obadiah Johnston, the Clover Hill overseer. William had left him behind to watch over the women, the house and fields, a formidable task.

Johnston shook his head. His pale skin had been burned a reddish-brown years before, but he still flushed every time he was spoken to by one of his employer's "wimmin folks."

"No'm, Miss Jessamy," he said. "Not yet. All's I know is, the Yankees say the battle of Bull Run —that's what they're callin' Manassas—is over with. I heered that th' Yanks broke and run like skeered rabbits when our boys give out with th' Rebel yell. But I ain' heered yet 'bout Mister Windsor or th' boys."

Jessamy's brow furrowed with worry. "Do you think they are all right, Obadiah? Would we have heard yet if they aren't? You can tell me if you know. I know that you hear things before we do, sometimes even before the papers find out."

Flushing even redder, Johnston hesitated, then said in a slow voice, "Miss Jessamy, war is powerful strange. One man can be hit by a ball, while the man next to him is left standin' thar untouched. I cain't say 'bout Mister Windsor and the boys, but I do know that the Confed'rates won that battle. That's all I know."

Jessamy sighed. "I suppose you're right, Obadiah. I'll just have to wait until we hear. At least the telegraph lines are still working, and newspaper reports are fairly accurate, if a bit slow. It just seems to take so long."

"Yes'm, that's right. But even an hour is a long time when it concerns somebody you care about."

A smile curved her mouth, and Jessamy nodded. "That's very true. I think I'll go and wait with Mother. She must be even more anxious than I."

"I'll let you know th' minute I heer somethin', Miss Jessamy," Johnston called after her as she went back into the house.

Jessamy gazed at her mother for a long moment, wondering how Abigail could seem so outwardly serene when their entire world was in danger.

"Hold up your hands, Jessamy," Abigail said softly, and Jessamy obeyed, allowing her mother to wind a skein of yarn from one hand to the other. Abigail was constantly in motion, knitting socks or rolling bandages, or sewing new uniforms for "our brave boys." She never seemed to rest, even at night. Jessamy frequently heard her soft steps in the hallway, and the muted mutter of voices in the night. Celine had told her that Miss Abigail was trying to attend to the business matters of the farm as well as their war efforts, and that Jessamy should do everything possible to ease her mother's burden.

Swallowing some of the guilt she felt at her own selfishness, Jessamy asked, "Do you think we'll hear from Papa soon?"

"As soon as he is able to write us, he will." Abigail gracefully wound another loop of gray yarn around Jessamy's hands. "Neither his name, nor your brothers' names, was on the lists the paper printed. I'm convinced that God has kept him safe for us, and that he is finding it difficult to get word to us."

"Then he might be captured!" Jessamy blurted out, then wished she hadn't. Abigail smiled up at her.

"No, or we would know that. The lines of communication are not swift and certain in wartime, dear. He might have written and the letter gone astray. It happens."

"But I don't know why it has to happen to Papa," Jessamy muttered resentfully.

"I'm certain that every daughter, and every mother, and every sister, feels the same way you do." Abigail's voice was slightly reproaching, and Jessamy sighed.

"I suppose you're right, but it does seem that we have been singled out for misfortune lately, doesn't it to you, Mother?"

"We have our health, and we have our home, and we have food to eat and clothes to wear. No, I cannot agree." A soft smile curved her lips again as Abigail said gently, "I know how hard it is for you to accept trials, dear. You've always had trouble with being patient. But you're nineteen now, and a grown young woman."

The implication was that Jessamy was old enough to accept the realities of life, and she sighed. It was true. Even if she had never married, never wanted to marry, she was past the first flush of womanhood. In another year or two, she would be considered an old maid by the standards of the county. Even Maribelle was engaged now, to Stuart Armstrong, a bashful young man from Hardeman County.

She could feel her mother's gaze resting on her, and looked up. "I may have to accept it, but I don't have to like it, do I?"

Abigail laughed. "No, I don't suppose you do!"

If it was an anxious time for Jessamy and her mother, it was even more so for young Bryce, Jessamy's twelve-year-old brother. No one wanted to cloud his young mind with dark thoughts, so mention of mortal danger was not allowed in his presence. Celine stood firm in guarding him from the oftimes brutal truth about the realities of war.

Yet young Bryce knew differently, and he resented being treated as an ignorant child. He besieged Jessamy with questions until she finally took pity on him.

His thin face was tight with anxiety when he confronted Jessamy at the back door, and his voice strident.

"I want to know the truth, Jess! Papa isn't just gone off to trade a few shots with the Yanks, is he? He's in danger, and I know it!"

"Oh, Bryce, I don't know why you want to know all the details, but if you'll just stop pestering me, I'll tell you the little I know about it!"

Folding her legs, she spread her skirts, sank wearily to the hard comfort of the back stoop, and stared at him in irritation. Bryce's fair hair fell over one eye, and he pushed it back as he waited with ill-concealed impatience. That a mere girl should know more than he!

"Then what, Jess? I heard from Winston Cleaver that there was a battle, and that Papa was in danger."

Jessamy's irritation evaporated in the face of his pain and worry. She felt a surge of affection for the thin boy who was staring at her so steadily, and managed a soothing smile. "There is danger anytime there is a battle, Bryce."

"But I thought Papa was not in the middle of the fighting! And I thought that Yankees weren't supposed to be able to hit a barn with a stick, much less what they were aiming at with a rifle!"

"I wish that were true." She reached out to grab his wrists, pulling him down to the stoop beside her. "We should have told you the truth, I guess. Sometimes the imagination conjures up things a lot worse than the truth." Pausing, she saw from his wide blue eyes that she was right, and her voice was soft and kind as she said, "Yes, they're in danger, Bryce. But we must pray that they will be safe, and come home to us soon. There is little else to do but wait for word of them."

Bryce's face paled, and he gave a tight nod as he rose and went back into the house. For a moment Jessamy wished she had not told him, then consoled herself with the assurance that he had to know sometime. It looked as if the war would drag on much longer than anyone had thought, and Celine and Abigail could not keep Bryce away from the newspapers and knowledgeable peers for much longer. It was inevitable that he know, and he might as well know from her.

"Well," she told Maribelle later, "he had to know! And it's not as if we've got Yankees on our doorstep or anything like that, for heaven's sake!"

Maribelle shuddered, and stared at her cousin in the soft lamplight. They were in Jessamy's bedroom, and the tall windows had been swung open to allow in cooling breezes. It was late July, and the air was hot and muggy. Maribelle wished again that she could go home, and didn't understand why her father remained in Maryland if it was so much safer here in this remote area of Tennessee instead of Baltimore where the Yankees roamed the streets at will. She worried about him as the war escalated.

News reports had boasted of the recent Confederate victory in Missouri. The Confederacy badly needed Missouri, and a Rebel force of Texans, Louisianians, Arkansans, and Missourians advanced on Springfield. Eleven thousand of them were under the leadership of one Major General Sterling Price, who had deferred the command to Brigadier General Ben McCulloch of Texas. Fifty-four hundred Union soldiers under General Nathaniel Lyon marched under cover of darkness to surprise the Rebels camped at Wilson's Creek ten miles southwest of Springfield.

Five hours and twenty-five hundred casualties later, the battle ended with General Lyon dead and the Federals retreating. It was another

Southern victory, but Missouri remained within the Union.

War haunted the days and nights of those waiting women. War had come to the tiny hamlet of Wilson Creek—could it come to Cloverport or even Clover Hill?

Crinolines rustled as Maribelle leaned forward and whispered, "But do you think the Yankees will come here, Jess? To Clover Hill, I mean?"

Jessamy stared at her as if she had just suggested they run naked through the town. "Don't be a goose, Maribelle! Of course the Yankees won't come here! Why should they? There's nothing in Cloverport or at Clover Hill to interest them. It's not as if we're an important town, or a seaport, or have huge warehouses filled with ammunition and supplies!"

"But neither was Manassas," Maribelle pointed out, and Jessamy fell silent.

"Well," she said after a moment, "they still won't come here."

September arrived in a fierce spate of rain and wind that scoured the black earth and filled the creeks and rivers to overflowing. It rained for six days straight, and Jessamy thought she would go mad before it stopped. Had the sun completely disappeared? Would it ever shine again and dry out the roads? Even the house smelled musty, and everyone crept around like shadows.

Fretful at the forced inactivity, Jessamy ranged like a caged beast from room to room.

The only bright spots in her days were the letters the family had finally received from William Windsor. They were all fine, he'd written, except for being wet and miserable. But no one had ever said war was comfortable.

Hugging her arms around her body, Jessamy gazed out the kitchen window at the wet green lawns, restless and filled with an energy she couldn't channel into sewing or rolling bandages. No, she had to get out of the house, had to get away from the pall of war and worry that hung over them all before she went crazy.

Turning abruptly, she mounted the stairs to her bedroom and jerked her riding habit out of the wardrobe. A good ride across the fields would clear her head and release her pent-up energy and anxiety.

Celine quickly put an end to that. "Your *maman* would be frantic with worry! I cannot allow you to do that!"

"It's only a ride, Celine," Jessamy began patiently, but the Creole would not hear of it.

"Non, non! There is too much danger!"

"All right, all right!" Jessamy snapped. "I don't need to hear any more, Celine. I'll stay in, but if I die of boredom, it's all your fault!"

Celine nodded. *"Bon!* I'm willing to risk it."

Frustrated and irritable, Jessamy smoldered. "I'll bet you are! I suppose you think it's just dandy that we sit around here all day every day with nothing to do but stare at the four walls."

"There's plenty to do if you choose to do it," Celine said calmly. "I find no lack of activity, and neither does your *petite cousine.* She does not complain about sewing uniforms or knitting socks, and even her small sisters help to roll bandages for the soldiers." She tilted her head to one side and stared keenly at Jessamy. "I think you are fighting your own battles on the inside, no?"

"No!" Jessamy said with a flash of ill temper. Then she flushed, realizing how immature she sounded. "I sound just like Carrie Sue or Sarah Jean, don't I?" she asked ruefully and Celine smiled.

"Yes, you do. But they are only six, and can be excused for bad manners, while you should know better."

"Oh, I know it, Celine, but at least the twins have the comfort of being too young to realize all the true horrors of what is happening."

"And because your little cousins are young, you think they are lucky, no?"

As Celine stared at her closely, Jessamy had the dismaying thought that everyone had to grow up. She had grown up when she hadn't even realized time was passing so quickly. So had Maribelle, and the Mullen twins would have to do the same. It was inevitable.

"Well, maybe not," she conceded. "It wasn't too long ago that Maribelle and I were the same age. Even Bryce is out of the nursery now."

"So, what will you do?"

A faint smile curved her mouth as Jessamy surrendered. "Roll bandages."

Celine gave a solemn nod as if she had expected no less from Jessamy. "They're all in the front parlor, as usual. Even the twins. I am sure they'll be glad to see you."

"I'm sure they will," Jessamy muttered with a sigh.

While rolling strips of clean linen into bandages, Jessamy stared out the parlor windows at the rain-swept lawn. Red buds of clover were sparse and soaked with rain, and the road beyond the grounds was a mire of mud. She thought then of her father and brothers, and wondered if they were forced to march in the rain, or were sitting somewhere with the rain dripping down on their heads. Or if they were still alive. . . .

She bit her bottom lip, and flipped the clean swathe of linen she was holding into a bin. Best not to think of that right now. She had too much time to think, too much time to worry, and she wished suddenly that her cousin would say something distracting, anything to keep her mind from wandering. Even the six-year-old twins, Sarah Jean and Carrie Sue, were dutifully rolling bandages in silence like their older sister.

Jessamy glanced over at her, noting Maribelle's solemn expression as she neatly rolled bandages. It irritated her that Maribelle could appear so completely absorbed in such a mundane task as rolling strips of linen, but she shook it off.

"Maribelle, didn't you say that you got a letter from Stuart Armstrong?" Jessamy asked brightly, forcing her attention from the rain to her cousin.

Maribelle looked up with a pleased smile, glad to have Jessamy's attention. Her cousin had been so moody lately, pacing the floor and grumbling, that she had not dared speak most of the time. Perhaps Jessamy was finally growing accustomed to remaining in the house instead of rambling about outside at will.

"I didn't think you were listening, Jess! Yes, I got a letter from Stuart. He and his brother Robbie are over in Memphis right now."

"Memphis! Why, that's only seventy miles from here."

Maribelle nodded. "I know. Stuart wrote that he might get to come home for a few days if his commander, Colonel Forrest, will allow it."

"Colonel Forrest? Isn't he the wily old coot who's got all the Yankees stirred up like a fox in the henhouse?"

When Maribelle nodded confirmation, Jessamy's lips turned up in a pleased smile. "Good! As smart as he is, there ought not to be much danger to Robbie and Stuart. I mean, Forrest is said to strike quick as a cottonmouth, then slither off into the underbrush without a trace. I heard as how the Yankees are swearing and cussing him for being a lot smarter than they are."

"You heard right," Maribelle said. "Stuart said in his letter that Forrest is the next thing to God as far as he's concerned, because he doesn't risk his men needlessly, and he always seems to get them out of trouble."

Jessamy rolled the last strip of linen and stuffed it into the box to be shipped to wounded men. For a brief instant she wondered about the men who might need one of the bandages she had rolled, and tried to visualize a weary blood-stained soldier wearing something she had created for him. It gave her a start, and she shivered.

"Let's hope Forrest keeps it up," she said to Maribelle.

Maribelle's round face was earnest and eager,

and there was the sheen of ardor in her brown eyes. "Oh, I do, I do! I hope he hounds those Yankees right back up North where they belong."

"I hardly think he'll manage that on his own, though it'd be a lot more convenient if he would," Jessamy observed with a tart edge to her voice. "I'm already sick and tired of this wretched war, and it's only been just over four months since Fort Sumter fell."

"Well, it should be over soon," Maribelle consoled her. "Stuart thinks that it won't be any time before the Yankees get tired and just go home."

"Since when did you become so knowledgeable about the war?" Jessamy couldn't help asking with an amused smile. "It seems to me that since you got engaged to Stuart Armstrong that's all you've been thinking about!"

Maribelle blushed, her fair skin suffused with a bright pink color from her neck to her eyebrows. "You can say the meanest things!"

"Mean? What's mean about marrying Stuart? I think it's about time you started liking something besides your silly needlework," Jessamy said. "Besides, I was only funning you and you know it."

Maribelle's embarrassment passed quickly. "Oh, I guess you're right, Jess. It's just that I feel . . . funny . . . sometimes when I think about Stuart. Do you know what I mean?"

"No. I have no idea," Jessamy lied without a qualm. She was unwillingly reminded of Alex Steele for some reason, and she could not imagine why. It certainly wasn't because she was attracted to him, or had the same feelings for him that Maribelle had for Stuart, for heaven's sake!

Maybe it was just that he had managed to make her forget her vow never to think of him again, not once in a blue never. Yet she thought of him a lot, always remembering the feel of his mouth on hers, and the glitter in his dark eyes when he had looked at her in the moonlight the last night she'd seen him. She gave another shiver, and didn't know why.

Chapter 6

THE RAIN HAD FINALLY STOPPED, leaving only a fresh cool scent behind to herald its passing. The sun shone across Clover Hill again, bright and golden, sparkling in lingering raindrops that clung to leaves and grass.

But with the September sun came an unexpected danger early that morning—Yankees.

At the sight of the sun Jessamy's spirits had lifted, and as soon as breakfast was over she went outside on the wide front porch with Maribelle and Bryce. The world looked scrubbed clean, and when the sun had dried the roads from their implacable muck to a surface that wouldn't suck at her mare's hooves, she intended to go riding. It was a good way to work off the restlessness that had inhabited her spirits lately.

Spreading her sprigged muslin skirt in a perfect circle as she sat on the wicker settee with Maribelle, Jessamy gazed out over the green lawns. Now that the rain was over, she could regard life with optimism, and her eyes sparkled.

Celine had brushed her hair that morning, absently scolding her for neglecting that duty, and the pale tresses gleamed like newly minted gold. In spite of the humidity, she looked as cool and fresh as the clover springing back up from the wet earth. And she felt even fresher. Impatient for the soggy ground to hurry and dry enough for her to ride, she gave a long sigh.

"What's th' matter?" Maribelle asked languidly, fanning herself with a French fan from New Orleans. It stirred up a slight breeze that reached Jessamy.

"I'm pure-dee bored, Maribelle. It's been days since I've done anything but roll bandages or play whist with Bryce, and I'm sick of sitting here. Aren't you?"

Maribelle's eyes widened slightly with surprise. It had never occurred to her to be bored. After all, her hours were filled with activity, even if it wasn't the whirlwind of activity that usually filled Jessamy's hours. Sewing and listening to her mother's chatter was enough for Maribelle. Her hours passed with serenity and peace, and she had no desire to throw herself into something that might cause her hair to muss or her skirts to wrinkle. Or interfere with thoughts of Stuart.

"No," Jessamy answered her own question, "I suppose you're not. One of these days I suspect you will turn into a porcelain statue, Maribelle, and it will be days before anyone notices."

Maribelle's brow knitted in perplexity before she recalled that a young lady should never purposely abuse her face with expression. It would cause wrinkles. That was how her aunt Abigail had retained such a smooth, unlined face all these years—by refusing to become flustered or allow any calamity to mar her features.

Only Maribelle's voice showed her indignation. "I suppose you think it's best to run about like a hoyden? Mama says that you were always a tomboy, and that you will never truly be a lady until you become more genteel."

"Is that so?" Jessamy glared at her cousin with irritation. "I hardly think much of the opinion of a woman who chatters incessantly and can't talk without chirping!"

When Maribelle gasped, Bryce saw the way the conversation would end if he didn't intervene.

"You two sound like a couple of squallin' cats," he remarked. "Isn't there enough fightin' without you all bein' so argumental?"

Jessamy and Maribelle rounded on him, glaring. It was one thing to fuss with a female cousin. It was completely another to be reprimanded by a younger brother!

Bryce grinned, not at all abashed by their combined anger. "See? Wait till the Yankees get here to fight—"

"Yankees!" came the wailing cry, startling the three on the porch into sudden silence. "Yankees!" sounded again, and they turned to stare down the curving drive.

It was Old Billy, and he was running as if all the hounds of hell were after him. His ebony face was gray with effort, and his skinny legs pumped furiously as he propelled himself up the drive. Jessamy recovered first.

Leaping up, she lifted her skirts with both

hands and stepped lightly down the wide steps to meet Old Billy on the lawn. Her heart was pounding, and her mouth was dry with a sudden, cold fear.

"What is it?" she demanded when he reached her, his chest heaving with effort.

"Yankees!"

The chilling word hung in the air for a moment, and Jessamy could barely comprehend what it must mean. It was ludicrous that Yankees should be so close to Clover Hill, simply impossible. Why, there were no men there to protect them, and . . .

Whirling about to face the frozen Maribelle and Bryce, Jessamy ordered swiftly, "Fetch Mother! Hurry, you gooses, before I slap your silly faces!"

Abigail would know what to do, but right now Jessamy felt she should ask some kind of questions. "What else, Old Billy? Did you see them? Are they near here? How many?"

The old man was stumbling over his words in his fright, and it never occurred to Jessamy to ask what he had been doing down by the crossroads. Not then.

Abigail Windsor was not at all flustered by the news that Yankees were approaching. She had already prepared for such an unlikely event. Unexpected emergencies were Abigail Windsor's forte, and she would handle this with the same aplomb that she handled cuts and broken bones.

"Hide the valuables where I told you, Moses. Celine, gather the others and go to your places. You remember where I told you. Old Billy, take all able-bodied men and as many of the stock as you can quickly gather and go down to the shacks by the swamp. You recall the hunting blinds? That is where you shall hide until the Yankees have gone. We will send someone for you when you are all safe from impressment into their army."

Relief showed in Old Billy's dark face, and he bobbed his head. "Yas'm, Miss Abigail. Ah knowed you'd tek keer o' things. Ah knowed it."

"Then go swiftly," Abigail ordered as she turned to see to other tasks. Old Billy departed toward the neat, whitewashed slave cabins while Celine and the others hid the silver and other valuables behind a secret panel. Every house had one, and Clover Hill was no exception.

Jessamy struggled for control of the fear that was so strong it was almost incapacitating. She must regain control of herself! The past months had been hard enough, provoking her into childish tantrums at some times, and fits of despair at others, but now with the danger of the enemy arriving on their doorstep, she could not allow herself the luxury of giving in to her moods.

Aunt Pretense was having nervous fits, and Jessamy remarked calmly, "She'll have a complete rigor if she finds out that Mother intends to talk to the Yankees."

"Talk to Yankees!" Maribelle stared at her cousin. One never talked to Yankees. Why, even though she hadn't met any, she knew that one just didn't talk to them! They were rude, crude people with a brash way of talking, and their nasal voices offended the ears. And they talked so quickly that no one could understand them, especially someone more accustomed to the soft, drawling Tennessee voices. But that was all hearsay to Maribelle, who had never been confronted with such a horror.

"I don't believe it," Maribelle said flatly. "No lady of breeding would stoop to speak to Yankees!"

"What do you expect her to do—write them notes asking them what they want?" Jessamy shot back.

They were upstairs in the bedroom with the younger children, where Celine had sent them for safety. Who knew what those dreadful Yankees might do to pure Southern women? It was said that they had abused more than a few during the past months, and horror stories that the girls weren't supposed to hear but did anyway came back to mind now. There had been the mountain girl in East Tennessee who had been ravished repeatedly and left to die, and there had been . . . but not now. Now was certainly not the time to think of those things. She had to think instead of protecting her mother as best she could. As the oldest Windsor child left at Clover Hill, she had a duty to perform.

That was why, when Jessamy heard the muffled clatter of hooves on the front lawn, she could not stay hidden in the upstairs bedroom. She had to know what was happening. But when she peeked out the window, Maribelle moaned dreadfully and told her not to disobey.

"Don't be a ninny!" Jessamy hissed. "Do you think I'm going to call out to them? Be still and stop that silly blubbering before I slap some sense into you. . . ."

Startled into silence by Jessamy's harsh words

and tone, Maribelle's sniffs subsided enough for
the exchange downstairs to be heard.

"Good day, madam," came the clipped words
from the blue-coated man riding at the head of
a large band of Union soldiers. His back was
ramrod straight, and his youngish face was
creased into a stern expression of self-impor-
tance. He said, "I am Captain Nelson, of General James Foote's command."

"Good morning, Captain," came Abigail's
unruffled, cool voice. She said nothing else, obviously waiting for the Union captain to state
his business.

Jessamy peeked over the windowsill, and
gasped at the sight of the mounted soldiers.
There were so many of them! Sunlight glittered
from bluish rifle barrels and the hilts of
sheathed swords, and she felt a wave of indignation. How dare they come to Clover Hill! How
dare they ride their horses across the smooth
lawn, cutting it to muddy pieces?

"Madam," Captain Nelson was saying, "we
have orders to appropriate your home for the
use of the United States, and we order you to
render yourselves and your goods to the benefit
of the Union."

Jessamy felt a hot wave of anger. Appropriate
Clover Hill? Not in a million years! Not as long
as she had breath in her body would Yankees
defile her home with muddy boots and nasal
twangs!

Forgetting her promise to remain out of sight,
Jessamy fled out of her room and down the
stairs, ignoring Maribelle's pleas to stop. Fury
rose in her as hot and wild as a summer storm,
and when she burst through the doors and out

77

onto the porch, her face was flushed and her eyes snapped with hot blue sparks.

Abigail had acceded to the captain's demands with quiet dignity, recognizing the futility of argument and hoping that such a concession would save her home from being abused or destroyed. Pretense had gasped and fainted, and the Union captain had leaped from his mount to assist Abigail. His efforts were waved away by Celine, a staunch protectress with the eyes of a tigress.

"Canaille! Do not touch her! No Yankee will soil Miss Pretense while I am here!"

"Celine," Abigail said softly, "go into the house and fetch the vinaigrette, please. Captain Nelson can pull up the settee for Pretense."

Though her narrow face was creased with righteous indignation and dislike, Celine would not argue with Miss Abigail. She never had, and she would not begin now, even though her disapproval was written all over her face.

Jessamy pushed past Celine at the door, and burst onto the wide veranda. "Don't you touch her!" she spat, startling the captain who had dragged over the settee. "I swear I'll . . . I'll shoot you if you try!"

After his rapid glance assured him that this fiery threat held no weapon, the captain smiled in amusement. The girl looked like an avenging Fury, arrayed in wrath and sprigged muslin. These Southerners were a hotheaded lot, he mused as he shoved the settee forward.

Abigail was momentarily nonplussed by her daughter's appearance, and gave a soft sigh of endurance as she felt Pretense begin to stir in her arms. "Jessamy, help me with your aunt," she said in the same cool tone she always used.

But Jessamy—for the first time in her life—deliberately disobeyed a direct command from her mother. She stood her ground, glaring at the Union captain with hatred.

"Get off our property! You have no right here!"

Drawing himself up, the captain met her glare. "I have more right than you at this time, miss. I have the entire United States government behind me."

"And I have God and right behind me!" Jessamy shot back at him.

"God always seems to favor the victors, which lessens your claim a great deal," the captain returned tightly. He looked back at Abigail. "Madam, I suggest you teach this young lady the proper role of the vanquished, or she might be put out a great deal in the next few weeks!"

Abigail straightened, letting Pretense rest against the settee. "Captain, I yield to your demands for occupation, but I do not need your suggestions on how to educate my daughter. Now, if you will be so kind as to allow us to gather up our family members and a few belongings, we shall not remain in your way."

As usual, Abigail's cool dignity defused the situation. The captain, smarting from her rebuke, nodded stiffly and stepped back to his mount.

Tears welled in Jessamy's eyes, and she turned to her mother. "You can't just let them do this!"

"Do you suggest we exchange fire?" Abigail asked. "I cannot imagine how you think we can defend ourselves other than with outward compliance. Now, quietly, help me with Pretense before she wakens and becomes flustered again."

Obadiah Johnston vacated his cabin, and Abigail, Pretense, Maribelle, Jessamy, Bryce, Sarah Jean, Carrie Sue, and Celine moved in. It was crowded. The three-room house was hardly big enough for Obadiah Johnston, much less eight people. But it would have to do. The Yankees inhabited the big house.

The two youngest children were bewildered by the move, and could not understand why they now slept on pallets on the floor. But that was their biggest worry, and Jessamy envied them.

She stood on the rude porch in front of the overseer's cabin and gazed up the hill with hot, resentful eyes. Hate for the Yankees burned in her heart as she saw the cut-up lawns of Clover Hill, lawns that had been smooth and green but were now rutted, dried tracks. The fowl that usually clucked and clacked over the lawns had mostly been eaten by the hungry Union troops, and only a few of the scrawniest still ranged in comparative freedom. What pigs and cattle that had not been hidden—and those were few—had graced the long, elegant dining table in the house. The gardens, heavy with ripe vegetables, were barren now. Even the orchards had been plucked clean, leaving little for those living in the overseer's cabin. Blue uniforms speckled the gracious halls of Clover Hill like blueflies. They had even taken the women's jewelry, including the birthstone ring Jessamy had received on her sixteenth birthday.

"Hush," Abigail said when Jessamy loudly proclaimed her hatred. "It does no good, except to make them laugh at us. Hold up your head and hold your tongue. Don't let them know how you feel."

That was hard for Jessamy to do. She wanted to let them know how she hated them, how much contempt she held for them all. They were crass, boorish men, with no manners and no finesse. Accustomed to the courteous, soft manners of the boys she'd grown up with, Jessamy curled her lip each time one of the soldiers dared address her. Her contempt did not endear her to them.

"Hullo, fire-eater," one of the lanky soldiers called to her one afternoon when Jessamy had gone to the well to draw up a bucket of water. She ignored him, with her nose in the air and her chin stubbornly set. Abigail and Celine had cautioned her against speaking to the soldiers, and had attempted to keep Maribelle and Jessamy inside as much as possible. If not for the fact that it was nap time and she was thirsty, Jessamy would be inside the hot, muggy cabin with the others. The inactivity was just as stifling as the heat, and she had crept from the cabin to fetch some cool water to drink.

"Let me pass," she said coldly when the soldier stood in her path.

"Too good to speak to a soldier?" the man taunted. His hand flashed out to grasp her by the arm, and his fetid breath fanned across her cheek.

Jessamy turned her head, swinging her other

arm up at the same time, bringing the bucket full force against the soldier's head. It was a reflex action, without thought, and when the man swore and dropped her arm, she fled.

Her long skirts tangled around her legs, slowing her flight. The Union soldier caught her easily, swinging her around to face him. He held tightly to her arm and dragged her close, lifting her to her toes. His features creased in a furious scowl.

"Here now! What the hell do you think you're doing, assaulting a Union soldier? You could be shot—or worse."

Jessamy could not imagine much that would be worse than being shot, but at the thinning of the soldier's eyes she suddenly realized that he obviously could. A cold lump formed in her throat, and she tried to jerk away. He held her fast, and Jessamy resorted to a trick she had always used with her brothers.

Dropping to the ground as a dead weight, she jerked the surprised soldier with her. As he tried to catch himself her knee came up, aiming for his vulnerable stomach.

This man was tall and lanky, and her aim was off. Her knee caught him in his groin, and he gasped in pained surprise. He also released her arm, which was all that Jessamy really wanted. Scrambling to her feet, she lunged forward, only to meet with an implacable blue-clad chest.

The world was reeling by in a blur, and at first a frightened Jessamy could only feel a new threat. She reacted with wildly swinging fists. A muttered curse hissed in her ears, and as her hands were caught in a bruising grasp she heard, "Be still, Jessamy! It's me—Alex."

Alex? At first she didn't comprehend, only grasped at the offered straw. Alex. It was someone she knew, someone who knew her well enough to call her by her Christian name.

Pausing and gulping in air to steady her pounding heart, Jessamy stood trembling and quiet. Alex . . . Alexander Steele. But wasn't he with the Union army? Alex . . . Alex here? Her head jerked back, and she met Alex's amused gaze.

The dark eyes regarded her swift change from fright to anger, and Alex shook his head. "Don't," he said softly. "It will only make things worse."

"As if I care! As if things aren't bad enough already, I have to be . . . be held hostage in my own home by a traitor! Don't you talk to me!"

But Jessamy was grateful that Alex had intervened, and heaved a sigh of relief when he explained to his superior officer that the young lady had been accosted by the enlisted man. She had only been defending herself, and the soldier had acted against strict orders.

Drawn outside by the commotion, Abigail Windsor took her daughter's arm and quietly thanked Captain Steele for his intervention. But Jessamy refused to acknowledge by word or glance that she appreciated his actions. He was, after all, a traitor to the South and she would never forgive him. Never.

She felt his dark eyes resting on her as she stood stiff and silent at her mother's side, refusing to look at him. Her heart lurched, and her throat was so tight that she could feel the ache all the way to her toes. How dare he be so handsome? How dare he be here, at Clover Hill, in the uniform of the enemy? She wouldn't look at him, would not recall the last time she had seen him, when he'd kissed her in the moonlight and made her dreams so disturbing.

Alex watched her straight-backed figure march away at her mother's side, and smiled. He'd known she would feel that way, which was one of the reasons he had remained in the background. It would have only fanned the fires of her wrath to see him at Clover Hill as a conqueror. If not for the soldier's confrontation with her, he might have been able to remain unseen. Now that was impossible. And maybe that wasn't so bad.

Chapter 7

CAPTAIN ALEXANDER STEELE'S COMMAND had been ordered to seize and destroy any harbors of safety or sanction for the Rebels. That included Clover Hill, and he knew it. And he also knew that when the moment came, Jessamy Windsor would never forgive him for the part he played.

Alex was right. It was hard enough for her to forgive him his sympathies. To forgive him his occupation of Clover Hill was impossible.

At night, when the cabin was dark and the only light came from the moon and the campfires dotting the lawns outside rude tents erected for the soldiers, Jessamy lay thinking. She envied Maribelle her untrammeled mind, and the sound sleep that claimed her each night as soon as her head hit the pillow. Though now burdened with tasks once performed by the slaves, and weary to the bone most of the time, Jessamy still found enough energy to hate.

She had two dresses, and only two sets of undergarments. The Yankees had not allowed enough time to choose much clothing from the house, but had hurried them out as if afraid they might seize contraband. There had been time to grab a few things of her father's, and some articles for her brothers as well as a change of garments for herself, but other than that, everything was left behind. It made her heart burn, and she frequently found her hands clenched into tight fists without even realizing it. It was just a natural reflex, a reaction to the presence of the invaders.

Days drifted into weeks, and still the enemy lingered with no sign of moving on. Patrols went out almost every day, and in the mornings, instead of waking as she once had to the soft sounds of laughter, Jessamy woke to the sound of a tinny bugle. Metal harnesses would jingle and leather would creak, and horses blew and snorted in the frosty morning air. Men swore, laughed, shouted.

Oh, how she hated them! Abigail cautioned her against showing it too openly, afraid that her daughter would offend them so greatly they would take some kind of action against her. Celine had no such qualms, however, and she showed them her contempt at every opportunity.

"They are detestable! Huns, all of them! I spit on their feet!"

Celine's narrow face would quiver with indignation, and she would sputter and fume about the injustice of enduring rude, crass men.

So Jessamy remained silent, and there was no repeat of the incident with the Yankee. No one accosted her as she went about her daily tasks, fetching water and helping her mother and Celine care for the others. Aunt Pretense was more of a burden than a help, just moaning and swooning and saying how upsetting it all was. Oh, why hadn't she gone back to Baltimore as she should have?

The tension made everyone's nerves taut, stretched to the breaking point at times. Jessamy actually quarreled with Bryce, something she hadn't done in years, their customary spats and exchanges of barbs growing sharper, until finally Abigail forbade them to speak to one another. And surprisingly, Jessamy agreed. After all, these were bad times, and she was too old to be squabbling with a younger brother.

Bryce became a silent shadow, staring at the blue uniforms with an intensity that worried his mother. He was quiet, too quiet, too withdrawn. Whatever his mother asked him to do, he did without comment. He gathered wood for the fire, dug turnips and potatoes and whatever else the Yankees would allow them to have. And he took a fierce pleasure in thwarting the Yankees whenever he could. He found fresh eggs and hid them from the bluecoats. He found a mother hen and her chicks and hid their nest. He slid away at dusk to go down to the swamp and fish. Bryce was now the man of the family, and he was determined to provide for them as best he could.

It was Bryce who brought Jessamy the news that her mare was gone, her prized Barbary mare, the one she loved above all.

"Gone?" Her face paled. "How? Where?"

He shrugged. "I don't know. She's not in the

stable, and I haven't seen her with the Yankees. Maybe . . . maybe she died or something."

"Old Billy would know."

"But Old Billy's down in the swamp, Jess. I daren't risk going down there, 'cause the Yankees might see me."

"Then I will!"

"No, no! You've already made 'em mad at you. I'll do it. You'll just have to wait till the time is right."

So she waited, and within a few days Bryce told her that he had talked to Old Billy.

"You're not going to like it, but Sultana's gone. He was out chasing her the day the Yankees came. That's how he saw them at the crossroads. She'd busted out of her stall, and he'd gone after her."

Jessamy felt a dull weight settle in her chest. "Then the Yankees have her?"

Shaking his head, Bryce shrugged and said, "I don't know. I sure haven't seen her around here, and you know if the Yankees had her they'd be sure and rub it in."

Jessamy's mouth set; it was one more reason to hate the Yankees. Sultana. Her prize mare, fleet of foot and clean of line, with her proud head and dished nostrils, the bright clear eyes and arched neck, would make some clumsy lout of a Yankee soldier a fine mount to ride into battle. They had stolen her, as they had stolen everything else.

September passed into October, and still the Yankees lingered. Jessamy wondered why. Were they waiting for some momentous battle, hoping to surprise Confederate forces? She wished she could get word from neighbors, or ride into town, but of course, the Yankees did not allow them to have so much as a single word with any other Rebel sympathizer.

The only way to get information was to ask a Yankee, and she only knew one. And she'd be tarred and feathered before she'd bring herself to ask Alex Steele one blessed thing!

Abigail held no ill will toward Alex, saying merely that every man had to do what his conscience bid him, but that was Abigail. Jessamy did not agree with her mother's conviction. And she did not believe that God sided with the right either, or He would have sided with them.

And God would have eradicated Alex Steele if He was truly on their side, too. Jessamy hated Alex most of all, hated the way he laughed at her, his eyes dark crescents in his tanned face and his teeth flashing at her in mockery. Oh, and his sardonic manner of bowing mockingly when he saw her made her want to slap his face! Her palms often itched to crack smartly against his cheek, and she would have to curl her fingers into her palms until her short nails dug deep in order to keep from following her inclination. It was all she could do to keep from telling him how she hated him, but she refused to give him that satisfaction.

Alex correctly read her sentiments in her mutinous eyes and dagger glances. He watched her when he had time, his dark gaze clinging to her slender figure as she went about her tasks. It was his duty to guard them, and while he chafed at being confined to camp instead of going out on patrol, he didn't really mind watching Jessamy.

As Alex was a distant relative of the family,

his commanding officer had suggested that he might be able to communicate any intelligence that he discovered.

"These Southerners seem to have a network of information that is more sophisticated than that of Washington," the general grumbled. "Work on them, Steele. See if you can find out about patrols in the area, et cetera. You're a cousin, aren't you? They'll talk to you before anyone else."

Alex had not bothered to inform General Foote that he was not exactly held in high esteem at this time. It should have been obvious.

The October sun had not been up long one morning when the door to the overseer's cabin creaked open and Jessamy stepped onto the shallow front porch. A light shawl lay over her shoulders, draping around her to ward off the chill. The sharp smell of smoke from a dozen campfires bit the air, and Jessamy gazed out across the now unfamiliar lawns of Clover Hill.

Where once stretched sleepy buds of red clover nodding in the sunshine, now there was only bare ground. The grass and clover had been trampled into the dirt and mud, and when it rained there was nothing to stop rivulets of water from raking furrows in the ground. The rosebushes were gone, the sweet williams and marigolds and chrysanthemums and other fall flowers shredded by hooves and boots. Some of the stately cedars had been chopped down for firewood, leaving ugly stumps where there had once been shade. Even some of the fences had been used, as they were made of weathered wood and burned better than the green trees.

And the house—the sprawling, glistening white house with the gracious porch that wrapped around three sides—was the officers' headquarters. It was bedecked with blue uniforms instead of familiar black faces wearing clean, starched clothing. Instead of the slurred, drawling voices, the house now rang with nasal twangs and the harsh, discordant clang of swords. Jessamy shuddered each time she thought of it.

Her home resembled a battlefield, littered with pieces of military equipment, trash, and tents. She felt as if she were living in a foreign land, and wondered wearily when the Yankees would leave and they could get on with their lives.

Lifting up the water bucket, she rubbed sleep from her eyes. She didn't sleep well anymore. The pallet on the floor was hard and unyielding, and for a moment she thought longingly of her soft feather mattress on the half-tester bed in her room. She'd never really appreciated it, but if she was given another chance, she would!

Jessamy's gaze swept across the lawn, paused on a familiar frame lounging nearby, and glittered with hatred. Alex. He was always there, lurking just beyond the fringes, watching, constantly watching, her watchdog. She knew he had been given the duty to guard them, but instead of excusing him it only made him more blameworthy in her eyes. Alex—his lean frame clad in a blue uniform, his boots polished and his leather holster gleaming, the sword dangling at one side—should have been in a gray uniform.

He saw her watching him and straightened, his body bending slightly from the waist in his familiar, mocking bow. It never occurred to Jessamy that Alex disliked his role. She saw his presence in only one light—that of the enemy. Her mouth pursed with contempt, and she was glad to see his eyes narrow. Good! Let him know how much she despised him!

Ignoring him, Jessamy stepped slowly down the steps, pushing at the hair in front of her eyes, sleep-tousled and irritable as she crossed the yard to the well.

Alex followed. She looked tired, and reminded him of a small child who can't understand why her world has been turned upside down. For some reason, Alex wished he could wipe away that look of pained confusion that often crossed Jessamy's face.

"Here, I'll carry that for you," he said when she had drawn up the water. He reached for the bucket handle, but she slapped his hand away.

"Leave it alone! Leave me alone! Go back to . . . to whatever you were doing and stay away from me!"

Alex's hand dropped. "I was just going to help."

"I don't need Yankee help!" Stormy blue eyes glared at him, and her soft mouth quivered for a brief instant before she steadied it into a thin, hard line.

Alex looked at her, noted the fine lines of tension around her eyes and mouth, and noted too the soiled, torn dress that she wore. It was all she had, probably, and he couldn't help remembering the way she had looked the night she had lured him to the gazebo, with a wide straw hat perched saucily atop her blond head, and her bodice stuffed with strips of linen. He'd thought her the most irritating, amusing scamp he'd ever known. Impish blue eyes had glittered with the joy of life.

Now her face was wan and her eyes sparked with hatred and impotent anger instead of pleasure. He silently damned General Foote for being such a hard-nosed officer and taking out his own prejudices on the innocent victims of war, but there was nothing he could do to change it.

"Yankee!" Jessamy spat again, loathing and contempt lacing that one word and making it sound as if she had said worse.

"Jess, I'm still a Southerner, Virginia-born and bred," Alex replied softly. "But I'm also an American. I refuse to apologize for my sympathies or beliefs."

Water sloshed over the sides of the heavy bucket, and Jessamy tightened her grip. Her fingers curled around the metal handle, but she hardly felt it cut into her palms. She was furious. One hand lifted to push aside the hair straying into her eyes, and she gave Alex a cutting glance.

"Wouldn't do you any good to apologize anyway, *Yankee*. A Rebel insult is better than a Yankee apology any day."

Her throat was so tight it ached, and she wished he would go away, fade into time and memory and be gone with the rest of the invaders occupying her home. It was hard to watch Clover Hill be treated with no regard. Hard to watch as soldiers cut up the clover-studded lawns with their marching feet and horse hooves. And even though she hadn't been in the house since the first day they'd come, she knew it was not faring well. Some of the curtains were gone from the windows, and she'd seen scrapped furniture tossed out back into a heap.

As if reading her mind, Alex said, "I have done my best to keep the house from being ruined."

"Have you? Not so's anyone would notice."

Staring down at her rebellious, mutinous face, Alex nodded. He understood, and he knew he would feel the same way if it were his childhood home being destroyed by the enemy.

"How's your mother?"

"What do you care?" was the harsh rejoinder. "If you truly cared how she was, you'd have stopped *them* from putting us out of her home. Now there are eight of us living in that three-room cabin, while Yankees soil our home with muddy boots and hatred."

"It seems as if Yankees don't have a monopoly on hatred, Jessamy."

"Don't you dare use my first name! I've given you no right to be so familiar!"

A slow smile curled Alex's mouth. She reminded him of a tawny kitten, all hiss and holler, her eyes blazing with defiance. In spite of himself, Alex reached out and cupped her chin in his palm.

"Let me be your friend, Jessamy. It's to your advantage to keep the enemy close."

Her slender body stiffened, and though she did not try to knock his hand away again, her face was rigid. "Just how close does the enemy intend to stay, Captain Steele?"

Alex's mouth squared into a grin. Jessamy's heavy black lashes lowered slightly, hiding her eyes, but Alex knew better than to be deceived. His thumb rubbed gently against her smooth cheek, and he could feel her tremble with anger beneath his touch.

"I intend to stay as close as I can, Miss Windsor. After all, we were childhood playmates once."

Her lashes lifted and she gazed directly into his eyes. For some reason that she didn't quite understand, his touch was making her tremble with more than anger. It made her stomach lurch, and there was an odd fire that flared when she met his gaze. Admittedly, Alex was handsome, and he had been a charming if somewhat infuriating playmate when they were children. But now they were grown-up, and now he was not only the enemy, but her jailer.

Sweetly, she whispered, "I hope that you do stay close, Captain Steele. I hope you are still here when General Johnston arrives and whips you damn Yankees all the way back to Ohio!"

Wrenching away from his gentle grasp, she whirled abruptly, not caring if the water in the heavy bucket drenched her skirt and shoes. Jessamy stalked away with her head held high. She could hear Alex laugh, and her cheeks burned with fury.

Alex leaned back against a tree and watched with genuine appreciation. She would not yield an inch, not Jessamy. Pride and hatred burned like an eternal flame, and they sustained her right now. He hoped that when the flame was finally quenched, she would have something else to sustain her. She'd need it.

He raked a hand through his dark hair, and his mouth twisted. This war was making enemies, and he damned the reasons behind it. War never solved anything. It never had, only made enemies out of neighbors. And no matter the victor, both sides would lose in this war.

He couldn't help but recall his mother's face when he had told her he was enlisting with the Union, could recall how his stepfather had been enraged. But none of that had changed his mind, for he knew he was right. He had to be, or all of this was for nothing. How could dissolution of the United States not be wrong? United, America was a great power. Rent asunder, she would fall to the greedy foreign powers that waited like huge vultures to feed on her natural resources. Disaster would result if the South won, and Alex knew it. Yet he felt at times as if he were a traitor, and it saddened him.

As he watched Jessamy stumble up onto the porch of the small cabin that was now her home, he thought about her mother, and how gracious she had been in spite of the invasion of her home and having her husband and sons fighting on the opposite side. Alex had felt compelled to extend his regrets to Mrs. Windsor for being in any way responsible for her eviction from Clover Hill, but she had stopped him.

"It isn't necessary for you to express regrets, Alex. I know that this isn't of your choosing. Still, I appreciate your being kind enough to tell me of your sentiments."

A rueful smile had slanted Alex's mouth. "Mrs. Windsor, my mother was right when she said you were a fine lady, and I fear she was right when she said I would not be able to straddle the fence."

Abigail nodded. "Charity has always been known for her perspicacity. War ofttimes causes the most enthusiastic of men to pause and think."

"Or straddle."

A faint smile curved Abigail's austere mouth, just the slightest deepening of her lips at the corners, as befitted a lady. "That, too." Straddle. Her cheeks pinkened at the crude word. It brought to mind unsavory images.

Alex had recognized her reticence at the word and thought of his mother. Charity was not as . . . well . . . He hesitated to apply the word *prudish* to Abigail Windsor. Perhaps *proper* would be more appropriate, though Charity Allen Steele Windsor had never been guilty of impropriety a day in her life. It was just that Charity was a little more worldly than Abigail, a little more aware. His mother was a Kentuckian, and didn't follow the same strict social code as did those old families from along the Maryland and Carolina coasts. She was a little more relaxed, a little less inhibited in calling a spade a spade, where the Maryland Fontaines that had bred Abigail were not. And certainly no one had ever accused William Windsor of disregarding the proprieties. He lived by the code which also guided his wife, though the rules were slightly different.

All of which had often made Alex wonder where the Windsor brood got their spirit. He knew all about William, and how he had come to America as a youth to work his way up in the world. He knew how William had fought in the Texas War and been wounded, and he knew how William had defied most of Baltimore society to wed aristocratic Abigail Fontaine. Yet William had always observed social rules to the letter. What puzzled Alex was the complete wildness of their children. He could well recall Nicholas as a child, and his utter disregard for safety or danger. The twins, James and Charles, were almost as bad, and their sister—Alex grinned at the memory.

Jessamy had been the first to take a dare, the first to swing sixty feet above a dried-up creek bed on a flimsy vine. She'd been the first in foot races, and had ridden the wildest ponies and climbed highest in the trees. Alex had never felt a part of the family anyway, and to watch his cousins cavort had seemed dangerous enough. He'd never felt the need to join in, never felt the need to prove himself. Oh, he knew that Nicholas and the twins had often thought him a spineless sort of boy, but that had not mattered then or now. Alex was never afraid of their opinion. He would do what pleased him, regardless of anyone's opinion.

Which was probably the reason he had flown in the face of his family's disapproval to join the Union army with complete equanimity. He had remained composed and unruffled as always, while Charity had openly expressed dismay and his stepfather had blustered about the disgrace. Alex had been mildly surprised at Huntley Windsor's reaction. It had never occurred to him that Huntley might feel so strongly about the issue. To see the normally reserved Huntley grow red in the face and roar had been an unusual spectacle. And it had been slightly daunting, which had surprised Alex.

He'd never thought much about his stepfather, just been acutely aware that he had married Charity and moved them from Virginia to Kentucky. Resentful at first, Alex had eventually reconciled himself to the fact that his father was dead and another man had taken his place. But it had left him with the conviction that nothing was irreplaceable in life.

His Virginia home had been replaced with a Kentucky home, and his Virginia relatives had been replaced with English relatives, and cousins from Tennessee, Mississippi, and Maryland. Fathers could obviously be replaced, Alex had concluded bitterly.

His childhood had been spent pretending not to mind things, as he'd instinctively known his mother wanted. He would not have hurt Charity by allowing her to know that he resented her decision to remarry. Now that he was an adult, he saw life a little more clearly, but his early resentment and bitterness still lingered in indefinable traces.

Perhaps that was why he was attracted to that half-wild hoyden who didn't hesitate to flirt in one breath and curse in another. She said bluntly and directly what she felt. It was a trait that Alex admired.

And beneath her heavy-lidded eyes he had seen something else, a spark of latent sensuality that intrigued and lured him to her like a moth to the flame. He'd first seen it the night in the gazebo, and had instantly recognized what she did not. Jessamy, lovely, willful Jessamy with the tawny hair and flashing blue-gray eyes, had caught his imagination and made him dream of her at night.

His dreams were not the innocent dreams of a childhood playmate, but the adult dreams of a healthy soldier. Alex did not try to convince himself that he had chivalrous thoughts about his cousin; he knew that he wanted her.

Chapter

8

"COUSIN ALEX SURE DOES WATCH you close," Maribelle commented. She and Jessamy were sitting on the small porch of the cabin, trying to stay cool in the still-warm noontime. A nice breeze had sprung up from the south, and it filtered across them, stirring hair and skirts in a gentle whisper. Alex Steele worked close by, his shirt off and his muscles flexing in the sunshine as he chopped wood. Jessamy felt a strange warmth in her throat as she watched Alex lift the heavy ax and bring it down in swift, smooth motions, his arms bulging with the movements. His bare chest was broad and muscled, and furred with a light pelt of hair that grew from his neck down to his belt. She turned her gaze back to Maribelle.

Maribelle lifted a brow and repeated, "I said, Cousin Alex sure does watch you close, doesn't he?"

Jessamy gave her cousin a frowning glance. "He's not our cousin!" she said sharply, then added more calmly, "And I'm sure he watches me so close because he knows who's to blame for the pepper in the general's supper."

"Did you do that?" Maribelle asked with a wide-eyed stare. "Oh, Jess, how dangerous!"

"You don't think I'm going to let these Yankees get by with destroying my home without some kind of retaliation, do you? And besides, the general doesn't know who to blame. He's got the Cahills' old groom doing his cooking for him. I think he's too stupid to know a house servant from a field servant."

"Did Captain Steele say anything to you?"

Jessamy shook her head. "No. Maybe he doesn't know any different, either. Or maybe he's afraid I'll carry important secrets to Lee's army!"

Maribelle giggled, then asked more seriously, "Do you think you could ever do something so daring, Jess?"

"What? You mean be a spy and carry secrets?" Jessamy turned to look toward Alex Steele. The notion had never occurred to her before, and she briefly pictured how Alex's face would look if he found out that she had managed to save the Confederacy from the hated Yankees. It sounded romantic and adventurous, and she envisioned herself in a disguise, risking life and limb to carry important documents to Jeff Davis himself.

"Yes, I'm sure I could! And wouldn't it be a pip to see Alex Steele's face if I managed it?"

Somewhat alarmed at the sudden light in Jessamy's face, Maribelle stammered out that she hadn't meant to actually suggest her cousin do such a foolish thing. "Why, th-they *hang* spies, Jess!"

"And you don't think the Confederacy is worth dying for, Maribelle?"

"No, and neither do you," Maribelle retorted with rare acuity. "I've heard you say a thousand times that you wish this silly war was over an' that ever'body would just go home where they belong. Spies are supposed to be more ardent than that."

Jessamy gave her cousin a thoughtful glance. "Spies are supposed to want the war to end with their side winning."

"Perhaps they are, but I still can't imagine you runnin' around in a disguise and duckin' bullets."

"Do you think I'm a coward?"

Maribelle shook her head so hard her brown curls danced madly. "No, I just think you're smarter than that."

Somewhat appeased, Jessamy relented. "Well, you're right about that, Maribelle. At least, I hope you're right."

Silence fell, and a bee buzzed nearby, droning on in an irritating symphony. The warm weather had produced an Indian summer, and even though the mornings were still frosty, the days were as warm as spring. If the Yankees hadn't been there, and the entire world hadn't turned upside down, there would have been lots of parties and festivities. Now, most of their neighbors were either displaced by Federals or afraid to come close to those that were. If not for the Negroes' grapevine, few of those who were displaced would know what was happening outside their sheltered little world.

The darkies were the only ones allowed to travel freely, and the Yankees seemed to think they could be trusted not to carry information. Fools! Jessamy thought with contempt. Didn't the Yankees realize that most of the slaves were treated as family, and regarded themselves as such? If they didn't, they should, she thought smugly.

Alex thought the same thing. He'd tried to explain to Captain Nelson and General Foote that the Negroes were quite loyal to their families, but Nelson and Foote had not understood. They would find out soon enough that their efforts to release some of the Negroes from bondage were met with suspicion and belligerence. Not all of the slaves were treated badly, and Alex did his best to persuade the officers to take that into consideration.

By forcing them away from their families, they often forced them into a poverty that they'd never known. On the larger plantations, everything was provided. They had warm, secure places to live, new suits of clothes twice a year, plenty of food and medical attention, as well as a love and security they would not find out in the rather frightening world into which they'd been thrust. Oh, it wasn't that way with all the slaves, but even the others still needed more preparation to be on their own. It was similar to forcing children out of the home before they were old enough or ready, and Alex could not help but think disaster was ahead. He visualized freed Negroes roaming the streets without work, food, or hope, and he knew what that would cause.

But no one would listen.

Instead, they freed the slaves at every plantation or small farm. First jubilant, then bewildered, Negroes soon found that they were expected to fend for themselves. In a war, with work to be done, they were often found doing for the Yankees what they had been doing for their Southern owners. It was trading one form of bondage for another as far as Alex was concerned.

That was one reason he had not spoken up when they arrived at Clover Hill and found only a few servants in residence. He knew there were many more Negroes at Clover Hill, but he also knew that they had been given an option to stay or go by William Windsor. Most had stayed. Only a few opted for freedom.

Alex suspected where the servants might be hiding, but he kept it to himself. Abigail sensed his discretion and was thankful for it. She understood him well enough to keep her gratitude to herself, knowing that to mention it would put Alex in the position of choosing sides.

It was Jessamy who didn't understand, fiery-tempered, volatile Jessamy who almost gave everything away.

Sitting on the porch that noon, Jessamy saw a shadow flicker just beyond the line of hickory trees fringing the far edge of the road. Her glance sharpened, and she quickly looked about to see if anyone else had noticed. No one had, as most of the Federals were out on a patrol. Only a handful had been left behind to guard the house and the women. Even Alex had disappeared into one of the tents.

Rising slowly, Jessamy made a show of stretching, and lazily announced her intentions of going for a walk. "Care to go, Maribelle?" she asked, knowing the answer before it was voiced. Maribelle was not a girl given to any form of exercise.

"No, you go ahead. I think I'll take a nap with the others."

"Fine . . ."

"Are you sure you'll be all right?" Maribelle asked anxiously, suddenly recalling her cousin's confrontation with the Yankee.

"I'm not going far, and besides, all I have to do is holler."

Jessamy's heart was pounding furiously as she ambled across the yard, skirting piles of brush and trash. She'd recognized Old Billy behind a far tree, and knew that it had to be something important to bring him this close to the Yankees. Walking casually, she kept a watchful eye out for soldiers, especially Alex, who always seemed to be near when she stepped more than a yard from the cabin.

But on this occasion, she did not see even Alex, and wondered briefly where he had gone. He'd been there only a short time before, but was now nowhere in sight. For some reason, this made her feel vaguely uneasy. At least with Alex watching her as if she were his next meal she'd had some sort of security. She hadn't worried about being accosted again.

"But that's silly!" she scolded herself. With Alex gone she had a precious moment of privacy.

When she reached the edge of the hickory grove, Jessamy paused, then began to wonder if her imagination had played a trick on her. There was no one there, and in the grove it was shadowed and quiet. She would have seen some-one if they'd been there, wouldn't she?

No breeze reached the grove, and the air was so soft and silent that Jessamy began to grow uneasy. Ridiculous! She had played in this grove a thousand times as a child. Why should she feel uneasy now? It was still the same grove where she'd hacked notches into a sapling with Nick's penknife. She could still remember how angry Nick had been that she'd dulled the blade.

Running her fingertips lightly over the still-visible cuts in the bark of the tall tree, Jessamy glanced around. She hesitated to call out, fear-ful that she had been wrong or that someone would hear.

That was when a hand descended upon her shoulder, bringing a gasp from her.

"Oh, doan yo' go an' holler now, Miss Jess!" came the quick plea. Old Billy put a finger to his lips, and his eyes were wide and frightened. "Ah done almos' got caught a'ready, an' Ah ain' hankerin' fer ta git in th' Yankee ahmy!"

"You scared me," Jessamy said when she could speak. Her legs were trembling, and she clenched her hands tightly to keep them from shaking.

"Yas'm, Ah kin see Ah did. Ah's plumb sorry 'bout dat, Miss Jess. Ah jus' cain' tek no chances dat some sojer maht of seed yo' come in hyah."

She grasped his arm, realizing that the old man was very frightened. Recalling the mean trick she and Nick had played on him with sheets years before, she knew it had taken a great deal of courage for Old Billy to brave the hickory grove again.

"What's so important that you left the swamp?"

Old Billy glanced around, then stepped closer. There was a furtive air about him, and he whispered as if the trees could tell tales.

"Cuhn'l For'est, he's a-comin' ter de rescue, Miss Jess! Ah seed him wif' mah own eyes!"

"Colonel Forrest? But he's in Memphis!"

"No'm, he ain'. Leas', not raht now he ain'. Ah seed him wif' mah own eyes!"

Jessamy's mind was working swiftly. "Do the Yankees know?"

"Lawdy, Miss Jess, Ah hopes not! Dere's bound ter be sum fightin', an' Ah knows Ah needed ter cum tell yo' ter watch out."

"Thank you, Old Billy. I'll tell Mother and the others. Now, you need to get back to hiding before you're caught out. Do you need anything?"

"No'm, Miss Jess. We done took all dat we needed w'en we went inter hidin'. We's all doin' fine, 'cept w'en it's early mawnin' an' de frost git inter mah bones. Den Ah wish Ah had a nice fiah ter warm me."

"Well, if Forrest is near, you'll soon have a nice fire anytime you want one. And we can all . . . Oh, run quick now, Old Billy! We can talk later."

After the old man had slipped back into the woods, Jessamy waited for several minutes in the grove. She perched on a fallen tree, and gazed at some of the raw stumps where the soldiers had "appropriated" trees for their fires. Soon it would be over. Soon the Yankees would flee Clover Hill and life would be normal again. How could she have ever thought she would long for days with nothing to do but roll bandages in the sunny parlor? Or lie abed and read, or even embroider around the fire on a chilly fall evening? But she did, and now that it was all close to coming about again, she felt a surge of joy and even sympathy for the Yankees.

Poor, foolish bluecoats! They did not dream that they were about to be run out of Clover Hill, and hopefully, out of Tennessee! But they were, and she was wildly glad.

Even Alex Steele would have his comeuppance, and she felt a fierce anticipation at seeing his face when he learned the news. Oh, it was almost too good to keep to herself, and she wished she could have the pleasure of being the one to tell him.

But that was impossible, of course, and now she had to warn her mother, and Bryce, who was prone to rambling about the woods scavenging food. He would need to stay close for safety's sake.

Abigail took the news as she took everything else life had dealt her, calmly and with fortitude.

"Then we must remain here without allowing the soldiers to know why," she said, and inclined her head in the direction of Pretense and Maribelle. Jessamy understood immediately, and had thought the same thing herself. To tell Pretense would be tantamount to announcing it directly to the Yankees, for the nervous little woman would most likely babble it out in near hysteria.

It was difficult keeping them all close without telling them why, and even more difficult waiting. Jessamy prayed that Forrest would hurry, and each time there was a loud noise or she heard a soldier shout, she would give a start.

"You're as nervous as a cat on thin ice," Maribelle complained once, and Jessamy silently agreed though she denied it with an air of surprise.

"Why do you think that?"

" 'Cause you've got the fidgets, that's why! All you've done all day is pace back and forth and jump out of your skin every time there's a noise. What's the matter with you, Jess?"

"Nothing. Just tired of Yankees, I guess."

"Aren't we all? But there ain't nothin' we can do about it now, except put up with 'em!"

Jessamy nodded, wishing for a brief instant that she could tell Maribelle and see her eyes grow wide with fright. It would serve the silly goose right for being so sanctimonious when she didn't have enough sense to pour . . . Oh well, that was one of Nick's phrases, and she'd best not even *think* it or she was liable to say it one day. Abigail would be horrified, and Celine would never let up scolding her. For men to use certain bawdy phrases was one thing, but for a properly reared young lady to do so would cause a scandal. Too bad she was a girl, for Jessamy would have dearly loved to use some of the phrases she'd heard Papa use when he was angry. There was a certain amount of satisfaction to be derived from spouting a ripe word or two in times of stress.

So she paced, and she fretted, and she exchanged glances with Bryce, who also knew.

Alex Steele noted her nervousness, and he began to ponder the reason. Jessamy, suddenly afraid? That was ludicrous. She'd faced them all down with fire in her eye and determination on her face, so he saw no reason for her to be nervous now.

He decided to confront Jessamy at the first opportunity.

"Are you ill, Miss Windsor?" he asked in his most solicitous manner when she went to the well for water. She gave him a quelling stare.

"Do I look ill, Captain Steele? If I do, it's only because I'm forced to endure the presence of Yankees—you in particular!"

"How upsetting for you."

"Yes, it is. Now if you will excuse me, I did not come to the well simply for a chance to talk to you. I have to take water back to my mother."

Alex's hand fell on her arm, and he felt her quiver at his touch. "You will pause a moment, won't you?" he asked pleasantly.

"Do I have a choice?"

A small smile touched his lips. "Not really."

Jessamy let the water bucket slam to the ground, then crossed her arms over her chest and gave him a stony stare. "Then go ahead and browbeat me, Yankee."

"You're a fiery little Rebel, Jess—"

"Miss Windsor to you!"

"—but I noticed that you seem to be under a great deal of strain today," he continued without pause. "Has someone been bothering you?"

"Yes—you!"

"Besides me."

"The entire Yankee army, President Lincoln, Sherman, Grant—"

"Jess, Jess, Jess! I had hoped for a more intelligent response from you."

"Sorry to disappoint you. Close association

with Yankee soldiers must have rubbed off on me."

"Such a quick tongue you have! I am agog with admiration, as I am certain you meant for me to be, but my question still remains unanswered. What is causing you to act so nervous?"

There was a brief flicker in her eyes that Alex could not quite interpret, though it seemed to him for a moment that it was triumph. What was the little minx up to now? He had no doubt she was up to something, though he didn't know what.

"Have you salted our water bucket again, Jess? Or put burrs under any more saddles?"

There was a flash of guilty surprise in her eyes for a moment before she sniffed and said, "I'm sure I don't know what you're talking about!"

"If it wasn't you, it had to be Bryce. Maribelle is scared of her own shadow, and no one else would think of such tricks. I have a long memory, and close association with your pranks. Now confess—what have you done to irritate and goad the Yankees today?"

"Breathe?"

Alex grinned. "All right. I can see that you have no intentions of cooperating, but I just thought I'd warn you: Don't put any more doses of pepper in our cooking pots. The general coughed and sputtered for a half hour, and if he'd known it was you, he'd have tanned your hide, female or no female."

"I shudder at the thought, but I still don't know what you're talking about."

"Have it your way, Jess."

"Oh, I will, Captain Steele, I will!"

There was such a note of certainty in her voice that it gave Alex pause, and he frowned down at her. Jessamy quickly lowered her lashes to hide her eyes, but it was too late.

Reaching out, Alex jerked her to him, his fingers digging harshly into her upper arms and making her gasp with pain.

"What have you done, you little fool? Nothing that will endanger your life, I hope, because before God, Jess, if you have I don't know if I can save you!"

He gave her a rough shake that made her head snap back and forth and her teeth bite down on her tongue. Fright swept through her, and she hoped that she had not somehow given anything away. Had she? Did he suspect what she knew? And how did Old Billy know about Forrest if the Yankees didn't know?

"Let . . . me . . . go!" she managed to say when he stopped shaking her for a moment. Wrenching away, she stared up at him with blazing eyes that had darkened to the color of wood smoke. Her soft mouth trembled with fury. "You damned Yankee! You traitor! Don't you ever, ever put your hands on me again! There's not enough hot water in the world to wash your touch away. . . ."

That was as far as she got before Alex reacted. He had not thought she could get under his skin so easily, but the glare of contempt pricked him into jerking her close again.

"You mean like this touch, Jess? If you've got to wash anyway, let me give you something else to wash away."

Before she could avoid it his mouth came down over hers and seared across her lips, half smothering her. He had pulled her so close her hands were trapped between their bodies, and she could do no more than clench them impotently. His lips were warm and hard, pressing against her mouth in a kiss that was hot and consuming. She hadn't realized men could kiss like this, this invasion that drew all coherent thought from her mind and left her limp in his arms. It was vaguely humiliating, but at the moment all Jessamy could feel was the slow kindling of a fire deep within her. She tried to tell herself that it was only Alex, her playmate cousin and now a hated traitor, but somehow the message did not reach her brain. Somehow, her body was leaning into his, her breasts pressed against his chest so hard she could feel his brass buttons bite into her tender skin.

It wasn't until he released her that she realized she had been kissing him back, and the sudden knowledge stung like the lash of a whip. Without pausing to think, Jessamy swung back her arm and slapped Alex across the cheek. The imprint of her palm and fingers left white marks on his tanned skin, and she didn't say a word as she glared at him.

A whoop of laughter assaulted her ears, and Jessamy finally noticed the blue-coated soldiers who had gathered to watch. Her cheeks flamed as she heard their jeers.

"Tame the little Rebel, Cap'n!"

"Show her that the Federals can do more than jus' fight, Cap'n Steele!"

"That's the way!"

For an instant, Alex was sorry he'd yielded to impulse. He hadn't wanted to humiliate Jessamy, but she would never believe that now.

And when he saw her small chin lift with wounded pride, he knew that the damage had been done. It was best to retreat and reconnoiter.

"You've made your point, Captain Steele," she said stiffly, "but I shall still wash your kiss away."

Alex grinned, then gave her that familiarly hateful half-bow that mocked her anger. "Try washing away your response," he said softly before pivoting on his boot heel and stalking away.

Jessamy stood by the well for a moment. She could feel the interested stares riveted in her direction, and knew that her shame had been witnessed by Yankees and family alike. Damn them—especially Alex Steele!

Chapter
9

PRETENSE HAD FAINTED dead away at the sight of her niece clutched in the arms of a Yankee. Even Abigail's assurances that it was Cousin Alex did not alleviate her horror. Of course, Pretense could not understand why a nice boy like Alex had done such a terrible thing to his family, when everyone knew Yankees were ill-mannered and horrible. Weren't they?

Abigail soothed Pretense, while Celine tapped her foot on the planked floor and waited for Jessamy to return to the cabin. Her brown eyes, so mild and kindly most of the time, flashed fire, and her stolid face was set in a grim mask reminiscent of a bulldog.

"Hush that snickering!" Celine snapped at Maribelle, who subsided with only a nervous giggle or two. To have seen Jessamy kissed so thoroughly was as fascinating as it was horrifying. Now her reputation would be ruined if any of the neighbors heard about it, which they

surely would. Gossip traveled faster than light-
ning bolts in Hardeman County.

"Has Jessamy been . . . *ravished*?" Maribelle
dared ask, and Pretense immediately went into
another swoon. The exact definition of ravish-
ment still escaped Maribelle, and so it was left
to Celine to explain.

When Jessamy stepped up on the porch, she
met Celine's stern gaze steadily, daring her to
say anything. The old woman's mouth opened,
then shut with a snap, and she shook her head.

"Sacrebleu! Nothing that happens will surprise me anymore," Celine was heard to mum-
ble as she turned and went back into the cabin.

Jessamy's chin lifted. Well, they all should
have stayed in the house like they were supposed to. She couldn't help it if Alex had behaved so badly, could she? And it wasn't as if
she had done anything on purpose.

Only Abigail seemed to understand, which
surprised Jessamy more than it did anyone else.
Abigail said nothing, nor did she look at her
daughter with that sorrowful gaze she used
when Jessamy had transgressed. It was puzzling, but Jessamy accepted it gratefully.

Pretense's two youngest daughters were wailing softly, not understanding why their mother
was so upset or why they were being ignored. It
was Bryce who calmed them, giving them a
cornhusk doll he had fashioned for them and
making them promise not to cry anymore.

"It seems that I've caused an uproar," Jessamy murmured with a wry smile, and Bryce
grinned.

"As usual. But don't worry—if you can kiss
your horses you can kiss a Yankee."

"Bryce!"

Abigail's stern reproof made him duck his head, but he was not a bit abashed by it. Jessamy childishly put out her tongue at him, and Maribelle giggled again.

"I think Alex suspects something," Jessamy whispered to Bryce later when everyone had calmed and the house was quiet.

Bryce stared at her gravely. "He'd be a fool if he didn't, and Alex is no fool."

"We don't share the same opinion on that score, but just the same, I hope he doesn't suspect the truth."

"Me, too."

They were quiet for a moment, listening to the now-familiar sounds of the Yankees stirring about. Jessamy was restless, and could tell that Bryce was, too. It was the waiting that was getting to them, making their tempers short and their nerves raw. If only Forrest would hurry up and get there so it would all be over with!

"Does it seem to you that there's a bit more noise than usual?" Bryce asked after a few minutes.

Jessamy listened. There were shouts, and the sound of creaking caisson wheels and horses, and she slowly nodded.

"Yes, it does."

"Maybe they've heard . . ."

Conjecture was unnecessary a few minutes later when Alex appeared on the porch. He rapped sharply on the door, then swung it open. Jessamy wasn't aware that she had stood until she felt his gaze on her, and she backed away a step or two at his approach.

Outlined against the fading afternoon light,

Alex looked even bigger than his six feet two, and she felt an odd leap of fear.

"Don't worry, I won't harm you, though I do wish you'd told me," he said to her.

"Told you what?"

"Don't fence with me now, Jess. You know what I'm talking about. You should have trusted me."

For a moment nothing was said, and the tension was thick enough to touch. Then Jessamy laughed, a harsh sound in the heavy silence.

"Trusted *you*? Trust a Yankee?"

His mouth thinned to a taut line. "Yes. I am family, and it might have saved . . . saved a lot of pain."

"What are you talking about, Captain Steele?" Abigail asked. She stood up, her aristocratic face composed and waiting.

"I'm sorry to have to be the bearer of bad tidings, but the general has ordered that the house be burned upon our retreat. As I am sure you are aware, Colonel Forrest is in the area, and we cannot leave any shelter or supplies for the enemy."

"Burn our house! Burn Clover Hill!" Jessamy cried, her feeling of triumph disappearing. "But you can't do that!"

Alex's face was grim, but his tone cool. "We not only can, but we are. I'm sorry."

"Sorry! Sorry! Why, you damned scoundrel of a Yankee goat—"

"Jessamy!"

She heard her mother's shocked voice, but goaded beyond control, Jessamy could not stop.

"I hope you're shot, Alex Steele, and I hope that they hang you as high as the sky!"

His mouth twisted wryly. "They very well may, so you might have your wish if I don't leave with the rest." He turned to Abigail. "Again, I am deeply sorry, Mrs. Windsor. I would not have caused you this pain were it up to me."

"I'll bet!" Jessamy spat. "It was probably your idea!"

Alex bent slightly from the waist in a bow, and this time it was not mocking. He hesitated a moment as if he wanted to say more, then shrugged and left, closing the door behind him.

White-lipped and wild-eyed, Bryce whirled to face his sister. "I'll kill them first," he said in such a low, fierce voice that it frightened her. "I'll kill every one of them!"

"Bryce, don't be foolish," Jessamy said in spite of her raging desire to do the same. She swallowed hot words that she wanted to say about the Yankees, knowing it would only fuel her brother's pain and wrath and goad him into acting foolishly. "There . . . there's nothing we can do."

An odd light was falling across the yard, and they all went out onto the porch and gazed up the hill toward the elegant white house. Smoke billowed into the sky, and tiny flames could be seen licking at the upstairs windows. The sharp smell of burning wood filled the air, and the burning of the house was so great a loss that Jessamy never even noticed when the last Yankee soldier rode out of sight. She felt empty inside, and filled with such bewildered despair that she wondered if she would ever recover. Perhaps it wasn't right to love an object built of wood and stone, but she felt as if every brick, every joint and mortice had been crafted with her father's love.

What would William Windsor say when he came back home and discovered there was no home there? What would he say when he saw the pile of charred rubble that had been his dream, his reward for years of work and effort?

And what if he didn't come back? Jessamy couldn't help but wonder.

She felt a dull throbbing pain, and looked down. Her fingers were dug into the rough bark of the log cabin, and whitewash had embedded in her skin. She swallowed, and it was like swallowing a persimmon.

Bitterness rose in her in an engulfing wave, and Jessamy wondered how her mother could watch her home burn with such a calm expression. Aunt Pretense had fainted again, fortunately, and Maribelle was weeping softly. The twins were wailing against Celine's narrow bosom, and tears streaked the achingly familiar face as she held them. Bryce quivered with rage and pain, and Jessamy shut her eyes against the sight of her family's suffering. She couldn't bear it. She just couldn't bear it.

The Yankees were gone and they'd taken Obadiah Johnston with them, impressed him into their army against his protests. It was either fight or be a prisoner, and he'd had to choose. The thought of a Yankee prison was worse than the thought of being shot, and so he'd gone, leaving the women without a man for protection. Except for the servants hidden down in the swamp, there would be no one there should danger threaten again.

Grinding her teeth, Jessamy kept her eyes

shut as she damned the Yankees with bitterness and hatred. They'd taken everything they could, left the Windsor women without anything to sustain them during the coming months, and she wished she could tell them how much she despised them.

Hoofbeats thundered across the yard, and Jessamy opened her eyes again. It was a Yankee soldier, and he was lifting a burning brand from the blazing house. Seeing her watching him, he wheeled his horse toward the cabin. Jessamy recoiled. It was the lanky soldier who had accosted her that day by the well, and he wore a look of triumph on his face as he swept one arm out toward the burning house.

"Well now, missy, what do you have to say to that? Who is gonna win this war now?"

"If you continue to do battle against women and children, you just might have a chance," Jessamy grated, "but I notice you Yankees turn tail and run like hounds when you find out Colonel Forrest and our brave men are in the area!"

The soldier's face flushed an angry red, and his eyes narrowed to spiteful slits. "Yeah, and Forrest just might find himself with no place to go, too!" He brandished the burning torch he held, a piece of the scrollwork from the porch. "I'm using this ta burn the bridge behind us, so ole Forrest ain't got no way to follow, missy!"

"It'll take more than that to stop Forrest or any other Confederate over five years old!" Jessamy snapped back, though she felt her spirits flag. She took several steps forward, hatred making her lose her caution. "You better get used to running, Yankee! You're going to be doing a lot of it!"

The Yankee urged his horse forward, and he might have been rash enough to take action if not for the sound of a bugle calling him. He hesitated, and when it blared again, he wheeled his horse around and spurred it in the direction of the bridge.

Jessamy felt a movement at her elbow. "If the Yankees hadn't taken my rifle, I'd shoot him in the back," Bryce said softly. "But at least you told him, Jess. At least you told him."

"Yes, I told him."

Bryce was silent for a moment, then said, "I wish I could ride after them with Forrest."

"You're too young. And besides, Forrest won't be going far once he finds out the bridge is burned."

Bryce nodded forlornly, his eyes glittering with unshed tears. Jessamy thought of her father and brothers, and she thought of the gracious home that would never be again. And she thought of the dusky night when she had waited for Alex Steele in the gazebo. Why hadn't she seen him for what he was then? It might have saved them all some pain.

Jessamy went to stand in the long curving drive that now led to nothing. She wanted to be alone, and she knew that if she remained in that depressing cabin one more moment she would go mad.

No one tried to stop her, and as she walked she let her tears flow. Her throat ached with misery, and she felt as alone as if no one else were within miles. Fine ashes were blowing through the air, carried on the gentle breeze to settle over grass and trees. Holding out her hand, Jessamy watched as her palm was coated with the black dust. What part of the house was now resting in her upturned palm? Her bedroom, perhaps? The parlor? Or maybe the small alcove where the staircase clock had chimed the hours of their lives for over twenty years? Smoke and tears stung her eyes, and she choked back a sob.

Damn them! If only she could help Forrest in some way, help him catch those Yankees and punish them for what they'd done!

Then it occurred to her—she could. Didn't she know this area better than she did the back of her hand? Didn't she know every ford in every creek within a twenty-mile radius? Sure she did! And she could lead Colonel Forrest to a ford that would allow him to catch up with the Yankees before they got two miles!

Jessamy was waiting when Colonel Forrest and his troops rode past the crossroads. She stood in the center of the road, her arms at her sides and her chin set.

"What can we do for you, miss?" a man asked, and she saw from the chevrons on his gray sleeve that he was only a sergeant.

"I want to speak to Colonel Forrest."

The man seemed amused. "What makes you think he's riding with us?"

"I know he is, and I must speak to him. It's important that I do."

Sweeping off his cap, the man hesitated. "Well, I don't know about thet, miss. The colonel might not want to be bothered, and—"

"Jessamy Windsor!" a voice shouted, and she

turned to see Stuart Armstrong ride up behind the sergeant. "Jessamy, I can't believe it's you!"

She smiled. "Hello, Stuart. Yes, who else did you think you'd find out here in front of Clover Hill?"

Stuart glanced up at the smudges of smoke still hanging in the air. "Well, I kinda thought that maybe you'd left. Gone to Mobile or Atlanta."

"No, we stayed."

"Maribelle still here, too?"

"Yes, but Stuart, it's important that I speak to the colonel at once! I have some vital information that might help him catch the Yankees who did this. . . ."

Within the space of a few minutes, Jessamy was in front of Colonel Forrest, a handsome man with a small beard and twinkling eyes.

"So you think you can help us catch Yankees, miss?"

"I know I can."

"How?" He leaned forward on his horse, saddle leather creaking and his smile still indulgent.

"They burned the bridge behind them, but I know another way to cross that creek."

At that, the colonel's eyes sharpened, and he sent a man off to verify that the bridge was burned.

"If you want to doubt me, fine, but it's only a waste of time. Why would I lie?" Jessamy half turned, sweeping out an arm to indicate the still smoldering ruins of her home up on the hill. "I've no love for the Yankees, Colonel Forrest."

For a heartbeat the colonel stared at her, then

he nodded. "All right, miss. Show me the ford. Have you a horse?"

When she shook her head he reached down, and she took his arm and swung lightly up behind him. Heedless of her bunched skirts or exposed legs, Jessamy directed Colonel Forrest past the crossroads and through a patch of woods that bordered the rushing creek.

Halfway there they met the returning scout, who verified that the bridge was burned. The scout glanced at Jessamy seated behind Forrest, his surprise evident.

"Colonel Forrest, sir, the enemy has cannon set up on the opposite bank. There is no way to cross the creek."

"This young patriot knows a way," Forrest said, and he turned to Jessamy.

The troop moved through the woods more quietly than Jessamy had thought possible. Raindrops still dripped from leaves and branches. In the trees a few birds chirped or fluttered, and there were vague rustlings in the underbrush that made her think an enemy was behind every tree. Hoofbeats were muffled on fallen leaves, and there was the occasional clink of sword or rattle of metal harness. Other than that, the woods were silent.

Jessamy's heart pounded furiously in her chest, and her mouth was dry. What was she doing here? Had she gone mad? Those Yankees wouldn't hesitate to shoot her, or let an anonymous cannon ball blast her into oblivion.

But she steeled herself against such cowardly thoughts when she recalled Clover Hill. Nothing was too great to dare to make those Yankees pay for what they'd done.

When they neared the burned-out bridge, a cannon boomed in warning. Horses neighed shrilly and men cursed, and Jessamy felt her throat tighten with terror. A tree crashed to the ground only yards from Forrest, and he was compelled to calm his mount by sheer force.

Jessamy clung tightly to the colonel, squeezing her eyes shut and praying as she had never prayed before. Loud pops sounded, and tree branches broke and fell in a shower of leaves. She winced and stifled a cry, grinding her teeth together to keep from calling out. Her fingers were tightly clenched in Forrest's coat, and she swallowed hard. More cannon boomed, and Forrest spurred his horse back up the path.

"Here, I cannot allow so brave a lady to be endangered this way," he said to Jessamy, but she shook her head.

Through white lips she grated, "No! I will not let them win!"

A glitter of admiration flared in the colonel's eyes, but he shook his head. "You are too fair a flower of the South to be risked," he began gallantly, and Jessamy cut him off.

"Sir, there are many flowers that will be ground under the feet of our oppressors if I do not take a small risk! I refuse to be sent back until I have shown you the way to cross the creek."

Rain-swollen currents flowed swiftly, sometimes pouring over the banks of the creek. Forrest looked at the rushing water and hesitated, but he saw the necessity. Above all else he was a soldier and a leader and he gave a tight nod of his head.

"Very well, brave lass—your courage shall not go unspoken. Lead us to the ford."

Jessamy led the Confederate soldiers along a narrow path that ran parallel to the creek until they came to a steep bank.

"This is it."

"Here?" an officer asked dubiously, standing in his stirrups to peer over the edge. His mount danced nervously on the bluff, blowing and snorting, its eyes rolling wildly as the officer tried to calm it. "It looks dangerous."

"I never said it was easy, I just said it could be done without harm!" Jessamy snapped, and Colonel Forrest laughed.

"Well said," he approved. "And now we ride on, young lady. Will you be able to find your way home from here?"

Nodding, Jessamy was swung down. She stood in a pile of damp leaves, her face flushed, her eyes glittering, and the colonel smiled at her.

"What can I do to repay such bravery and gallantry, Miss Windsor?"

Her chin lifted, and there was a militant gleam in her eyes as she said, "You can capture the Yankees who burned my home, Colonel Forrest! That will be ample reward."

The colonel sat back in his saddle and laughed. "See the brave women of the Confederacy, gentlemen? This is what we are fighting for! What do you say—shall we capture the enemy and bring them low?"

For the first time, Jessamy heard the bloodcurdling Rebel yell, and she understood how it could strike terror into the heart of the enemy. A chill pranced down her spine with icy fingers, and the colonel saluted her with his sword, then whirled his mount and rode away.

Robbie and Stuart Armstrong rode past, grinning like monkeys and waving at her, and she waved back. They looked like boys on a Sunday outing instead of soldiers bent on killing, and Jessamy thought for an instant of her brothers off somewhere up North, probably doing the same thing.

She stood there for several minutes after the troop rode over the edge of the bank and crossed the shallow ford to the other side. Then she heard pistol and rifle shots, and the scream of wounded men. Shuddering, Jessamy realized that she was not as brave as she'd thought. She picked her skirts up high as she ran for home.

Chapter 10

SHUDDERING, Maribelle stared at her cousin in awe. "I cannot believe that you actually rode with Colonel Forrest, Jess! Or that you . . . you even dared go near cannon and such! If it was me—why, I'd have fainted dead away!"

"Now you're beginning to sound like Aunt Pretense."

"No, I mean it! You often said you'd be brave, but I never believed you till now. I think you *could* carry secret papers to Jeff Davis if you wanted!"

Jessamy didn't bother telling Maribelle how terrified she'd been. It was too nice having her look up at her with big cow eyes full of admiration. She'd enjoy it just a little bit before she confessed that she'd been almost frozen with fear when the cannons were booming and men were shouting.

And there were moments when she couldn't believe it herself, couldn't believe that she'd been bold enough to offer her services to an officer of the Confederate Army. But she had, and Colonel Forrest had shown every evidence of appreciating her actions, not been shocked like Celine said.

Celine had rolled her eyes and shaken her head, allowing as how "proper young ladies do not act like the white trash that lives down by the swamp!"

"I did not. I saved our brave men time and trouble, and maybe made it possible for them to capture the Yankees who burned our house!" Jessamy had refused to back down, and returned Celine's gaze without flinching.

"Sacrebleu! You could have let your brother show the soldiers where to go, instead of riding astride with your skirts up around your knees and showing your legs!"

"Bryce wasn't there and I was. Besides, this is war, Celine, and there just wasn't time for some of the proprieties."

"I think I agree," Abigail had surprised everyone by saying. "Now, Celine, Jessamy is a heroine, and should not be scolded for what she has done."

It was help from an unexpected source, and Jessamy was suddenly, fiercely, glad she had acted as she had. If her mother approved, then it was an endorsement.

Old Billy and the others had been recalled from the swamp, and the men were now trying to salvage what they could from the wreckage of the house. The charred ruins were still too hot to sift, but the piles of discarded furniture and items the Yankees had thrown outside yielded a few usable articles. One of the kitchens was still standing, though the other had caught on fire and burned. The stables were left, but the storehouses were mostly gone but for a few, and those few looted.

The occupants at Clover Hill slowly began to try and put back together the threads of their lives. Though the Yankees had left their home in a shambles, they had not destroyed the indomitable spirit of the survivors.

That was evident the following day, when the tinny call of a bugle sounded on the road winding past the ruined lawns. Old Billy was sifting through the remains of the house when he heard it, and he ran for one of the rifles he had taken to the swamps with him. Bryce ran too, demanding that Old Billy give him a weapon.

"I can shoot it, and I will!" he said so fiercely that the servant nodded and wordlessly handed him a rifle.

There was not enough time to flee. The soldiers were stirring up a cloud of dust at the crossroads.

Jessamy stood on the porch of the overseer's cabin with her mother and the others, feeling angry and anxious at the same time.

"Maybe it's our boys," she said, and no one spoke. It was too great a hope to be voiced aloud.

Then Abigail took a step forward, and her normally cool voice quivered with just the faintest trace of emotion. "It *is* our boys! I see their beautiful banner. . . ."

Jessamy's knees sagged with relief, and she grasped at the rough bark of the porch post to keep from plopping to the ground. As the line of gray uniforms rode up the drive in triumph, she also saw blue uniforms, and realized that Forrest had made good on his promise.

Colonel Forrest confirmed this as he rode up to the rough cabin and reined in his mount, gallantly sweeping off his hat and smiling down at the ladies.

"As you can see, Miss Windsor, your fair courage infused nerve into my arm and knightly chivalry into my heart. I was inspired to follow your cries for justice, and I have, indeed, done so. Note, if you will, the enemy that have been captured."

Jessamy turned to look, and was glad to see that Forrest had managed to capture about thirty men, a great many of them officers. It was his greatest coup to date, and he was very pleased with himself.

She smiled up at him. "Colonel, it was my privilege to have inspired you, and I see that you outdid even my hopes for justice."

"And without losing more than three men!" Forrest said. "I count those three in my heart, and regret their passing, but know that they died for our Glorious Cause."

At the moment, Jessamy did not mind sparing three men for the Cause, but when she discovered that one of the three had been Robbie Armstrong, she paled.

"Not Robbie! Oh no . . ."

Maribelle wept when Stuart told her, his face grave and tortured. It was a bitter blow for young Armstrong. He and his brother had never been separated for long, and now they would be separated forever. He clung to Maribelle, and no one said a word about it, even Aunt Pretense.

They stood in the yard outside the small whitewashed cabin, while weary men draped themselves over the area so recently vacated by the Yankees. Campfires were built again and slave cabins occupied by soldiers. Tents were hastily thrown up, and a surgeon's tent lay close to the overseer's cabin and the well. Moans and cries drifted from the tent.

Jessamy stood, her arms wound about her body in a tight knot, her face rigid as she tried not to look around her.

All around lay wounded men, bleeding and suffering, men in gray and blue uniforms alike, and Jessamy had the brief thought that it was odd the enemies' blood should be red. Somehow, she had ceased thinking of them as Americans, even as human. A blue uniform contained an enemy, a man who was responsible for pain and death and the destruction of her way of life.

"Oh Jess!" Maribelle cried, seeing the strained expression on Jessamy's face. "You must be sufferin' so! I'd forgotten that you an' Robbie—that you were good friends."

Turning, Jessamy stared at her cousin blankly. She had not thought about Robbie, and she felt a guilty twinge. She had been so busy thinking about the enemy and how she hated them that she'd not mourned the death of a friend.

She looked away, anywhere but at Maribelle's comforting face, her tear-streaked cheeks and soft eyes oozing sympathy. A flash of irritation made her voice sharp when Maribelle tried to hug her, and she pushed her away. "Don't! I—I can't think about it right now. And besides, we weren't . . ."

Jessamy paused. Her averted gaze had chanced to fall upon a pair of dark eyes and a familiar face staring at her with an interested, half-mocking expression. Alex. He was looking at her with a black brow cocked and a smile curving his mouth, and for a moment she did not notice the bloodied bandage around his chest and arm. All she could think of was that he was there, now a prisoner instead of a victor. Life did have its compensations at times.

Bewildered by Jessamy's rebuff, Maribelle followed her gaze. "Why, it's Alex Steele! And he's wounded!"

Now Jessamy noticed the wide bandage wrapped around his chest, the uniform shirt that was torn open and hanging. She felt a flicker of concern, but it passed quickly as she remembered that he was still her enemy.

"So he is," Jessamy said coldly, and turned away. She could hear Alex laugh softly, and that made her furious. He did not care that she did not care, and somehow that made her even more angry. He was supposed to be devastated that she wanted him dead, that she enjoyed his capture. Instead he laughed at her.

In the days that followed, Jessamy refused to help with the wounded enemy. She did her best to nurse the boys in gray, following the surgeon's instructions with a queasy stomach and weak smile, but she bluntly refused to assist one man in blue.

"No. I will not compromise my beliefs," she said firmly when her mother reminded her that her father and brothers might need help from a Yankee woman. "And I am certain that Papa would rather die than take help from a Yankee!"

Abigail gave her a keen look. "Is that what you want for him, Jessamy? That he die in pain and alone, with no one to hold his hand or pray for him?"

Jessamy shifted uncomfortably and could not look at her mother. "No, but neither do I want to help the man who might be the very one to kill him, either!"

There was a brief moment of silence, then Abigail nodded her head wearily. "Very well. Do as you think right, daughter. I suppose I cannot guide your heart, and at the moment, I do not know what is right. I am just doing what I think is best for me." She laid a cool hand against Jessamy's cheek and smiled. "You're strong-willed, my dear, and I admire that. Your brave heart will carry you through times that may subdue others."

Jessamy received Abigail's light kiss on her forehead gratefully. There were moments when she felt as if her mother truly understood her, and accepted her in spite of it. It was comforting, and there was so little comfort these days.

Especially for Bryce. The twelve-year-old was steadfast in his hatred for the enemy, and dogged the colonel to allow him to go with them when they left.

"I'll fight! I've got my own rifle and I'll steal a horse if I have to. . . ."

Colonel Forrest, his customary smile fading, grew sober and grave. He put out a gloved hand and placed it on Bryce's shoulder, staring down at the boy's earnest face.

"The South does not yet need the lifeblood of its youth, son, though I respect your desire to join us. You are more needed here at home with your mother at this time. She has no one, and must depend on you."

Angry tears glittered in Bryce's eyes, and his small chin jutted out fiercely. "She has Old Billy and Moses to care for her!"

"How old are you, son?"

Bryce tried to make himself appear taller as he drew his slender frame up, sticking out his chest and throwing back his shoulders. Straight dark lashes like his sister's blinked rapidly to clear away the tears, and he deepened his voice.

"Twelve years old, sir!"

Colonel Forrest smiled. "Wait, son, until you are a little older. There will be a position for you with me when you are fifteen, should the war still be going on, which, hopefully, it will not."

Bryce made a manful attempt at swallowing his disappointment, not wanting the colonel to think he was a child begging for a denied treat.

"Very well, sir, but if I cannot fight, I can beat the drum or sound recall on the bugle."

Pulling at his small beard, Forrest regarded Bryce for a long moment. "We have no need of a drummer boy now, but if your mother agrees, I shall take you with me."

A grin split Bryce's face, and he nodded eagerly. "I shall tell her now, sir!"

"She must agree," the colonel cautioned, but Bryce had already begun running toward the whitewashed cabin and his mother.

To his utter sorrow, Abigail would not hear of it. "No, I cannot risk all my sons," she stated so firmly Bryce knew there was no hope she would change her mind.

For several days, he was a despondent figure on the front porch, his head in his hands, his blue eyes cloudy with disappointment. An occasional soldier would try to cheer the boy, ruffling his light brown hair or telling him a joke, but nothing helped. The only time he would brighten was when he sat with the gray-clad men around the campfire at night and listened to the retelling of battles they'd fought, skirmishes in which they'd battled the enemy and won.

"I spoke with Captain Steele today. He cautioned that we should watch Bryce more closely, and not let him become too enamored of war," Abigail commented with a slight frown one evening. It was late and she was tired from nursing soldiers and seeing to her family all day. The hours were long, and even at night in front of the fire she did not rest, doing light needlework, mending socks or shirts. The fire in the stone hearth flickered brightly, chasing away the chill in the drafty cabin, and she pulled her shawl more snugly around her shoulders as she glanced around at her family. They were all there except for the two youngest girls asleep on their cots, and Bryce, who was, as usual, with the soldiers.

Abigail looked into the leaping flames and sighed. "I hope that Captain Steele is wrong in his belief that Bryce might try to join them."

"I cannot imagine why you listen to anything that traitor has to say!" Jessamy said more sharply than she intended. She flushed when Abigail turned to her in surprise. "I mean, he's the enemy, and he just wants you to worry."

"Why, Jessamy, I don't think that is it at all. You must remember that Alex is still family, and even if he chooses to fight on the side of the enemy, he would not want to see Bryce harmed."

Jessamy's chin thrust out, and her eyes darkened. "I disagree, Mother. Didn't he burn Clover Hill? And didn't he take us all prisoner, taking all our food and calling it contraband? Oh, he spouted off disclaimers, saying if it was up to him he wouldn't, but he did it just the same."

"This is war, and in war men must do things they would not ordinarily do," Abigail said gently.

"War just gives them a good excuse to behave like animals with no morals! I don't see where Alex Steele can excuse himself for a moment, though he sure does try."

Abigail's needle punched through the thin cotton shirt she was mending, and for a moment nothing was said. Aunt Pretense was huddled in a rocker, creaking back and forth like an old granny, and Maribelle nodded sleepily by the fire. Celine sat like a stone near the door, posting herself as watchdog. Only Jessamy was filled with a restless energy, longing to escape the confines of the cabin and her family.

Maybe it was the crisp November night, or the full moon that cast a light almost as bright as day over the land, but whatever it was, she felt as if she would scream if she didn't get away.

Standing abruptly, Jessamy said, "I'm . . . I'm going to the privy."

"Take a candle, dear," Abigail said, and Jessamy went to the rickety table against the far wall. Several tallow stubs lay in a neat row, and she fit one into a wooden holder to take with her, feeling Celine's sharp eyes on her the entire time.

"You do not need to be out there by yourself,

Jessamy. It is dangerous," Celine said with suspicion heavy in her voice.

"Good heavens! It's only a few yards away, and these are our boys here, not those wretched Yankees!"

Her disclaimer did not mollify Celine, who watched her narrowly. *"Oui,* I know that very well, but we cannot be too sure that some of those Yankee soldiers might not be sneaking about, either!"

"With all our boys sitting here? Don't be silly, Celine! You're getting nervous as an old guinea hen!"

Jessamy lit the candle, avoiding Celine's gaze, and opened the door. "I'll be back shortly," she said as she ducked out the door.

"See that you do!"

It wasn't until she was several yards away from the cabin that Jessamy drew in a deep breath and blew out her candle. She didn't need it. It was almost as bright as day outside, with the moon throwing silvery light across the lawn and the campfires blazing high. Several soldiers touched their caps and nodded to her as she passed, and she felt at ease. None of these men would do her harm. They were gentlemen, not like those rascally Yankees who had watched her with sly leers.

Somewhere close by a soldier was playing a mouth organ, and the plaintive melody sent a shiver through Jessamy. She paused to listen beneath the bare branches of an oak, one hand against the rough bark. It was an old Negro hymn, soft and melancholy, its lyrics bringing to mind visions of heavenly angels perched in chariots.

Swing low, sweet chariot, comin' for to carry me home, she sang softly, and couldn't understand why there were tears in her eyes. She sniffed, and used the edge of her shawl to wipe away the tears. This was ridiculous, and she shouldn't be standing here thinking sad thoughts. She should be rejoicing, for hadn't Colonel Forrest captured a great many of the enemy and set the rest to flight? If more Confederate leaders could do the same, the war would be over in just a few months.

A shadow drew her attention, and Jessamy looked up to see a gray-clad soldier approaching. She smiled, suddenly grateful that he was there instead of a Yankee.

"Hello . . . Corporal," she said, identifying him by the two bars of the chevrons on his sleeves.

Pausing, he doffed his cap, smiling back at her. "Hello, miss." Another pause, then he said awkwardly, "It's a fine night."

"Yes, it is." She recognized the admiration in his gaze and smiled again. Moonlight streamed down over the soldier's pale hair, making it gleam, lighting up the world with an eerie glow. "You look almost like a ghost," she said then, searching for a casual topic. She waved a hand. "Because of the moonlight, I mean."

"Well, I'm not a ghost," the soldier replied as he twisted his cap and stared at her. There was something—expectant—in his gaze, as if he were waiting for her to say something else, and Jessamy tried to think what it might be.

She couldn't think of anything that might be relevant, and so she smiled again, lowering her lashes the way she had seen Maribelle do, the way she had seen countless Southern girls do when they wanted to appear demure and shy.

To the young soldier, however, far from home and his sweetheart, this lovely girl seemed to be flirting with him and he was both surprised and excited. She just stood there with her lashes lowered and her face faintly flushed, and he thought he had never seen anyone so lovely in his entire life. And when she lifted her lashes and gazed up at him again, the soldier lost all thought of propriety.

Almost dropping his cap in his eagerness, he reached out to grasp Jessamy's arm, clumsily trying to press a kiss on her hand. But instead of reacting with pleasure or shy acquiescence as he had expected, she gave a small cry and tried to pull away. In his surprise, the soldier kept his grip, his fingers digging into her arm as he tried to think what had gone wrong.

"Let me go!" Jessamy cried out, wrenching away from him with a quick twist of her arm. Her heart was beating fast, and she panted for breath, frighteningly reminded of the Yankee soldier and another confrontation.

"Hey! I—I'm not . . . hey!"

The hapless soldier's misfortune was compounded by the sudden arrival of another soldier, this one clad in the hated blue uniform of the enemy. Seconds later, the Confederate corporal found himself lying on his back nursing a bruised jaw, staring up at the dark-eyed man straddling him.

"Are you all right?" Alex asked Jessamy, who gazed at him angrily.

"Of course I'm all right!"

Alex straightened, unclenching his fists.

"Why is it I seem to be constantly rescuing you from overeager admirers, Miss Windsor?"

"Because you leap to conclusions as fast as you leap on enlisted men!" she shot back. Now that she was rescued, she saw that the poor corporal had only been trying to relate his admiration for her, and she felt foolish. She had overreacted to his advance, when he had only been trying to kiss her hand.

"I see," Alex was saying, his head tilted to one side as he regarded her without smiling. "Then you were enjoying your little tête-à-tête? I apologize for interrupting your mauling, Miss Windsor." Reaching down, he helped the bewildered corporal to his feet. "Carry on, Corporal," Alex said, then pivoted on his heel and stalked away.

Jessamy gazed after him angrily. "What is he doing running around loose anyway?" she asked aloud, and the corporal regarded her warily.

"He's an officer, and all the officers were asked to give their word they wouldn't try to escape."

"And Colonel Forrest believed him?"

The corporal shrugged. "I don't know, miss. But I do know that even if he does escape, it won't make much difference. He doesn't know anything important."

What the soldier meant was, no correct information had been released. Not that it would have mattered to Alex, for he had not given his word. He alone of the captured officers had managed to avoid giving his word of honor. They had not noticed, and that gave him an edge he fully intended to use.

Jessamy stared into the shadows after Alex, trying to compose herself, wondering why he had suddenly appeared at her side. She barely noticed when the corporal backed away, his cap in his hand, his dignity and ego bruised.

Leaning back against the oak, Jessamy thought about Alex for several minutes. Odd how she thought about him even when she didn't want to think about him, how he would just pop into her head all of a sudden. It had happened too many times to count, and she supposed now that it was because she couldn't understand why he had to be a traitor. He was born a Southerner, born in Virginia and brought up in Kentucky—what had happened to twist him into a man who would deny his own blood? And her mother was wrong about him being a relative, because he wasn't. Not a blood relative, anyway, and that was what really counted. Though she had a hatful of cousins who weren't really cousins but were given that title through courtesy and lack of another label to put on them, it wasn't the same.

Like Uncle Bertram, who had married Abigail's sister and wasn't really her uncle except through marriage. Bertram Weaver had a brother who had sired seven children, and all of them were called her cousins, though technically they weren't. Families could be so complicated at times, and if she thought of Alex Steele as her cousin, she felt disloyal. And if she thought of Alex as her cousin, then she couldn't think of him as . . .

But that was ridiculous!

Straightening, Jessamy thought with a trace of panic that she had gone moon-mad. Lunacy! Sheer lunacy to think of that disreputable, disgraceful, disloyal traitor as anything other than a despicable beast! What if her mother should find out that she had been rescued by him again? It would be embarrassing at the least, and she could not think of anything else quite so humiliating.

Perhaps that was one reason why, when she returned to the cabin, Jessamy remained silent upon discovering that Alex was there. She sat stiffly on the low bench by the door, her eyes riveted on the fire as if fascinated by the leaping flames. Alex and Abigail were speaking softly so as not to wake the others, and even Celine had gone to bed. No one else stirred in the small cabin.

Jessamy tried to ignore them, tried to pretend Alex was at the far ends of the earth, but it was almost impossible. She could hear his low, soft voice, his Virginia accent that made him sound so different from Tennesseans. After all his years in Kentucky, he still spoke with a slight Virginia drawl.

"So, Captain Steele, how is Charity?" Abigail was asking.

"Please, call me Alex. We are still family. My mother was fine, judging from the last letter I received. You know that there was a bit of fighting close to our home."

"No, I didn't. Is everyone all right? Huntley, and your home?"

"They're all fine. Some of the crops were trampled, but that's all."

Jessamy could stand it no longer. Her heart beat with fury, and she was trembling all over. "How fortunate for you, Captain, that your home was spared while ours wasn't! I suppose you've congratulated yourself for your cleverness in avoiding it!"

"Jessamy Ann Windsor!" Abigail never used her full name unless quite put out with her, but Jessamy could not stop.

"Well, why shouldn't I say something? Did he spare our home? His home is still standing!"

"You must recall that it is your uncle Huntley's home as well," Abigail pointed out.

"But Uncle Huntley has no sons, so it will go to this blackguard someday, while we have nothing—"

Alex stood, his voice even, his gaze steady. "I know that you blame me for the burning of your house, but it was not of my choosing, Jess. I told you that."

She stood, her entire body quivering with hurt and rage. "And I told you that I do not believe you! Why should I believe the enemy?"

Alex took two quick steps forward, reaching out to grasp Jessamy by her arms. "You shouldn't believe the enemy, but I'm not your enemy. When will you learn that?"

"Any man in a blue uniform is my enemy!"

"That's like saying all dogs bite."

"Don't they?"

"Only if provoked." Alex gave her a slight shake when she would have twisted away, wincing slightly at the pain it caused him. "Listen to me, Jess, before your hatred festers your soul. This is war, but don't make it a private war. Keep it impersonal, or you will be consumed with bitterness one day."

"I'm consumed with it now!" she flashed, and succeeded in wrenching away from him. When he flinched again she was glad she had caused him pain, and hoped that it was twice as great as the pain she had suffered when Clover Hill burned. "I shall never forgive you, Alex Steele, no matter what you may do."

A slight smile flickered on his lips. "Never say never, Jess. It always comes back to haunt you."

Never say never! It already haunted her, had shrouded her days and nights even when she tried desperately to push it from her mind.

"I won't forgive you until never turns blue!"

Alex laughed softly. "Then, until the blue never, Jess—"

Whirling, she yanked open the cabin door and stepped outside, snapping, "I shall stay out here until that foul odor leaves our cabin!" The door slammed behind her, cutting off Abigail's expression of reproach and Alex's grim amusement.

Almost immediately, Jessamy wished she had not been so hasty. The night air was decidedly cool now, and if Alex had not been there, she would have gone back inside. But he was there, and so she stood shivering on the porch, thinking it would be just like him to linger in the warm cabin while she grew blue with cold. One more thing to fan the fires of her wrath.

By the time Alex left the cabin, Jessamy's lips were purple and her teeth were chattering. He took one look at her and burst into laughter.

"So, has the night air cooled your fire, little Rebel?"

"Go . . . to . . . hell," she said between clacks of her teeth, and hoped that Abigail could not hear.

Shrugging out of his coat, Alex tried to drape it around Jessamy's shoulders but she ducked.

"No! I—I'm going inside, and I wouldn't wear that blue coat if I was dying from the cold!"

With surprising strength for a wounded man, Alex put it around her shoulders, buttoning it over her flailing arms. "I want to talk to you a minute, and I don't want your mother to hear. You can't pay attention if you're shaking like jelly, so be quiet."

"Be quiet? Just who—"

"I said be quiet, Jess," Alex repeated, this time more harshly, and as he was dragging her from the porch and out into the yard, Jessamy concentrated on where she was stepping instead of answering. Some instinct told her that this was important.

She was right.

Alex stopped beneath the same oak where he'd found her earlier, and his voice was urgent. "Jess, do you know where your brother is?"

"Bryce?" She shook her head. "No, over listening to the soldiers, I suppose, like he usually is. Why?"

"Because he's not there. I've looked for him. Do you have a horse?"

Jessamy stiffened. "If you think for one minute that I'm going to help you escape, you can just go fiddle! Why, I wouldn't help you even if I liked you, which I surely don't, so you can—"

He gave her a hard shake, his voice quick and cold. "Stop being so ready to fight, and start thinking! Bryce is gone, you little idiot, and I think I know where."

"Bryce? Gone? I don't know what you mean. . . ."

"I'm not a bit surprised, but that doesn't matter. He is not in camp, and he has not gone to

149

run any errands for your mother. In my usual discreet manner, I have asked her. She does not yet know he has disappeared, and until we have to tell her, I think it best not to do so."

Jessamy's head whirled. "But Bryce wouldn't just run off by himself. I mean, where would he go? He ought to know I can't do all these chores by myself, and . . . why?"

Alex gave her a look of contempt. "Don't you ever think about anyone else but yourself? Did it ever occur to you to give your brother some comfort, that he has been hurting just like you have been? Think for a few minutes how he feels."

"Don't presume to tell me about *my* brother!" Jessamy flashed, though she thought with a start of guilt that he was right.

Dragging her so close his face was only an inch or two from hers, Alex ground out, "And you call me selfish? I have rarely seen such a self-centered, inconsiderate—"

"All right!" Tears sprang to her eyes, and with a sense of distress she felt them begin to fill her nose. She hated to cry, for it made her nose red and runny and she looked like a fool. But now she was worried about Bryce, really worried, and she had the distressing conviction that Alex Steele was right. She had been selfish, and she had ignored Bryce. Now he was gone and she had no idea where or why.

"But Alex, where could he be?" she asked so plaintively that he softened.

Loosening his tight grip on her arms, he pulled her to his chest, letting her put her head against him and weep softly. She could feel the strong thud of his heart beneath her cheek, and she tried not to think about the fact that it was Alex who held her as she let him pat her head and say comforting things.

"I think he followed Forrest's command. Remember, he wanted to be a drummer boy or bugler."

She drew back, staring up at Alex in confusion. "But Colonel Forrest is still here, Alex!"

A slight smile slanted his mouth, and for some reason she had the distracted thought that when he smiled he was very, very handsome.

"No, Forrest wants us to think he's here, but he left behind only a very small contingent of men to see that we prisoners are exchanged. The lit fires and multitude of tents are all for show."

"Oh."

Alex pulled her into him again, and at the feel of her small firm breasts against him he felt the old stirring of desire. It overrode everything else, his plans, Bryce, his wound, everything but the girl in his arms. She smelled like woodsmoke and felt like heaven. And when he lifted her chin with his finger and began to kiss her, she kissed him back. He'd half expected it, sensing her attraction to him before she did, but he was still surprised at the intensity of her kiss.

Jessamy couldn't understand it either, couldn't allow herself to examine her reaction. There was something about Alex's touch that made her normally cool brain lose all control, and she found herself leaning into his embrace.

Alex slipped his hands beneath the coat Jessamy wore thrown over her, pressing them against the small of her back and holding her tightly against him. In spite of the night air and his thin shirt, he felt as if he were on fire. His mouth moved across her lips with swift certainty, and he kissed her hungrily, lingering, tasting the velvet sweetness of her. She moaned, her head falling back, and he reached up to cradle it with one hand, his other hand still holding her close against his lean body.

It was a startling discovery for Jessamy. She wanted him to keep kissing her, and she wanted something else, though she wasn't quite certain what. There was a slow, coiling fire inside her, burning and searing and making her legs weak and her breath harsh and rapid. She was confused. She didn't understand how her body could betray her like this, when under normal circumstances she would never have dreamed of allowing Alexander Steele within a yard of her.

Yet now she wanted him to keep kissing her, wanted him to caress her cheek, and the line of her throat, as he was doing, wanted it to go on forever. Alex smelled of woodsmoke too, and leather and tobacco, and even a trace of whisky. Instead of being repelled by it she found his scent tantalizing, and didn't know why. Why she should be drawn to him now remained a mystery she didn't even want to consider. Not now. Now there was nothing but Alex, nothing but the fire burning hotter and hotter, and she could think of little else.

It was Alex who finally drew back and took a deep, steadying breath, Alex who set her firmly from him before he took more liberties than he should. He smiled at the confused expression in her eyes, and at her small moan of protest.

It was no use telling her that he was more miserable about it than she was, no use trying to explain that if he didn't stop now, he wouldn't stop at all. How could he tell Jessamy any of that?

Drawing in another ragged breath, Alex pulled his blue coat more firmly around her shoulders. His fingers held the edges together, hiding the tempting sight of her young body. Best not to fan the flames any higher. . . .

"Jess, I'll try to find Bryce for you. Do what you think best about telling your mother. It's your decision."

Jessamy was trying to rearrange her disordered thoughts into some semblance of order, trying to cudgel her stubborn body into submission. She was still shaking, and could not quite control the quiver in her voice.

"I . . . I will."

He smiled. "I know. And look, about your house. I want you to know that—"

Stiffening, Jessamy's eyes flashed, as she realized with increasing horror that she had just kissed the man responsible for the burning of her home. How could she have been so weak!

Alex knew at once that he had said the wrong thing, and gave a sigh of resignation as she twisted out of his grasp, leaving him holding the blue coat as she fled. Her words floated back to him, and he could not help a rueful smile.

"You're still a damn Yankee, Alex Steele!"

The slamming of the cabin door punctuated her defiant shout, and Alex slid his arms back into his coat. He winced again, damning the bullet that had sliced into his chest and deflected from a rib to ricochet into his upper arm. He was still sore, and would be sore for some time. It was going to be a damnable nuisance while he was carrying out his plans.

Chapter 11

MOONLIGHT SHIMMERED EERILY over the quiet grounds of Clover Hill. It pricked through the tiny chinks between the logs of Obadiah Johnston's whitewashed cabin, the slivers of light tracing the fretful lines creasing Jessamy's face. She was waiting, and she hated waiting.

Abigail had still been awake when Jessamy returned to the cabin disheveled and with her lips bruised, but she did not notice her daughter's state. She was still waiting up for Bryce. Time passed, and the moon rose higher in the night sky and the soldiers' fires burned lower. Still he did not come home, and Abigail rose abruptly from her place by the hearth.

"I shall wake the others. Someone must know where he is or when he will return."

Biting her lower lip, Jessamy did not argue. She didn't know what to do. Should she tell her mother, or let her fret? Or hope that somehow Alex Steele would arrive at their door with a recalcitrant Bryce? She waited and hoped.

But after the others had been woken and questioned, and Abigail grew even more fretful, Jessamy was forced to tell her mother what Alex had said. For the first time in her life she saw Abigail Windsor slip into a faint. She did it quietly, without the fuss and fanfare that usually attended Pretense's faints, leaving them all staring at her crumpled form.

It was Pretense, strangely enough, who recovered first.

"Sara Jean, get my vinaigrette bottle! Maribelle, fetch a cool cloth. You, Jessamy, help me with your mother."

The girls leaped to help, and as Abigail lay on a thin cot with her eyes closed and her face composed, Jessamy had the thought that it would be much kinder if she were allowed to sleep for a long time. Waking was such a brutal thing when one woke every morning to a world that was in tatters, with nothing the same.

"Oh, *a pauvre petite!*" Celine crooned, staring down at Abigail anxiously. "This has made her ill! And Bryce, he's a bad boy to stay out like this, and worry his *maman* so! I am tempted to use a hickory switch when he gets back. . . ." In her distress, she slipped into the French patois of her youth.

"That doesn't help now," Jessamy murmured, and moved close to her mother's bed. "It would help more if she slept until he got back. Or until someone brings him back."

"Perhaps that is so, but it is not wise," Celine said soberly. "She might get the brain fever if she sleeps too long."

So Jessamy gently patted her mother's hand and put cool cloths on her forehead while Pretense waved a bottle of smelling salts beneath Abigail's aristocratic nose. Poor Pretense. Her normally flustered face was even more flustered now, with her corkscrew curls bobbing wildly and making her look half mad in the dim light of the cabin. Yet oddly enough Pretense had never before seemed so much like Abigail. Jessamy had often wondered how the two could be even distantly related, much less sisters. But now, in a time of crisis when there was no one else to take the reins of command, Pretense rose to the occasion. It was as gratifying as it was vaguely puzzling.

Abigail did, of course, recover. After all, she was made of sterner stuff than to collapse at such news, but it was still hard to see the distress in her fine eyes and the faint web of wrinkles that fanned from the corners. She looked up at her daughter, her voice soft.

"Where do you suppose he has gone, Jessamy? Do you think that Colonel Forrest will know?"

Jessamy mumbled that the colonel had ridden out, but that she would ask him when he returned.

Nodding, Abigail lay back on her cot, closing her eyes. It was then Jessamy decided on her course of action.

Long after the others slept, when the moonlight began to soften, she crept from the cabin. She was wearing her father's sweater and her brother Nick's pants, with Bryce's good shoes on her feet and a straw hat on her head. In one hand she carried the light rifle that had been in the swamp with Old Billy. Bryce's hunting rifle was gone.

Determination shone from her eyes as Jes-

samy made her way to the edge of camp. The
sentry dozed, and she silently cursed him for being a disgrace to the Confederacy, but was glad
he slept at his post. He might have stopped her
even if he'd known who she was, but in her disguise, she would certainly have been stopped.
Nothing must delay her. She intended to find
Bryce and bring him home.

The familiar woods in the daytime were
friendly, with landmarks to guide her and curious creatures that scampered away at her approach. Night was an entirely different matter,
Jessamy discovered.

She paused, listening to the vaguely sinister
rustlings in the underbrush, and stared at the
deep shadows shrouding the trees and yawning
ahead of her like bottomless caverns. She
scoffed at her fears and surged forward, tread-
ing as lightly as possible, wincing at every crack
of a twig or branch beneath her feet. It was
more frightening than she had thought while
lying safely in her cot and waiting for the others
to fall asleep. Reality was much darker than the
fantasy had been.

Moon shadows wavered in front of her, shap-
ing the normally friendly landscape into a col-
lage of beasts and hideous creatures of the
night. Jessamy's courage faltered, then she
boosted it by visualizing her mother's face as
she had last seen it. How could she even consider turning back when she remembered the
faint lines that had creased Abigail's brow? She
couldn't, of course.

But it was still hard to force her feet forward,
to swallow the fear that rose in her throat at the
smallest sound. Memories of the Yankees re-

turned to haunt her, and memories of the depre-
dations suffered by others at their hands
ballooned in her mind from vague rumors to
certainties that clawed at her fears. The rifle
felt clumsy and useless in her hands, and with a
sense of despair, she recalled that she had forgotten balls and gunpowder. What good would it
do her now?

Jessamy slapped at a low-hanging branch. It
snapped back, sending her hat flying from her
head and dousing her with droplets of dew. She
shivered as it splattered her face in a chilly
shower.

"Dammit!" she said aloud, and felt oddly com-
forted by the sound of her voice. "Dammit," she
said again, softer this time, rolling the swear
word off her tongue without fear of reprisal. A
faint smile curved her mouth as Jessamy wiped
the dew from her face. After all, who was out
here to listen and report to Abigail that her
daughter was swearing in a most unladylike
manner?

"Does your mother know you swear?" a deep
voice asked from the shadows to her left, drawing a high scream from Jessamy.

Whirling, she dropped the rifle in her haste to
flee, fear spurring her. She was abruptly
stopped by a harsh arm around her waist and a
hand over her mouth.

"You little fool!" the voice grated in her ear.
"Do you want to sound the alarm to every Rebel
in Tennessee?"

Alex. She recognized his voice, recognized the
rough inflection. She should have known that
he would somehow cause her trouble.

"Let me go," she said against his palm, her lips moving in muffled anger.

"Let you go to rouse Forrest and his eager brigade? Not a chance," Alex said into her ear, holding her back against his hard chest. One arm wound around her body in an iron grip, constricting her chest and making it hard for her to breathe, while the other pressed the back of her head into his shoulder. She could feel the rapid thud of his heart, and the labored breaths he took, and knew that his wound must be bothering him. Jessamy decided to take immediate advantage.

Lifting her feet suddenly so that she was a dead weight that would throw him off balance, she twisted at the same time. It did not have the effect she desired.

Instead of forcing him down to catch himself and let her go, Alex held her even more tightly, throwing his own weight back so that her feet were lifted from the ground. Jessamy's kicking feet lashed out, bruising his shins but doing relatively little damage and certainly not freeing her. She kicked so hard one shoe went flying through the air to land with a muffled plop in the bushes. Her only consolation was that it caused him some pain in his sore chest and arm.

A muttered curse sounded in her ear, and she winced at the harshness of his voice. She'd made him angry, truly angry, but at the moment she didn't care. How dare he hide out here in the woods and try to scare her, and . . . what *was* he doing out here so far away from his guards, anyway?

Jessamy stopped struggling. She stood still

and quiet and waited for Alex to remove his hand from her mouth so she could ask him that very question. It occurred to her as she waited that he could very well be escaping. What a feather in her cap if she could manage to capture him!

Common sense intruded into her fantasy with a rude twist of Alex's hand and his tightening arm across her chest.

"Little fool! You're lucky that branch knocked off your hat and I recognized you, because I was about to silence you the same way I did the guard," he muttered against her ear. A chill skipped down her spine at his words, and she recalled the guard she had thought was sleeping at his post. Instead of irritation at the guard, she now felt regret that she had thought him a slacker. If she had known—but she hadn't, and now here was Alex, a very different Alex from the laughing-eyed man who teased her into sulks. This Alex was quiet and deadly, and she could feel the taut strength in the tensed muscles holding her against him. This was not a childhood playmate, but a soldier, a man who was her enemy.

"Will you be quiet if I take my hand away?" he grated, but Jessamy did not agree. Pride stiffened her backbone into a straight line, and her feet began to dance again. Alex snarled another curse as her solitary shoe heel dug into his leg. "I can be rougher, you know!" he snapped. "I just thought you might want to behave like a lady and call a temporary truce."

Temporary. That was the key word. Jessamy paused in her mad flailing of his shin to consider the truce. She was tired and her lower jaw hurt where his palm was digging into her skin so hard. To continue fighting would get her nowhere, as he had the advantage. Not only that, she was thirsty and curious to know how Alex Steele had managed to get away from his guards.

"Truce," she mumbled finally, and was relieved when he took his hand away. Alex set her down and turned her around to face him, his eyes dark and unreadable in the bright moonlight.

"What the hell are you doing out here?" he asked finally. Jessamy glared at him.

"I could ask you the same thing."

"I think I'm more in a position to be asking than—"

"I wouldn't count on that!" she cut in. "Forrest and his men are within shouting distance—remember?"

"And what makes you think Foote isn't?" was Alex's cool rejoinder. That left Jessamy momentarily quiet. For some reason, it had not occurred to her that Foote might still be close. Perhaps it should have. If Foote was still in the area, and Forrest was still in the area—then both of them were liable to capture.

Seeing that he had made an impression of sorts on Jessamy, Alex relaxed against the broad trunk of a tree. He folded his arms across his chest, stifling a wince of pain at the discomfort that caused. Best not to let the little minx know that she had gotten the upper hand, even if only for a few moments.

"Well," Jessamy said at last, tossing back her head so that her hair fell from its clumsy knot down her shoulders, "what do I do now, Yankee?"

"My name is Alex."

"I know your name, but you're still a Yankee."

"And you're still a foolish little fire-eater! Don't you see that we're at an impasse, Jess? Neither one of us can afford to let the other go. So the main question is, what do *we* do now?"

"I rather think the question is—what do *you* do now?" she countered. "Only think—if I call out, the chances are that Forrest is much closer than Foote. And even if Foote arrives first, would they shoot a woman? No, more likely they would place me under military arrest and perhaps even slap my lily-white hand. But you, now that is a different story altogether. . . ."

She could see by the tightening of his mouth that he was already aware of the truth in what she was saying, and it pleased her a great deal. Alex's dark brow lifted, and his lips thinned into that predatory smile that she hated as he purred, "But if I decide to announce to Foote that you are a spy, my dear, you will meet the same fate I would meet at the hands of Forrest. And even Forrest may recognize my worth as an officer. Prisoner exchange is a favorite pastime, you know. Spies are hung immediately."

"And if I name you as a spy . . . ?"

"I am still an officer, and officers are expected to be spies."

Furious, and goaded into carelessness, Jessamy pivoted on her bare heel and ducked into the thick underbrush. Alex was on her in an instant, his long arms catching her by the waist and lifting her from her feet.

"You broke the truce," he observed.

Her feet swung above the ground, and her hair dangled in front of her eyes, obscuring her view of the shadowed ground and anything else. Escape was futile at this point, she decided.

"I didn't say I wouldn't attempt escape. A truce is just for negotiations, and you know it. Negotiations failed miserably," she said in breathless little pants as his arm tightened.

"Jess, Jess, Jess—are you really so foolish?" he chided. "Only think. What will you accomplish alone? And what are you doing out here in the woods at this hour? In those clothes? I have a hunch I know, but I just want to hear you say it."

"You must know what I'm doing," she replied sullenly. "If you'll put me down before my feet go to sleep, I can talk much more easily."

"As if I needed that," he said as he lowered her slowly to the ground. Keeping one hand curled tightly around her wrist, Alex propelled Jessamy toward a fallen log and forced her down on it. He bent close, his face in shadow, his voice tight. "You're going after Bryce, aren't you?"

"Yes. . . ."

"You're a fool! He's miles ahead of you by now, and I told you I'd find him."

"So where is he? I don't see him in your back pocket, Captain!"

Alex raked a hand through his dark hair, shaking his head and gazing down at Jessamy's upturned face. She looked so vulnerable sitting there staring back at him, the moon shining on her delicate features and revealing the slight sheen of tears in her eyes. Her mane of hair tumbled over her shoulders and framed her small face like a tousled lion's mane, and her slender frame was almost vibrating with reaction.

"Cold?" he asked unexpectedly, and she gave a violent shake of her head.

"No. Just annoyed because we're wasting time while my brother is getting farther and farther away."

Alex propped a booted foot on the log beside her and leaned his elbow on his knee. "Did it ever occur to you that you don't know which direction he took?"

"He went after Forrest—wherever he is."

A wry smile twisted his lips. "Right. And I suppose you intend to just flail about in the woods until you happen to run into Forrest—or maybe Sherman?"

The log was wet, and the night air was cold, and she hated the fact that Alex had logic on his side. Jessamy put her cold hands between her knees and said as steadily as she could, "If I have to."

"Ah, logic, thy name is not Jessamy!"

She snapped to her feet. "You're an uncaring wretch anyway, so why don't you just step aside and let me pass? I won't tell anyone I saw you, and you can do the same favor for me. I have to find Bryce and take him back to Mother before she becomes even more upset, and you are simply in my way, Captain Steele. Now please remove yourself."

"And you think it's just that easy? That you tell me to move out of your way and then you'll find Bryce and go home? Has anything in this damned war been that easy, Jess? Has it?"

Faintly disturbed by the sudden, violent emotion in his voice, Jessamy gave a slight shake of her head. "Nooo. . . ."

"You're right! And this isn't going to be easy either, because we're both caught in an awkward situation. If I let you go, I have no guarantees, and if you let me go, you have no guarantees."

"But your word as a gentleman should—"

"My word as a gentleman!" Alex yanked her close, his fingers biting into her shoulders, his thumbs forcing her chin up so that she had to look directly at him. "There are no gentlemen in war, Jessamy! Can't you get that through your hard little head?"

She tried to pull away but he was holding her too tight, and she felt a sudden surge of fear. There was an odd light in his eyes, and she wondered if his wound had caused him to get a brain fever.

Alex had a fever, all right, but he could have told Jessamy that it had nothing to do with his brain. It was his body that was burning, and she was the cause. As he held her he felt the familiar tug of his senses that he experienced whenever he was close to her. It had nothing to do with anything but the fine texture of her skin, her soft rounded curves, and the slow fires burning behind her sleepy eyes. Or maybe her mouth, the full lips that could be so sulky one moment and provocative the next. She was young, and she was headstrong, and she was so alluring that he thought he must have wanted her for a long time without knowing it.

Dark shadows played across Alex's face, hiding the fires in his eyes but unable to hide the fire in his touch. Jessamy realized that he wanted her, and oddly enough, instead of being angered or offended, she felt a strange sense of excitement.

Slowly, she became aware of his touch in a way she hadn't been before. The coiling of his fingers into her shoulders slackened, and his thumbs began to caress the sensitive underside of her chin, rubbing up along the curve of her jawbone to her ear. Jessamy could almost feel the pounding of Alex's heart, and for a moment wondered if it was hers. Her throat was tight, and there was a wild flutter in her stomach as his head descended, blotting out the moonlight and lacy shadows of bare tree branches, filling her world with nothing but Alex.

His mouth was soft on hers at first, gently touching, whispering over her lips in a kiss as light as a shadow. And when she moaned softly and closed her eyes, he pulled her into him, close against his chest, his arms going around her body to hold her in a fierce embrace. This kiss was deep, almost like the last time, an urgent touching of the souls instead of just the lips, and Alex could feel her response.

"Sweet Jess," he muttered thickly against her mouth. His voice was deep and rough with emotion, and Jessamy had the hazy thought that she should not be standing alone in the woods with Alex Steele. It was too dangerous, dangerous in a way that had nothing to do with the war or soldiers or right or wrong. This had to do with man and woman, and she knew she might be lost if she continued to kiss him back.

Yet it was hard to pull away, hard to refuse that languorous rush of heat that made her forget the chill night air, forget everything but Alex and his arms and his hard mouth on hers. And when he tilted her head back and kissed the base of her throat where her father's shirt did not button, Jessamy could not force him away from her. It was too sweet a feeling, too tantalizing, and she clung to him as if she were afraid of being swept away by the wind.

If she was so warm, why was she shivering? she wondered vaguely as his mouth moved lower, his fingers pushing aside the cotton shirt to bare a wide expanse of creamy skin. Though she had exposed more when she'd worn one of her pretty gowns, this was different. This was more intimate, more dangerous than wearing a dress with a neckline that plunged to the navel.

What was she doing? Here she was in the woods letting Alex Steele—a Yankee!—take liberties with her that no man had ever taken before! And though if she had to be honest she would admit she wanted him to keep kissing her, she knew that she couldn't. Her mother's frequent admonitions as to what a lady should and shouldn't do intruded, as well as a sense of guilt for liking how he made her feel.

Digging her fingers into his broad shoulders, Jessamy dragged her familiar barriers back between them, wrenching her mouth away from his hungry kiss.

"Don't! I—I need air. . . ."

It took Alex a moment to react. His body was too filled with urgency and desire for her, and though he lifted his head and stared down at her face, he did not release her or take his hands away from her sweet curves. His entire body was throbbing, and his normal responses slow. All he could think about at the moment was holding Jessamy even closer, of kissing her all over and making her shudder with pleasure.

When she succeeded in pulling completely away from him she stood panting a moment, her lips slightly parted and her eyes as gray as storm clouds. She wasn't angry. Not yet. She was puzzled by her fierce, sweet reaction to him, puzzled and curious. Why Alex and not someone else? It was an enigma that she could not decipher. Why did she have such a strong reaction to Alex's embrace and not to that of the young men she'd kissed before, young men whom she had liked much better? They were more like her, more like the brothers she'd grown up with, not Alex. Alex was too bold, too mocking, too . . . too male. He exuded masculinity in a way that just wasn't well bred, and she didn't give a fig that he came from a well-bred Virginia background. There was a black sheep in every family, and Alex Steele had to be the one in his. Why had her uncle Huntley ever married Charity Steele anyway? Why would a well-to-do bachelor wed a widow with an unruly son? It didn't make sense, and neither did her reaction to the grown-up Alex, the Alex who confounded her at every turn. He never reacted the way he was supposed to react, never behaved like a gentleman at the proper times, or treated her with the courtesy due the only daughter of William Windsor. And he was a Yankee, to boot!

As the fire in his blood cooled, Alex recognized the internal struggle going on in Jessamy's tousled head. If she knew how tempting she looked with her flowing ash-blond hair in tangles and her father's shirt unbuttoned. . . .

He cleared his throat and said coolly, "Go find your lost shoe, Jess. We've got some walking ahead of us."

Chapter 12

"I CAN'T BELIEVE you intend to do such a thing!"

Irritably, Alex gave Jessamy a slight shove between her shoulder blades. "Of course I do. I explained my reasons, and I don't know why you insist on arguing about it every step of the way."

"So much for your given word of honor," Jessamy spat.

Alex smiled. "I never gave my word of honor to anyone, much less a Rebel. It's their own fault if they assumed that I agreed without getting a direct reply."

"Oooh!" Jessamy gasped in rage. "You meant to escape all along, Alex Steele!"

"Of course. Wouldn't you?"

She stumbled, caught herself, and flung away his hand. The moonlight could not penetrate through the thick canopy of leaves overhead, and the path was too dark to see a foot ahead. Alex was forcing her on, her brother's rifle in his hand, his voice implacable. Childishly, she felt like putting her hands over her ears.

"Look, Jess, neither one of us can be trusted not to betray the other. I don't have the time or energy to take you back to Clover Hill, so this is the only way. If you hate being in my company so much, maybe you'll think about that in the future and not go sneaking off into the night."

"What will Mother say when she wakes up in the morning and I'm gone, too?" Jessamy countered in desperation. If he wouldn't let her go for her own sake, maybe he would for Abigail's. . . .

But Alex was unmoved.

"There's more at stake than your mother's distress. It is unfortunate that Abigail will be upset, but that's just the way it is."

"Damn Yankee!"

A faint chuckle sounded behind her, and Jessamy wished she could shoot him. He found her situation amusing when she could find no humor in it at all.

"I don't know why you chose the wrong side, Alex Steele, when everyone knows how atrocious the Yankees are! Look what they did in Virginia, your birthplace! And how that maniac Sherman smashed Fort Walker. . . ."

Alex's puzzled voice floated to her in the dark. "Fort Walker? Sherman?"

"Yes, Sherman, the *other* Sherman, Brigadier General Thomas Sherman." Her voice was spiteful as she said, "You must not have heard. There was a sea battle on the Carolina coast."

Alex's voice was dry. "No, you Confederates aren't too good at sharing information with prisoners. And I thought you folks didn't find out many war details in remote Clover Hill."

"We didn't while you Yankees were there, but it was simple enough once you were gone."

Wryly, Alex commented, "And of course, you are vitally interested in politics, Jess."

"No! Only in winning this hateful war and getting things back to normal!"

She slowed her steps, barely able to see the path in front of her, her throat suddenly clogging with unshed tears. How had this happened to her, to Jessamy Ann Windsor who had never wanted anything more than to ride her horses and maybe dance in the moonlight? Life had been quite satisfactory before this stupid war had begun, and she highly resented it being ruined now. Clover Hill was gone, her father and brothers were off somewhere doing only God knew what, and now that impulsive Bryce had gotten her involved more deeply than she had ever dreamed. Oh why, why hadn't she stayed at home and waited for someone else to find him? Now she was in the woods with Alex Steele, who had made it plain she would not be returned home until he had made it to safety. Well, guile might prevail where brute strength would not.

While she was watching her step and plotting a way to coax him into releasing her, Alex was thinking about the difference already made in less than a year. It was early November, yet political events had been set into motion that could only have far-reaching and disastrous consequences.

"Things will never be back to normal, Jess," Alex was saying quietly, and there was such a note of sadness in his voice that even Jessamy noticed. "War destroys lives as well as homes. There must be a better way. . . ."

Pausing, Jessamy turned to face him, straining to see his face in the dark night. Her voice was urgent, hopeful. "If you truly feel that way, can't we do something about it? Can't we just . . . just go our own ways and not join in? I mean, if we could make a difference. . . ."

Alex's hand descended upon her shoulder, and his tone was light. "You still think that just because you want something badly that you get it, like a new horse, or a new gown. Well, life doesn't work that way, Jess. It'd be nice if it did, but it doesn't. Grow up. You and I can't make a difference, not this time, not in this war."

"How do you know unless we try?"

"Do you want to be the first one to sashay up to Grant or Sherman and say, 'This is silly. Why don't you take your troops and go home?' That would be a great scene!"

"Oh, you know I didn't mean like that, Alex! Do you have to be so literal?"

His palm cradled her chin, tilting back her head. "Yes. It's my nature. Do you have to be so idealistic?"

Knocking away his hand, Jessamy turned. "Yes. It's my nature!"

"Then you need to remember that there are no heroes in this war, my idealistic friend. Brother is fighting against brother, and our united states are at each other's throats. It's not merely an inconvenience, nor is it romantic as some young fools thought. . . ."

"I suppose you're talking about John Anderson, or Ryan King, or my brother Charles when you say that?" Jessamy shot back. "You can talk about half of Cloverport if you want to, but those 'romantic young fools' are off somewhere fighting and maybe dying, and you . . . you're hiding out here in the woods with a woman."

"That's debatable. You seem more child than woman most of the time, but you're right about half of Cloverport—which constitutes maybe twenty people—off fighting and dying. Only, you seem to be forgetting that there are a lot of boys from small towns up North doing the same thing!" Alex's voice was tight with anger. "I've seen young men from Penn Run, Pennsylvania, with half their faces shot away, and boys with no legs or arms, and it doesn't matter if they're from the north or the south of America when it comes to dying, Jessamy."

Tears thickened her voice as she muttered, "I know. I know. It's just that . . . that . . ."

"It's just that you can't stand the thought of your friends being the ones to die," Alex interrupted in a much kinder tone. "I know. I feel the same way, Jess. Remember, I knew the Andersons, the Kings, the Mullens, the Weavers, the Leatherses. . . ."

A shaft of moonlight filtered through the thick canopy of leaves, revealing the silvery tracks of tears streaking her pale cheeks. "All family, Alex. Those are all relatives or neighbors of mine, and they're out there dying and I can't do a thing about it."

"That's the way it is in all wars, Jess."

She nodded, suddenly weary, suddenly too tired to take another step. Jessamy sank abruptly to the ground, her legs folding beneath her like wet paper.

"I can't move. Shoot me if you want, but just let me sit here."

A faint smile crooked Alex's mouth. "I won't shoot you. Not yet, anyway. Besides, you forgot balls and powder for your rifle."

Her voice was irritable. "I know! Why do you think I didn't shoot you?"

Jackknifing his long legs, Alex crouched beside her. "I kinda thought it was because you were too frightened."

"Of a mere Yankee?"

Chuckling, he said, "Of a mere Yankee! Ah, sweet Jess, you never fail to amuse me."

She leaned back against a tree and closed her eyes. It was too much. Everything that had happened was just too much for her to bear right now. Opening her eyes again, she scooped out a bed between the knobby roots of the tree, and covered herself with dead leaves. It offered a surprising degree of shelter, and warmth of a sort.

"I'm going to sleep," she announced. "If you want to watch me, go ahead."

Alex didn't say anything. His nerves were wound too tightly to sleep, and he knew if he let his guard down for a moment she would run like a rabbit.

Throughout what was left of the night he watched her sleep. There was plenty of time to think, and Alex found that most disturbing. The past month spent as a prisoner had been bad enough, but it had been a month without any information. Where was Foote? Where was Sherman or Grant? He had not even known as much as Jessamy, and God knows she tried to ignore the war as completely as possible.

And now he was in enemy territory, alone, saddled with a hostile prisoner, no ammunition and no idea of where to go. And on top of that, his chest wound was still unhealed. The brief struggle with the Confederate guard had opened it up again, and he could feel the warm trickle of blood wetting his shirt and dripping down his side.

Wadding up a ragged handkerchief, Alex stuffed it under the bandage wrapped around his ribs. That should soak up a little of the blood, he thought with a wince. In spite of the cool air he felt flushed, and he sucked in a deep gulp of air to steady himself.

With the first rays of morning light, Alex roused a drowsy Jessamy.

"Come on. We've got to move."

Her eyelids seemed so heavy, and she felt as if sand lay beneath the lids as she tried to open her eyes. "I can't get up," she mumbled, and Alex shook her again, his voice sharp with impatience.

"Come on! I've got no intention of being caught out here by Forrest or his band of merry men."

Reluctantly, she let him pull her to her feet, brushing away clinging leaves from her trousers as she stood. Weary lines were etched into Alex's face, and the pale sunlight accented the bluish tinge of his lips. It occurred to Jessamy then that Alex was in more pain than she'd thought.

"Are you all right?" she asked, narrowing her eyes at him.

"Don't I look all right?"

Ignoring his sarcastic tone, she shook her head. "No. You look perfectly dreadful."

"That should hearten you. Now come on. I don't have time to stand here trading compliments with you—"

"That's too bad," she interrupted, "because I was going to say that I'll tend to your wound for you."

Shaking his dark head, Alex lifted the useless rifle and slung it under his arm. "Don't bother. I'm strong enough to last for a long time."

Jessamy managed a careless shrug. Crossing her arms over her chest, she suppressed a shiver from the chill. "I thought you'd be stubborn, but it's your wound. I don't suppose you brought anything to eat with you?"

"I didn't have as much time to prepare as you did. I don't suppose *you* thought of food?" Alex countered.

When Jessamy would have denied forgetting food, she saw the faint glitter in Alex's eyes that told her he knew better. It would be no use to pretend otherwise, so she lifted her chin and glared at him defiantly. "It never occurred to me that I wouldn't go right back."

"What? You thought Bryce would be waiting for you around the corner?" Alex began to laugh, shaking his head, and Jessamy grew angry.

"I don't see a ham and a full sack of potatoes on *your* arm, Yankee!"

As Alex's stomach was growling ominously, he had to agree that he'd not been able to bring any food either.

"You're right," he surprised her by saying. "What are we going to do about it?"

"Since I'm not exactly certain where we are, I have no idea where to get something to eat," she admitted after a moment.

"I thought you knew this area."

"I do! It's just that I'm disoriented, I guess. I don't recognize anything, and as we're in the middle of the woods where there are very few landmarks, I hardly think I should be expected to give altitude and longitude."

Alex's lips pursed in a silent whistle, and his eyes crinkled in appreciation. "So you did learn something from your tutors, after all. Altitude and longitude? And here I thought you were completely ignorant."

She glared at him for a moment, aware from his tone that she'd said something unintentionally funny, then decided that there was no point in pursuing it. He would only laugh at her, and why allow him that luxury?

Snapping around on her heel, Jessamy stalked through the tangled underbrush and along the path. She felt a faint sense of uneasiness as she led the way. Nothing looked familiar. Hickory, oak, ash, and walnut trees thrust bare branches into the crisp morning air, and the path wound haphazardly through the woods. Broken and bent branches indicated something had passed this way recently, but it could have been a deer as well as a human. She could feel Alex's gaze on her back, and heard him following close behind.

As the day pressed on it would grow warmer. Though it was November, the days were still warm, with only a faint bite of chill when the sun was shining. It was when the sun went down that the air grew cold.

The trees thinned out gradually, melding into plowed fields that wore a thin blanket of frost over the hard furrows. A split-rail fence ran in a ragged line around one field, and Jessamy paused to get her bearings.

She'd ridden over this area so many times with her brothers, thinking of nothing but the moment. It made her throat ache to consider that she might never be so carefree again.

Clearing her throat, she pointed. "Just ahead is a farmhouse. It belongs to a Methodist minister. He's a staunch abolitionist, but a good man, and he will give food and shelter to any who come to his door."

Alex nodded. "Fine. Just remember one thing —don't get any ideas about trying to get the jump on me, Jess. I won't take it kindly if you go back on your word."

Her eyes flashed, growing cold and flinty as she glared at him. "I would not go back on my given word, Alexander Steele! Not even to a damn Yankee!"

A brief smile crooked his mouth, and he gave a tight nod of his head. "Good. As a 'damn Yankee,' I appreciate that."

"You should."

Starting forward with an angry jerk, Jessamy glowered. "It seems to me," she said over her shoulder, "that all you Yankees think about is betrayal. I don't suppose you think about what all you've done to us, the crimes you've committed against your own countrymen—or women."

"What are you talking about?"

Jerking to a halt, Jessamy swung around to face him, her cheeks flushed with anger and her eyes a smoky gray. "I am talking about Yankees, and the crimes they commit against helpless people who have no defense, or who have committed no crime worse than being a Confederate."

Alex's eyes narrowed, and his mouth thinned. "Look, you are getting worked up about something I have no control over, so there's no point in ranting at me about it. I do what I have to do, and that's that."

"Like killing the guard at Clover Hill? Did you have to do that after pledging your word of honor that you wouldn't attempt escape?"

"I told you—" Alex began evenly, but she cut him off.

"And what about that poor defenseless girl in Kingsport, the girl Yankee soldiers brutalized until she died?" Her voice was thick with scorn, and she tossed back the hair from her eyes as she took a step closer to him.

"I don't know what you're talk—"

"You know very well what I'm talking about! I'm talking about all the brutalities committed in the name of the Union, that's what I'm talking about! You Yankees are full of sanctimonious self-righteousness, but you don't hesitate to commit the worst atrocities on those who can't defend themselves!"

"And I suppose Confederate soldiers are gentlemen to the end?"

Alex's sardonic inflection was not lost on Jessamy. It was just like him to try to throw the blame on others when he knew he was wrong, she thought bitterly.

"Confederate soldiers do not take advantage of innocents in this war, Captain Steele. They are brave and gallant on the battlefield, but no true Southern gentleman would dare do the things you Yankees have done!"

Letting the rifle rest on the ground, Alex leaned on the barrel and studied Jessamy's flushed face for a long moment. Her chin was lifted in familiar defiance and her hair was thrown back in a shining ribbon. Her entire body radiated a challenge, and for a moment he was tempted to let it pass. Why tell her the truth when she so obviously wanted to believe otherwise? He'd already stated that war did not breed gentleness or gentlemen, but she would not believe him until she witnessed it herself.

Shrugging, Alex lifted the rifle and tucked it under his arm again. "Fine, Jess. You're right. Yankees are the only savages in this war. All Confederate soldiers are perfect gentlemen and only shoot back, never first. That's probably why they'll lose the war—"

"Liar!"

"About which part? Losing the war or being gentlemen?"

"I hate you, Alex Steele."

"And I've heard that enough already. Let's go. I'm hungry and your Methodist minister might decide to leave."

But when they approached the neat white frame house where the minister lived, they found him at home. Only, he had company—an entire squad of Confederate soldiers.

Jerking Jessamy to a halt, Alex slapped a hand over her mouth and dragged her to the shelter of a hedge. She clawed at his hand furiously, her body heaving against him, but it had no effect. Jessamy was forced to lie on the ground with Alex's heavy body slanted over hers, forced to watch as her countrymen dragged the minister from his home and proceeded to hang him.

A cold weight settled in her chest, and she grew still under Alex as she realized what was happening. She could tell by the tensing of Alex's muscles that he was holding himself back, and she shivered. This could not be—these could not be true Confederates who were laughing and taunting a man of God, shoving his weeping wife and children from one place to another, forcing them to watch as they hung him from a sturdy oak in his own front yard.

One gray-uniformed soldier looped a rope around the minister's neck, yanking it tight. "There now, preacher, does that new collar fit right?" he taunted.

The minister said nothing, merely stared contemptuously at the soldier until he turned away. Then the doomed man's gaze moved to his wife. "Have faith in God, wife, and do not let these minions of Satan defile your dignity."

The soldier pulled the noose even tighter, tightening it until the minister's eyes began to protrude. "Shut up, old man!" he snarled. "Here, Luke, you pull on t'other end of the rope."

The man called Luke hesitated, exchanging glances with the officer in charge, a lieutenant mounted on a dainty sorrel horse. Jessamy gave a start of surprise, recognizing not only the officer but the horse. It was Teddy Tyree from over in Shelby County, a man who had visited her house and danced in her ballroom many times. And he was riding her sorrel mare! Sultana!

Only Alex's heavy hand stayed Jessamy's urge to rise and fly at the soldiers in gray.

"Lieutenant?" the soldier asked.

The question hung in the air for an instant before the officer nodded and aimed a stream of tobacco juice at the ground. "Hang the abolitionist," was all he said.

Jessamy watched in horror as the rope was slowly pulled and the minister's feet lifted from the ground. It was to be no quick death, but a slow choking of the life from him. She buried her head against the cold ground, hearing the awful choking sounds and the woman and children's cries for mercy. There was to be no mercy this day, not for this man, and Jessamy hid her face in shame.

How boldly she had just denounced Yankees, and how fiercely she had defended the Rebels who were hanging an innocent man! Alex had tried to tell her, but she had not listened. Had it been only an hour before that she had so haughtily proclaimed all Confederate soldiers gentlemen? Perhaps this was her punishment for being self-righteous, this witnessing the horrible death of a man she knew.

She lifted her head again, drawn to watch though she could feel gentle pressure from Alex's hand on her head. But she had to see. Somehow it was important that she witness what was happening, though it sickened her to see it.

The minister's feet dangled above the ground, swinging slower and slower, finally ceasing their horrible kicking motions as he sagged in death. His face was a purple blotch and his eyes protruded in death. His wife threw her apron over the children nearest her so they would not see, and Jessamy turned her face back into Alex's shoulder.

As she shuddered against him, she heard the soldiers let the body fall with an awful thump, heard the wife's cry and the children's sobbing. And when Jessamy heard the cold voice of the lieutenant order that the body be left in the woods for the animals, it took every ounce of Alex's strength to hold her back from leaping from their hiding place and confronting the officer.

Once more Alex's hand held her mouth while his brawny arm kept its tight grip on her squirming body. Jessamy was so outraged she could not think of her own danger, could think only of the callous treatment being foisted upon countrymen by soldiers who were supposed to be fighting for them. Hot tears squeezed from beneath clenched eyelids as she finally surrendered to Alex's superior strength and lay still on the damp ground. The taste of dirt and leaves could not take away the bitter taste of disillusionment.

"You should have let me go," Jessamy said in a dull tone. She barely glanced at Alex. He was seated cross-legged, feeding small twigs and dry leaves into a low fire. It was dark again, deep shadows shrouding the woods where they had stayed hidden most of the day.

"And what good would that have done me? Then I would have been discovered too, and I'd hate to think I'd fill some scrawny fox's belly instead of a family plot."

Jessamy gave an impatient shake of her head, dislodging the leaves that clung to her tangled hair. "Why?" she couldn't help whispering, shaking her head. "Why?" It was a question she couldn't stop asking herself, a question that had no good answer.

Alex didn't even attempt to give her one. He just shrugged, as he had done every time she had repeated that forlorn word. Why? He couldn't guess why men were driven to such inhuman measures, but then, he couldn't imagine that he would ever be driven to such measures himself. War was war, yes, but perpetrating such horrors on civilians took a much darker nature as far as he was concerned.

Jessamy stared into the darkness beyond the small circle of light shed by the fire, her thoughts as dark and brooding as the shadows. Each time she thought of Teddy Tyree, she tried to reconcile him with the nice, courteous young man who had often visited her home. That Tyree had been a polite, well-mannered young man. The Tyree she had seen today had been a vicious, coldhearted man with no soul. And now she waited for Alex to say "I told you so." He could do so easily, of course, for she had so blithely and adamantly vowed that all Southern men were too gentlemanly to do exactly what Teddy Tyree had done. And to think that he had Sultana, too! It made her cringe to think of her lovely, spirited mare in the hands of such a brute.

Tucking her knees beneath her chin, Jessamy hunched her shoulders against the cold night

air. Alex's coat slipped slightly, and she tugged
it back over her shoulders. He had insisted she
take it, saying he didn't want to be burdened
with a sickly female, and she had gratefully accepted. The fire offered little enough warmth,
but Alex refused to make one too big for fear of
being discovered by lingering Confederates.
And after the day's events, she wasn't too certain she wanted to meet up with any soldiers
either, blue or gray.

"Here," Alex said, holding out a baked root
he'd dug from the ashes of the fire. "Eat something and you'll feel better."

Jessamy gazed at the root with dubious interest. "I am not at all certain I'll feel better if I eat
that."

"It's better than nothing."

"I'm not sure of that, either."

"Do you do anything besides carp and complain?" Alex inquired in a polite tone.

For the first time since that morning, a fire
flashed in Jessamy's eyes. "Yes! I sometimes
shout and swear!"

"A welcome improvement, I'm sure. Take it.
You'll need to keep up your strength for shouting and swearing." He waved the unappealing
root in front of her.

Jessamy snatched the baked root from Alex,
burning her fingers and muffling the hot words
that sprang to her lips. Why give him something
else to taunt her about? He was having too good
a time as it was.

"If you'd care for meat in your diet, I could dig
up some grubworms," Alex offered when the silence stretched between them. Jessamy gave
him a glare.

"Thank you, but no!"

"Are you sure?"

"Are you heartless?" She surged to her feet, tossing aside the gnawed-on root. "Don't you care what happened to that man today? Did you enjoy seeing a man of God hung and his body left for the wild animals?"

Alex rose to his feet, too. "No, but I don't intend to spend my time wallowing in fear and sympathy, either. He's dead. We're not. There will be plenty of time for regrets after this war is over, Jess, but there's no time for them now."

"You have no heart—"

His hands flashed out to grab her by the shoulders. "I have just as much as you do, but if I spend my time thinking about what happened, I'll be just as ineffective as you are right now! And we have to survive this, Jess. Can't you see that?"

Her bottom lip began to quiver, and her eyes filled with tears. "All I can see is . . . is that man choking to death in front of his family, and it hurts!"

She sounded so much like a grieving child that Alex forgot his anger. He folded her into his arms and began to stroke her hair as he would have a child's. When he sighed, his exhalation stirred Jessamy's tangled hair and it tickled his mouth. He could feel her slender body shaking beneath his too-large coat and didn't know if it was from grief or cold, and he didn't want to ask. It would be disastrous to let her dissolve into pity, self-pity or otherwise, but he couldn't keep from offering her small comfort.

Finally she disentangled herself from his embrace and stepped back, not wanting to admit that she did feel better for his comfort, and too confused to wonder why. Wiping her face on the sleeve of his coat, she managed a watery smile.

"I think I'll be all right now."

"You were all right to begin with," he said so softly that she stared at him for a moment. "It just took some convincing to let you know that you're all right," he added then, and she nodded.

"Yeah, I guess you're right." Shoving her hands deep into the pockets of her brother's trousers, Jessamy rocked back on her heels. She stared self-consciously at the ground and wondered why she felt so odd with Alex, why she couldn't just think about him as she had her brothers or other cousins, or any other boy. How did he make her feel so young and foolish?

Alex returned to the fire and poked it to a higher blaze. "Here, Jess. Sit close. I don't want to risk a bigger fire than this."

Nodding, she knelt close, holding her hands palms out to the fire, concentrating on the orange, blue, and yellow flames that leaped and soared in licking tongues.

"Maybe something happened to make Tyree act like that," she said after a few minutes, and Alex shrugged.

"Yeah. Maybe."

"But you don't think so."

"Did I say that?"

"No, but you think it."

He stared at her in exasperation. "Jess, don't put words in my mouth. There's lots of things that will make a man turn hard—"

"But you wouldn't, would you?"

Firelight played across his rugged features,

and she could see the faint tilt of his mouth. "I hope not, Jess."

She hugged her knees close and looked back at the fire. "I don't think you would."

Several minutes passed and the fire burned lower. It was late, and the thick copse of trees was far from the road, but Alex still would not relax his guard. He'd been surprised too many times in his life to take chances. That was why, when Jessamy stood and announced her intention of going to the small stream to wash her face and hands, he hesitated.

"That might not be a good idea, Jess."

"It's only a few yards away, and you can see me every step of the way. Besides, Alex, there are certain . . . things . . . that a female must do in private."

A hot flush stained her cheeks at her oblique reference to bodily functions, and she couldn't look at him. It was a delicate matter, and she hoped Alex would have enough courtesy not to press. He did, but she could see his reluctance to let her go alone.

"Walk slowly and carefully, and stay in sight. Tie a rag to any bush you hide behind"—he ignored her sniff of dismay and continued—"or I won't know where to find you if I have to. Understand?"

"Perfectly, Captain Steele."

He grinned. "I knew you would."

Jessamy turned and picked her way carefully across the hard ground, peering through the dark toward the glittering stream. There was no moon this night, just dark shadows and a hazy glow that gave everything a surrealistic quality. It was eerie, Jessamy thought as she trod upon a dry branch and heard it crack loudly beneath her feet. Even the air seemed to shimmer with expectance, and she shivered.

Pausing, she turned to glance behind her, and was reassured by the faint glow of the fire. Alex's dark shape could be seen beside it, and she turned back to continue down the sloping bank.

Her feet slid abruptly from beneath her, depositing her harshly on the ground. Jessamy's breath left her lungs in a silent whoosh of air, and frosted the night. Gingerly, she picked herself up from the ground and brushed leaves from the seat of her trousers. There was no shout of laughter behind her, so Alex must not have seen her fall. He would certainly have appreciated it if he had, she decided as she reached the stream.

The water was icy, and she washed her face in brisk, vigorous strokes, gasping at the shock. It made her skin tingle, and she began to feel alive for the first time all day. Shimmery droplets of water sprayed upward as she dipped her hands again, and a fallen leaf scudded past in a silent whirl. She watched as it quickly disappeared from sight.

Night birds whispered in the trees lining the bank, and she tilted back her head at the liquid music. The feathered creatures seemed to be trying to match the sound of water, and she smiled. These small miracles of life reminded her that it wasn't all in vain, that life went on even when the horror seemed to invade and destroy. Alex had been right when he'd said that she was stronger than she thought she was, and she knew it now.

Rising, Jessamy shook her hands dry and stepped behind a clump of bushes. Even in war there were certain things one could not avoid. Nature intruded, which made life seem normal again.

When Jessamy started back up the slope toward the fire and Alex, she saw that the blaze had died down to only a faint glow. An expression of annoyance creased her brow, and she walked faster. After the walk to the cold stream, she had looked forward to sitting once more beside the fire with Alex.

"Why did you let the fire go out?" she asked crossly as she stepped into the tiny clearing, but there was no answer. Alex lay stretched motionless upon his back, one arm thrown over his head. "Alex! Great guard you are," she began testily, and bent to toss another stick on the fire. "I could have been abducted by an entire regiment and you wouldn't have noticed! And there I was, beginning to feel safe with you as my watchdog, when all the time—"

"When all the time your watchdog was sleeping," a soft voice said, making Jessamy jerk around to stare into the shadows beyond the clearing. A figure stepped out, and the faint light of the fire reflected from the long barrel of the rifle he held in one hand.

One hand went to her throat, and instinctively she took a step backward. "What . . . what do you want?" she demanded in a surprisingly steady voice as she recognized one of the men from the minister's home. She pointed a shaking finger at Alex. "What did you do to him?"

"Aw, I didn't kill him, only gave him a little thump on the head," the gray-clad man said with a leering grin. "I thought the lieutenant might want to question him before we kill him."

Jessamy's brain whirled. "Do you mean Lieutenant Tyree?"

The man's eyes narrowed, and he paused in his slow approach. "Yeah. How do you know him?"

"I saw . . . today . . . he was riding a sorrel mare that belonged to me." Realizing that she had just admitted to witnessing an atrocity, Jessamy added quickly, "He was on the road south of the twin forks. I was hiding in a hedge and was too scared to call out."

"Scared 'cause your watchdog happens to be a Yankee?" was the sneering reply. "Or scared 'cause you might git shot for a Yankee yourself?"

Drawing herself up, Jessamy glared at him in spite of her jangling nerves. "I am as devout a Confederate as you are, sir, perhaps more so! My father and three brothers are riding with the Ninth Tennessee at this very moment, and you dare to question my loyalty? How bold you are!"

"And how bold *you* are, keeping company with the enemy. If you know Lieutenant Tyree, then you know that he don't cotton to keeping the wrong kind of company."

"I have not seen Teddy Tyree since before Christmas last," Jessamy lied, noting with a trace of panic that the soldier had begun his slow approach again.

"I'm thinking that you don't really know him at all," the man said. "I'm thinking that maybe you overheard more than you should. And I'm thinking that maybe you ain't a Confederate at all, but a Yankee sympathizer. Maybe even a spy."

"No!" Jessamy cast a desperate glance toward Alex, hoping he was still alive, wishing he would regain consciousness and rescue her from what was swiftly becoming a dangerous situation. "I—I am as loyal as you are, truly I am! I've rolled bandages, tended the wounded, said prayers for our Glorious Cause, and—and—"

"And you coulda done that for t'other side, too," he pointed out in a reasonable tone. Aiming a dark stream of tobacco juice at the ground, he wiped his mouth on his coat sleeve and stepped closer. He was so close Jessamy could smell the whisky on his breath, could smell that it must have been weeks—months—since he'd bathed, and could smell the sour odor of the tobacco he was chewing.

Holding up one hand, she flung a last, desperate glance toward Alex at the same time as she lifted her chin in defiance. "If you touch me, my father and brothers will kill you. There will be no hole where you can hide if they look for you—"

"Damn, lady! I'll probably meet 'em in hell long before they get wind of what I intend to do." He smiled, his lips curling back from stained, chipped teeth. "You know it too, don't you? I can see by the look in your eyes. It's the same look all you women get before . . . before. Yankee, Rebel, it don't matter none. You all get that same whey-faced look and start in bleating."

He said more, began to describe in great detail what he meant, but Jessamy blocked his

words from her mind. It was too horrible to con-
template, and she barely realized it when he
reached out for her, his fingers clumsy with the
cold as he jerked open the buttons to Alex's coat.
Perhaps he wondered why she didn't fight him
after her brave words, or perhaps he didn't care.
Her muscles were lax, almost flaccid with shock
as he tugged the coat away and began to unfasten the buttons to her father's shirt. Not even
the brisk night air across her bare breasts
pulled Jessamy from her stupor.

Her eyes struggled to focus, but her brain
blocked that, too. Jessamy stared blankly, was
vaguely aware of being laid down, of the sharp
pricking of the ground into her bare back, and
of a man bent over her, panting, his fetid breath
washing across her face in a revolting wave. It
was only when he tugged at the rope holding up
her brother's trousers that she reacted normally, one leg jerking up in a reflex action that
caught them both by surprise.

Jessamy stared dimly at the man as he rolled
on the ground, holding his groin and cursing
her, telling her what he would do to her in a few
moments. His lips were pulled back from his
stained teeth, giving him a feral look that made
her shudder in reaction, and his low, vicious
words finally penetrated her consciousness.

Shrouded in a fog of unreality, Jessamy was
only vaguely aware of Alex still yards away, of
his slight stirring at the soldier's curses. Her attention became focused on the immediate danger as her brain registered the threats from the
soldier.

"I'm going to make you good and sorry, little
girl. . . ."

Jessamy's distracted gaze shifted from Alex's pain-contorted face back to her attacker.

When he pushed to his knees and his lowered trousers revealed his intentions, Jessamy recoiled. Reality intruded then, and the fog that had protected her evaporated in a flash. Rage filled her, righteous rage, and fumbling blindly in the dark she picked up a thick branch and began flailing him with it. She whacked him again and again, fiercely glad to hear his cries of pain, glad to see the blood streaming from his ear and face.

If not for Alex's intervention, she might not have stopped until he was a shapeless mass, and Jessamy gave a cry of disappointment when he pulled her away.

"Jess! Stop it! He's dead! He's dead, I tell you!"

It penetrated finally, and Jessamy gazed down at the motionless figure on the ground. He was dead. She had killed a man, and that man her own countryman, a Confederate soldier. The bloodied tree limb dropped from her hand to the ground, and she looked up at Alex.

"He's dead."

Alex nodded, and reached down to lift his coat from the ground. That was when she realized that she was bare-chested, and that her trousers had slid half off, exposing her navel and half of her stomach. Yet at the moment she didn't care. As he pulled his blue coat around her, Alex gave Jessamy a critical stare.

"You need some whisky," he said in a matter-of-fact tone, and bent to rifle the soldier's body. Jessamy's blows had smashed his head and face, and had broken one arm and a bottle of whisky, but the soldier had carried a spare in his back pocket. Alex pulled the cork and forced the bottle between Jessamy's compressed lips. "Drink it. It will warm you up a bit."

She was shaking all over, as if she had the ague, and as reaction set in she began to cry. Tears mixed with the whisky that spilled down her chin, and she didn't care. The hot, burning liquor finally penetrated, warming her insides and making her lightheaded. Vaguely, as if she were in a dream, Jessamy became aware of Alex chafing her hands between his rough palms, his soft, soothing voice telling her everything would be all right, that she was a brave girl and had done what she had to do.

"Did I?" she echoed, blinking at him. "Is killing all right?"

"When it saves you from being killed yourself," was Alex's brisk reply. "Now here—lie down while I poke up the fire. We need to get away from here as quickly as possible in case our intruder's friends come looking for him."

Jessamy could not bring herself to watch as Alex dragged away the bloody body, could offer only a slight nod to acknowledge Alex's grim pleasure of the fact that the soldier had bullets and powder and a good rifle. And he had money, though it was only Confederate instead of greenback. It was all too horrible, and she tried not to recall the things the soldier had said, the things he had done before she had finally reacted. If she closed her eyes, she could see him over her, his leering face and hot eyes, and her stomach revolted when she recalled how he had slobbered over her bare breasts, leaving wet trails across her skin.

Leaning over, Jessamy emptied her stomach

of its few contents. Alex said nothing. There was nothing he could say. Time alone would ease this night, and he knew it.

"Ready to go?" he said several minutes later, and Jessamy looked up at him. For the first time she noticed the blood on his face.

"You're hurt!"

"Only where he whacked me. It'll heal. My pride's hurt more. I was so busy watching you, I never saw or heard him coming. Come on, Jess. We need to push on."

The night shadows closed behind them.

Chapter 13

IT HAD BEEN A WEEK since Jessamy's confrontation with the Confederate soldier. On several nights, she had woken from a fitful sleep, crying out and thrashing around. It had taken Alex's best efforts to calm her from her nightmares, but he had not lost his patience, only held her tenderly in his arms, repeating soft phrases until she finally quieted.

For Alex, it was pure torture. Knowing the shock she had received, he dared not press himself on her, but it was hard not to kiss or caress her. He wanted to. He wanted to hold her gently, kissing her and stroking her body until she kissed him back. It was even more difficult hiding his damned male reactions from her, and he wondered if she realized what she did to him when she lay in his arms.

Jessamy did realize, and oddly enough, it piqued her curiosity instead of frightening her. She'd endured uncontrolled lust with horror, but Alex's carefully controlled desire awakened her interest. How could it not, when he took such great pains to hide it?

They'd traveled over fifty miles since first leaving Clover Hill, and were near Pittsburg Landing, where boats carrying troops frequently docked. It was on a swift-moving curve of the Tennessee River, near a thriving little town. Along the way, Jessamy had used the wad of Confederate money taken from the dead soldier to purchase food and blankets. At least they were no longer hungry, and though they didn't dare linger too long in a town, they had warm blankets at night. Alex lingered on the fringes of towns in an effort to learn more about his command. He fully intended to rejoin them at the first opportunity, then make arrangements to send Jessamy home, but he hesitated to tell her. It would only start another argument.

By tacit agreement, neither suggested they seek lodgings. They preferred the anonymity offered by the countryside, and Jessamy—who until a few short months ago had spent all her sleeping hours in a luxurious feather bed—was the first to spread her blankets on the ground at night. Her hair stayed in braids for necessity's sake, since it took too long to comb out the tangles if she let it hang free. She still wore her brothers' trousers and shoes and her father's shirt, though Alex's coat had been replaced by a simple jacket. It had seemed more expedient to travel as a couple with no political preference, and so Alex had been persuaded to relinquish his blue uniform.

"Imagine that farmer's surprise when he finds his clothes replaced by a Yankee's uniform!" Jessamy had said with a laugh when

Alex had returned from his raid upon a clothes-line.

Alex had grinned. "He'd have been even more surprised if I had replaced his wife's lace drawers with my blue trousers!"

An easier relationship had developed between them during the week, perhaps nurtured by that one horrible day. Whatever it was, they now enjoyed a friendlier rapport. It was a welcome relief from the former tension. And it was intriguing as well.

Though the days were still warm, the nights were growing bitterly cold. Alex's wound was almost healed now, and he exercised his arm every day for an hour, a procedure which Jessamy watched with some amusement.

"You look very fierce," she observed, straddling a fence rail and munching on a late apple. Her coat was open, her hair free in the brisk wind that blew across the Tennessee pasture, and she was enjoying Alex's fencing exercises.

He turned, thrust with an imaginary sword, pirouetted, lunged, parried, and turned again, all with an expression of intense concentration on his handsome face. Jessamy took another bite of her apple, her eyes dancing with mischief. In a swift, graceful movement she tossed the apple core at him, laughing when he dodged it and sent her a flickering scowl.

Poor Alex. He was trying so hard to ignore her, and she thought that he looked perfectly silly alone in the pasture with only his boots and trousers on. Silly—and immensely appealing.

Sunlight gleamed on his chest, shoulders, and arms as they flexed, and the vivid purple of the scar on his side stood out in rigid contrast to his smooth, dark skin. Fascinated, Jessamy watched the ripple of his muscles, the hard-coiled bands tightening, briefly loosening, then tightening again. There was a dark pelt of hair on his chest that dipped toward the band of his trousers in a vee, but when her gaze followed, she jerked her eyes away and slid from the fence rail.

She stood uncertainly for a moment, not sure what she wanted to do, but knowing that she couldn't just sit there and gawk at Alex any longer. For some reason, she was having thoughts she shouldn't have, and it bothered her. Why should she think such things, let her curiosity wander where it had no business wandering? It wasn't ladylike, and it wasn't . . . well, it just wasn't right.

Feeling as if there were a bite of apple still lodged in her throat, Jessamy turned toward the abandoned barn where they were staying. It was a structure that had once been painted a clean white but now showed only weathered boards with chipped, peeling flakes of paint. The perfect refuge, it was filled with piles of hay and small creatures seeking shelter. Birds roosted in the loft, and a family of raccoons had burrowed homes in one far corner. Nighttime brought the muffled scufflings of the creatures as they scampered about, and Jessamy usually snuggled close to Alex's back while they slept. It seemed safer.

The barn was shadowed and festooned with draperies of gauzy spider webs, but it offered a form of security and she sank to a pile of sweet-smelling hay near the door. A brittle hay stalk provided an excellent chewing stick as she thought about her situation.

She wanted to go home. Nothing was working out right. She had no idea where Bryce was, her mother would be frantic with worry, and she was confused. Too many things had happened, too many of her ideals had been brutally shattered. It was dismaying to see that Alex had been right about so many things. How could she have known that men would behave like such animals, men she had known for years? It was still hard to reconcile Teddy Tyree with the hard-faced Lieutenant Tyree she had witnessed only last week. Maybe she'd never be able to adjust to that.

Tucking her knees up to her chest, Jessamy rested her chin on them and sighed, staring out the huge open door. This was a beautiful land, but she had never dreamed it could be so harsh. If not for the money they had, they would have starved. Alex supplemented their meager cash with his hunting, becoming quite proficient at snaring rabbits, and Jessamy thought that once she got back home she would never again look at a rabbit in quite the same way.

"Contemplating another apple toss?" Alex asked, startling her as he came to sit beside her. She smiled up at him.

"Maybe. Watch your head."

"I'll just watch you. That's easier. And safer."

"That's what you think." She lobbed a handful of hay at him, laughing when he ducked. With a mock growl deep in his throat Alex lunged at her, a brawny arm catching her around the waist and flinging her back into the pile of hay.

Squealing and struggling, Jessamy squirmed like an eel as she tried to avoid being pinned down, but it was useless. Alex was no novice at this, and he had straddled her in an instant.

"Give?"

She blew a tuft of hay at him. "Never!"

He began to tickle her, his blunt fingers digging into her ribs until she laughed so hard she was breathless. Again came the question: "Give?"

Breathlessly: "Never!"

"You're overly fond of that word, Jess," he teased. "Do you know moderation, areas of gray instead of black and white, one extreme or the other?

"I—I've heard of it!" she managed to gasp out.

One hand moved to her knee, expertly finding just the right spot to wring cries of laughter from her. "I could do this for days," Alex said in a solemn tone, "but I don't think you could stand it."

"Do . . . your . . . worst, wretch!" she gasped between unladylike snorts of laughter. Her hair was in her eyes, catching beneath her shoulders as she struggled, her hands pushing at his immovable frame with futile jerks. He just grinned down at her, one eyebrow waggling in mock evil. Jessamy could feel the tensing of his leg muscles as they squeezed against her sides.

"My worst?" Alex was saying in a thoughtful tone. "Hmm. I wonder what that could be. . . ."

In a surprise movement he leaned forward, his mouth grazing Jessamy's lips in a brief kiss so electric it startled both of them. He drew back instantly, releasing her, his dark brows drawing down into a knot. She stared back at him, quiet now, all laughter gone from her face.

For a few moments there was only the sound of two rapid heartbeats, then Alex leaned forward again, slower this time, his face blurring as he captured her willing lips with his. Jessamy closed her eyes. She could feel the hard thud of her heart, could feel the hard thump of his heart beneath her exploring fingertips as she touched him. It did not seem odd to be kissing Alex this way. For some reason it seemed just right.

And when he slowly lowered his body to slant across hers she didn't protest but put her arms around him, holding him close, letting her fingertips trace patterns over his smooth, bare back. She could feel the taut muscles flex, could feel his erratic heartbeat, could hear the ragged breaths he took, and suddenly she wanted more. She wanted Alex, all of him, and she wasn't quite certain what that involved. All she knew was that he was making her feel light-headed, making a coiling fire burn inside her, a fire that threatened to consume her and leave only ashes.

"You better push me away now," Alex said thickly, "or it will be too late."

Drawing back, he stared down at her, his eyes dark with hot fires, his expression so intent it took her breath away.

"I don't want to."

Her soft murmur was so low he had to lean forward to hear it, and then it didn't matter anyway because he was kissing her again, unable to stop, unable to hold back the passion that had been building in him since he'd been lured into the gazebo that soft spring evening.

Yielding to the sweeping fire that flared higher and higher in her, Jessamy forgot everything but Alex. Nothing else mattered right now, only the man who was cradling her body in his arms, unbuttoning her shirt and sliding his hands over her. He was still kissing her, his mouth moving against her parted lips with a fierce urgency that transferred to her. She was shaking with the same urgency, not quite understanding it, only wanting to explore it.

Shyly at first, then bolder, her hands moved across Alex's back, tracing his spine, spreading against his smooth hard flesh as if trying to memorize every inch of him. When he removed her shirt, tugging it gently away, he lifted his body, ignoring her soft moan of protest, sitting back on his heels to gaze down at her.

"You're beautiful," he said in such a husky voice that tears came to her eyes.

She'd been told she was beautiful before, but never like that. And it had never mattered before if she was. Beauty was only a means to an end, whatever end she happened to be seeking at the moment. But somehow it truly mattered now that she was beautiful. She wanted to be beautiful for Alex, wanted to keep that glow of appreciation in his eyes forever.

"You're beautiful, too," she whispered back, then blushed when he laughed and teased, "Men aren't supposed to be beautiful!"

"Well, you are!" she defended herself. Her hand moved up to cradle his square jaw, rubbing against the thick, dark bristle of beard that had grown in the past week without shaving.

Her fingertips traced the arch of his brow and the line of his cheekbone, that harsh slash across his face that should have been too hard but wasn't. It only made him look more rugged, more . . . dangerous. Jessamy shivered.

"Cold?" Alex asked softly, and she shook her head.

"No. Just . . . just curious."

Alex lay back across her, his touch gentle as he began to explore the small, firm curves of her body, the thrust of her breasts and the tight round of her hip. When he slid her trousers down Jessamy closed her eyes, a hot flush moving up to stain her cheeks and even her breasts.

"Don't be embarrassed, love. It's just me. It's Alex, and I wouldn't hurt you for the world."

Gazing down at her closed eyes, the slight trembling of her lips and the quiver of her long, straight eyelashes, Alex smiled. She was so young, so vulnerable, so lovely. He would never hurt her, never do anything that was wrong for her, but how did he tell her that? He wasn't good at that sort of thing. He'd never been in love before, never held a girl like Jessamy in his arms. There had been women, of course, but not innocents. And never anyone this special.

Softly, tenderly, Alex explored Jessamy's quivering body with loving hands. And when he put her hands on him, she flushed and jerked away.

Alex reached out and drew them back, sliding her palms down over his chest and stomach. "Don't you like to touch me, Jess?"

"Yes . . . no . . . oh, I don't know!" Her lashes lifted to reveal smoky eyes. She was trembling all over. To touch him so intimately seemed so strange, yet so right. How could that be, she wondered, biting her lower lip as he held her hands against him.

"Touch me, Jess, like I'm touching you."

"But . . ."

"Touch me."

Her quivering hands stroked lightly over the hard muscles of his chest, sliding down to the ridges of his stomach, letting the silky black hairs curl over her fingertips. She felt him shudder beneath her touch, and looked up into the hot glow of his eyes.

"There," he said thickly, "that wasn't so bad, was it?"

She managed a smile. "No. It was . . . nice."

"Nice?" He levered his frame back over her, pressing his chest against her bare breasts, his warm breath tickling her ear as he breathed, "Nice?"

Fragrant stalks of hay popped and cracked beneath their weight as Alex shifted, sliding his arms beneath Jessamy's body to cradle her. Neither of them felt the chill in the air as he began kissing her again, his mouth hovering over her parted lips and seeming to draw the air from her lungs. It was exhilarating, frightening, wonderful.

His mouth slowly roamed from tasting the velvet furring of her lips, sliding over her throat to the tiny pulse that beat below. Then he kissed her shoulders, his hands sliding down her slender arms to hold her hands, his mouth following in such slow, heated kisses that Jessamy squirmed beneath him. Her breath grew short and shallow, so that when he returned to kiss her lips she struggled to draw in air.

"Alex . . ."

"Yes, love?"

She shook her head, tawny hair falling into her eyes, eyes that were shadowed with confusion. "I . . . don't know."

Alex knew, but he wanted her to be ready for him. He wanted her to desire him as much as he desired her slender curves, wanted to feel her sweet body close around him, and wanted to hear her soft cries in his ear. He would not let himself rush it, though he wondered how long he could hold back.

"Kiss me, Jess."

Obediently she lifted her mouth to his. Her tongue slid between his lips, tentatively at first, then bolder, and she felt the heated press of him against her. It was almost frightening, and she dared not look down, flushing as she realized how different their bodies were.

"It's all right, Jess," he murmured against her mouth, obviously reading her sudden embarrassment. "Men just show their feelings more openly."

Then he was kissing her back, quick and hard, making her forget that she was embarrassed, making her forget everything but the sweeping fire that rushed through her veins.

When he held her beneath him and nudged between her thighs Jessamy took a deep breath and put her arms around his neck, looking up at him with trust and love. She was shaking inside and outside and wanting him to love her completely, and he recognized it in her eyes.

"Now, love," he whispered, and slid forward that first tiny bit. She tensed, her eyes opening wider as her back arched against him, and he began kissing her again, kissing her until the tension eased. Then, as she held him tightly Alex entered with a swift thrust that made Jessamy gasp and cling more tightly to him. He was immediately still, holding her and stroking back the hair from her eyes as he murmured soft words, words that didn't penetrate the haze of passion but gave her comfort.

It wasn't until she put her hands on his face and began to kiss him, her lips slanting across his mouth in a slow caress, that he moved again, his body rocking against hers in a rhythmic motion. For Alex it was slow torture, this holding back, but for Jessamy it was sweet suspense. It had never occurred to her that making love could be so tender and sweet and wonderful. She'd always assumed that it was just something married couples did in order to have children. But this, this was such a rapturous experience that she wanted to weep with the joy of discovery.

How had it happened, this sweeping rush that made her cry out and cling to Alex, holding him, wanting to absorb his every muscle and even his very breath into her body? If she could breathe him she would have, inhaled pure Alex and been ecstatically happy.

The shuddering release that left her both weak and yet invigorated was so new, so different from anything she had ever imagined that she wanted to do nothing but talk of her discovery.

"Alex?"

Lifting himself to one elbow, he gazed down at her with soft, dark eyes. His finger teased a damp strand of hair in her face, and a half-smile curved his mouth.

"Yes, love?"

She touched his chin with a finger. "Why didn't you tell me?"

"Tell you what?"

"How wonderful it would be."

A soft chuckle rumbled in his chest. "I never thought it would make much of an impression on you if I offered my enlightening views on a gratifying sexual experience, Jess!"

A frown puckered her brow. "You're probably right," she said so seriously that he laughed aloud, tucking her into his hard chest and holding her.

"You're a silly wench."

"But you love me anyway," she returned with such a confident air that his expression grew solemn.

"Yes, I think I do," he said. "I think I've loved you since you were six years old and swore at me for laughing when you fell off your pony."

"I didn't swear at you!"

"Yes you did. For a six-year-old, it was a pretty racy thing to tell a male cousin he was a jackass."

Jessamy's eyes glittered with laughter. "Well, I was only stating the obvious, and by the way— I did not fall off my pony!"

"You did, don't you recall? He threw you right into a clump of blackberry bushes."

Indignantly: "No he didn't! I just jumped when he stumbled—"

"You fell," Alex retorted with a firm kiss that left her quiet and dreamy-eyed.

"Well—maybe." A smile curved her lips as she

put her arms back around his neck and snuggled close. Alex had drawn a blanket around them, and they lay in their bed of hay and lovehaze, forgetting the world around them, forgetting everything but each other. Nothing else mattered now.

Slanting Alex a glance from beneath the straight line of her eyelashes, Jessamy caught her breath at the surge of love that washed over her. It wasn't just that he was so handsome—though she supposed that every woman in love had the same opinion of her lover—it was that he was so tender when she needed tenderness. Alex seemed to understand that she had doubts, that she had been, only a few hours before, a young, confused girl. Now she was a woman. A woman in love.

She smiled, watching him drift back into a contented sleep. One fingertip grazed his beard stubble, then rose to tease the dark hair that fell across his forehead. His brow twitched, and she took a tawny spool of her hair and swept it lightly across the tip of his nose. Alex didn't open his eyes but waved one hand across his face and mumbled a light protest. Jessamy smiled with delight, and dragged the tip of her hair over his face again.

This time his lids opened and he grabbed her so quickly she didn't have time to duck. Laughing, Jessamy could not avoid Alex's mock anger, nor the bruising kisses he pressed on her. Rolling over with her beneath him, Alex held her down with both hands spread out, levering his body across hers. He straddled her, a knee on each side of her slender frame.

"You are an evil wench," he said, leering

down at her. "Don't you believe in letting a man rest?"

Her head rolled back and forth on the hay. "No. I get lonesome."

"Try sleeping."

"I can't, Alex." She wiggled provocatively and watched his expression alter from laughter to a more serious stare, his eyes taking on that glow she'd seen before. Her own smile slowly faded as she recognized the light of desire in his eyes, and deliberately, slowly, she moved her hips up and against his lean body. He still held her arms outspread but when she arched her back he released them, moving down on her body, his chest slowly melding with her curves.

Catching her breath, Jessamy closed her eyes and smiled. This was so new, so delicious, and she shivered with delight when Alex began kissing her again. Desire sparked anew, flaring between them in a white-hot spurt of passion. Nothing mattered but the moment, and Alex taking her with him to those still unexplored heights. How could anything matter when they had each other?

It was a question that was to haunt Jessamy in the following weeks, weeks when she discovered that fate could often shatter the tenuous relationship between lovers.

Chapter 14

THE TRAIN LINES HAD NOT yet been cut,
and still carried passengers and supplies from
Kentucky through Tennessee and into Alabama,
Georgia, and Mississippi. Though largely unre-
liable, they did run frequently, with long pauses
for unexpected events. Jessamy and Alex stood
on a flat wooden platform in southwestern Kentucky and waited for the train.

Hot tears thickened her voice, clogged her
nose, and streamed down Jessamy's face.

"But why can't I go with you, Alex?"

Raking a hand through his thick, dark hair,
Alex sighed and managed a slight smile. "Ah
love, you know why. It's too dangerous. And besides, do you think your father or your brothers
—especially Nick—would be happy to see us together?"

"I don't care!" Her fierce reply vibrated into
the air, and Alex reached out to pull her to him,
one hand smoothing her tawny hair.

"Now listen to reason, Jess. I have to find my

command and you need to go home to your mother. You know she's worried sick about you, and with Bryce gone, too—"

"But we need to find him! He wouldn't listen to you if you did find him, so I have to go along and—"

Alex put her back from him. "No." His voice was firm and final, and she recognized the futility of further argument, though it didn't deter her. "We've talked about it and talked about it, and nothing has changed. I will find Bryce and send you a message as soon as possible. If I can, I will send *Bryce*." Alex's mouth twisted in grim amusement. "Though if Bryce is half as determined as his sister, I have a feeling he won't go anywhere he doesn't want to go."

Jessamy had the same feeling. To be honest, it wasn't just her concern for her brother that spurred her desire to go. It was her love for Alex. How could she bear to be parted from him, to wonder if he was alive, or wounded and needing her? And to wonder if maybe it would be her father or one of her brothers who might be responsible for his death? Or if Alex would be responsible for their deaths? Oh, dear God, it was too hard to think about, too hard to be the one left behind to wait and wonder.

She vibrated with intensity, and her voice was quick and urgent as she looked up into Alex's dark eyes.

"I could keep wearing boy's clothes, and I'll cut my hair and carry a rifle, and I can shoot, Alex, you know I can! I can shoot as well as any man, and I can ride, and I won't complain about cold or rain or no food, if only you will let me go with you. Oh Alex, please!"

It took all his willpower to shake his head, to keep his voice hard and cool.

"No, my love. I can't risk you. If the worst should happen, you wouldn't be safe."

Jessamy's shoulders slumped in defeat and she turned away. Alex reached out to touch her, but let his hand fall to his side. Sympathy would only make it harder.

"Jess, the train is coming. I hear the whistle," he said after a few moments, and she nodded. There was a tight knot in his chest as he watched her surreptitiously wipe away her tears, square her shoulders, and turn to face him with a watery smile.

"Be careful. Don't stand in front of any bullets." She gave a toss of her head, her shining hair ribboning down her back as she ignored the curious stares directed at her from several well-garbed matrons. Let them stare. Her world was disintegrating and she didn't care what those long-nosed women thought about her.

Alex gave her an encouraging smile. "I've kept you with me longer than I should have anyway, love. I'll be back for you. And I'll write."

"You better." She leaned close to whisper, "Even if you are a damned Yankee, you are *my* Yankee."

Grinning at her, Alex shook his head. "And you, my love, are a fiery Rebel. When all this is over, we won't have to take sides anymore."

She shuddered. "I hope not, Alex. The choosing is almost as bad as . . . as what I think at night."

"I know—" A whistle shrilled, drowning out the rest of his words, and he gave a grin and a shrug. Jessamy gazed up at him with intense longing, her heart in her eyes, and he tried not to see. It was too painful. "Guess you have to board now before the train leaves without you," he said when steam billowed out and the engine began to groan and whine as the big wheels ground slowly forward. He gave her a gentle shove toward the car where a conductor was hanging out and frowning at her with a watch in his hand. "Hurry, Jess."

"Are you sure you don't want any of this money?"

Alex shook his head. "No. You might need it. Besides, what would a damn Yankee do with Confederate currency?"

"You didn't mind that when we stole it," she shot back with a wan smile.

There was just time for a brief, hard hug and a kiss before he lifted Jessamy aboard the train. She clung to the door and stared back at the platform until the train rounded a curve and she could no longer see Alex's tall, broad frame. Only then did she give in to the harsh, racking sobs that tore at her. There was no one to give her comfort, no one who could kiss away her pain and fears. And it was then, when she thought of her mother, that Jessamy wondered what Abigail Windsor would say when she discovered that her only daughter had fallen in love with the enemy.

"It's been over two months," Maribelle whispered to her mother, "and she still sits at that window and moons! What do you think ails her?"

Pretense shook her head, and the corkscrew curls bobbed wildly. "Heavens! I have no idea."

Only Abigail knew what "ailed" her daughter, and she chose to keep that information to herself. When Jessamy had returned home tired, rumpled, and heartsore, only Abigail recognized the grief in her face for what it was. She had listened quietly, her face paling, but with no condemnation for her child in her eyes or heart. This was a precarious time, and if things had been different, Abigail had no doubt that Alex would have properly courted Jessamy. But this wasn't those safe times, and there wasn't much time. She cautioned Jessamy to keep her love to herself, or she would be ostracized.

"Not many would understand, Jessamy."

"You mean because Alex is the enemy?"

"No, I mean because you put the cart before the horse," Abigail had said softly, and there was no doubting her meaning. Jessamy's eyes had widened. She hadn't known she was so transparent, that her mother could see through her so easily.

Patting Jessamy's flaming cheek, Abigail murmured, "You aren't the first young lady to seek love outside of marriage, dear, but it isn't socially acceptable. I doubt that it will ever be. It is to your advantage to keep your love to yourself. One day, when this war is over, you will be able to shout it from the rooftops if you like."

"What . . . what do you think Papa will say?"

Smiling, Abigail pulled a worn, well-read letter from the pocket of her frayed shirtwaist dress. Her fingers traced the flourishes of his sweeping cursive, and a bemused expression lingered in her eyes.

"I think he will understand," Abigail said at last, and Jessamy didn't press for any more answers.

Everything was so mixed up, and no one knew where Bryce had gone. William Windsor had searched in vain, and there had been not a single word from Alex since Jessamy had boarded the train near Hopkinsville. No letter, no message, nothing from Alex. Only Captain Windsor wrote, and his news was not always good. Bryce followed Forrest, but somehow had been incorporated into another regiment. Though William tried, he had not yet been able to catch up with his youngest son. And the battle news was frequently as grim. Jessamy tried not to dwell on the dismal facts he sent them, tried to hold out hope for a quick end to the war.

Winter had passed in rain and cold winds, and the war limped on. On February 6, it was confirmed that General Grant was on the Tennessee River, and the frontier was in danger. Fort Henry fell after an hour's bombardment, and while the Confederate generals consulted at Bowling Green, Kentucky, their chance to concentrate the Confederate forces east and west of the Tennessee River literally went up in smoke as Fort Henry burned.

As the armies were systematically crushed and scattered, Captain William Windsor consulted with his fellow officers on the grave situation. Finally, Johnston decided to gather his scattered armies at Nashville, then withdraw if necessary through Stevenson, Alabama. Somewhere down the Memphis and Charleston Railroad, they would reunite with the West Tennessee brigades who were under Beauregard's command. The quickest route was across the bridge at Clarksville.

William wrote to his family of the danger and misery suffered by enlisted men and officers alike. And he wrote of the Rebel army losing Fort Donelson to a picket fence. Abigail read it aloud, her soft, cultured voice faltering in places, her pain evident as Jessamy, her cousins, and her aunt gathered around the fire to listen.

"There are strange things in war, dear wife, but one of the strangest happened at Fort Donelson. We had fought and fought well, against high odds. When word came that we were to surrender, we were aghast. That brave son of the Confederacy, Colonel Nathan Bedford Forrest, put out that he would not surrender, but that he and his men and whoever wanted to follow would go. Many did follow, your husband and sons among them. You see, Floyd's scouts had come back with word that Federal soldiers were packed as tightly as corn rows, and that we had no chance of defeating them. We had spent four days in the field, with cold and hunger as our enemies as well. The horses were weary, as were the men. It wasn't until we rode away, following Colonel Forrest and his younger brother, that the truth was known.

"The word to halt came down the line, and a subaltern and three men who had been reconnoitering rode up to report that the enemy was in a battle line directly in our path. It was an identical report to the one from Floyd's scouts. Forrest asked for a volunteer to verify this, but none of us was up to that sort of thing. Forrest did not hesitate. He turned his command over to Kelly with the orders that if he did not return, to carry the men out the best way he could but to get them out. He had promised a great many parents that he would care for their boys, and he intended to keep that promise. Abby, try to imagine if you will, that cold, gray morning, with the fog lying in tattered shrouds about the land, hiding trees and shrubs and gilding them with deceit. Dead men lay all around, their faces as gray as the fog, as gray as wood ashes, fixed in death and some with staring, sightless eyes. It was a scene to behold like no other. As was told later, Forrest and his brother pressed on in spite of this grievous sight, riding their shivering mounts amongst the rolling mists until they came to what looked like solid lines of men rising up from the fog. They paused, and noted that the long lines of men were too silent, too fixed, to be human. Moving stealthily closer, Forrest and his brother stared in amazement, for in front of their startled eyes rose—not specters of death or armed men but a neat, winding line of picket fencing!

"In the gray gloom of night and fog, Floyd's scouts had mistaken the fencing for fresh divisions of reinforcements. With that mistaken information, our fates were

sealed with the generals in command. 'Surrender' was the order and surrender we
did, excepting those of us who chose to follow Bedford Forrest. And it was too late to
do anything about it when Forrest arrived
back to where we waited. He met us where
the water overflowed the Cumberland City
road. As it lined the road with ice, the water looked most formidable. Once more
Forrest called for volunteers to test the water, and once more none stepped forward.
It's not that I am a coward, nor your sons,
Abby, but we did not then know this remarkable officer, nor his capabilities. We
were just on the threshold of discovering
how remarkable he was. Forrest himself
rode quickly into that torrent of water,
splashing through to the other bank, the
water rising no higher than his saddle
skirts. Many in our company then pledged
their undying allegiance to Colonel Forrest,
and know in him a confidence that we feel
for few other leaders. The colonel himself
solemnly reminded us that we had not lost
Fort Donelson to the strategy of the Federals or to Grant, but to a line of picket fence
and a gray mist. . . ."

Finishing, Abigail put the now-tattered pages
of the letter in her lap and lifted her face to her
family. Tears streamed silently over her cheeks
and dropped to her bodice as she whispered,
"How long must this go on?"

It was the closest she had seen her mother to
despair, and Jessamy went to her and put her
head in Abigail's lap. Nothing was said. Only

the soft crackle of the fire in the grate made any noise as the family sat lost in their own thoughts. William's letter had made a profound impression on all of them, had shown them how devastating and terrible war could be to the men who braved weather and wounds to fight for their beliefs.

In the days after, Jessamy frequently thought of her father and brothers, and just as frequently thought of Alex. Had he too had narrow escapes? She fretted constantly, and woke up at night in a cold sweat. Sometimes she would rise and wrap herself in a warm cloak and blankets and walk outside. There was something soothing about being able to suck in deep gulps of cold, frosty air untinged with woodsmoke and the close press of family.

All the soldiers—Rebel and Yankee—had long since abandoned Clover Hill to its fate, and it lay, a ruined, raped estate bare of sustenance but filled with hope and determination. Most of the Negroes had come creeping timidly back, home to Clover Hill, home to Miss Abigail and her soft voice and hands and sense of security. The harsh times were too much for Abby, and her health was slowly deteriorating in spite of the extra help.

Jessamy could see it, could see the dark circles under her mother's eyes, the lines of worry that began to mar that smooth countenance in spite of her every effort. It had begun with Bryce's defection, then worsened with her daughter's long absence. Jessamy felt pangs of guilt each time she saw those tiny lines in her mother's face, felt as responsible as if she had drawn them there herself.

It was late in March, and the nights were still long and cold, the north winds howling down at times with a fury. Those were the times Jessamy felt most restless. With the cramped cabin filled with people and the acrid sting of smoke, she would often seek relief outside in spite of the harsh weather.

She thought of her neighbors, and wondered if they were as tired and hungry as she was. There wasn't time or means for visits anymore; in fact there was no time for anything but work. Even in the winter when there weren't gardens to weed or fields to plow, there was still the cutting of wood to be done, the hunting that would bring in a scrawny rabbit or two for the evening meal. A few times, even Jessamy had taken one of the old rifles and gone into the woods to hunt.

On a recent visit into Cloverport, Jessamy had run into the Leathers sisters. They lived on a sprawling estate not far from the boundaries of Clover Hill, and they were suffering the same privations. All their Negroes had gone at first, then returned cold and hungry and penniless, with their hands out and misery in their eyes. Of course they had not had the heart to turn them out, though old John Leathers had died defending Fort Henry and there were no men left to help do the hunting. A cousin was a riverboat captain for the Confederacy, and he sent them small amounts of money from time to time to tide them over. Other than that, the Leatherses were entirely on their own, just like a dozen other families left behind. The Weavers, the Mullens, the Kings, the Andersons—all were bereft of their menfolk and forced to fend for themselves.

Jessamy blew out a breath of air, watching the frost cloud evaporate in the cold night. She leaned against the broad trunk of an oak, tilting back her head to watch the stars glitter in the dark sweep of sky that stretched overhead in a vast canopy. Somewhere beneath that sky were her father and brothers, and somewhere too was Alex. Where were they? Were they cold? Hungry?

As she wiped away a tear from the corner of her eye, she heard the faint, unmistakable sound of a horse's hoof on frozen ground. Jessamy grew still, straining to listen. Who would be riding this way so late at night, unless it was. . . .

Unless it was soldiers, perhaps, coming back to invade Clover Hill again. Her heart was pounding, and the breath hung in her throat as she sucked in another deep gulp of air, standing on her tiptoes and peering through the dark. Should she run? Hide? Warn the others? Who was it, and what did they want?

A thousand thoughts skimmed through her mind as she hesitated, poised to flee yet waiting to see who it might be on the road leading to Clover Hill. The blanket slipped from her shoulders and a chill ran down her spine as she stood shivering beneath the old oak tree near the road. To her right was the grove of hickory and ash trees, and to her left wound the split-rail fence, or what was left of it. Just in front was the road leading from the crossroads toward Cloverport.

As she watched, half-hidden in the shadow of the oak, the clatter of hooves grew louder and Jessamy finally saw a hazy group of riders. Her fingers dug into the bark, and she hoped they would pass by, hoped it was not the enemy. A faint spray of moonlight glittered on a brass uniform button, reflecting in tiny bursts, but she could not tell the color of the coat. Bits and metal curb chains rattled on the horses, and there was the sound of creaking leather and weary blowing of the horses as they trod slowly across the hard-packed rutted road.

It wasn't until they drew abreast of the tall oak tree and neared the spot where the curved drive to Clover Hill began that Jessamy recognized them. She saw the telltale glisten of white teeth in a dark face first, heard the soft, cultured, familiar voice of a Negro, and knew who it was. The tall, straight frame of the rider in front was as rigid as ever in spite of obvious weariness. Pushing away from the tree, Jessamy flew out into the drive just as they turned their mounts.

The lead horse reared immediately, snorting loudly, and his rider had to calm him with quick, hard pulls on the reins.

"Dammit, Jess, you spooked my horse!" came the irritable male voice, but she didn't care.

She reached up and tugged at the horse, a broad, happy smile curving her mouth. "You can fuss all you like, Nick Windsor, but I'm still glad to see you!"

"I wish I could say the same thing," was the disgruntled reply, followed by, "Oh, all right! I'm glad to see you, too!"

"It's a good thing he recognized you in the dark, Jess, 'cause I was about to shoot," James said, and she saw the bluish glimmer of his rifle barrel as he put it away. Behind James was

Charles, with William Windsor bringing up the rear. They were home at last!

Dempsey was grinning happily, his face bisected by the gleam of his teeth, his eyes shining brightly in the dark as he drawled, "We're very glad to be home, Miss Jess!"

"I'm glad to have you home, Dempsey," she returned with a welcoming smile that was softened by sudden tears.

Nick leaped lightly from his horse, and folded Jessamy into his arms. She pressed close, rubbing her cheek against his coat, inhaling the scent of many fires, of gunpowder and leather and horses. He seemed so different now, so much older, and when he put her at arm's length she saw that he was.

Jessamy's heart sank. Did Alex look that way, too? As if he had seen the fires of hell? Her gaze shifted from Nick to her father, and she saw the same watchful expression in eyes that had always been filled with a mellow light for his daughter. James and Charles looked different too, as if they had aged ten years in less than one.

"Come see Mother," Jessamy said quietly, and they followed. She heard Nick's soft curse as the ruins of Clover Hill rose up in the night, the still-standing chimneys pointing blackened, accusing fingers to the sky, an eerie silhouette on the hill. William said nothing, and the twins and Dempsey seemed too weary to make a sound. It was deathly quiet as they approached the whitewashed overseer's cabin, the muffled clopping of horse hooves providing a solemn accompaniment.

Jessamy felt oddly out of place when she saw

her mother fly into her husband's arms with a glad cry, saw tears fall unchecked down Abigail's cheeks. She felt like an interloper, and turned her eyes away. Her brothers did too, shifting from one foot to another, until finally they mumbled that they would help Dempsey put the horses away. Jessamy went with them, leading her father's horse.

Nick walked quietly, leading his horse, his jaw muscles clenched. "Mother wrote us about the house, but I couldn't believe it," he said finally. He paused and looked down at his sister. "Tell me about it."

She shrugged helplessly, not wanting to describe that terrible day, not wanting to remember it. Nick's dark eyes pierced her like knives, and she knew he was waiting, knew he would wait until she told him everything he wanted to know. Sucking in a deep breath, she pulled her blanket more tightly around her and looked directly into his eyes.

"It was Yankees—"

"Well, I didn't think it was Reverend Dooley!"

"Aw, go easy, Nick," James interrupted when Jessamy stopped and glared. "This has to be as hard for her to say as it is for us to hear."

Nick nodded tightly. "Sorry. Go ahead, Jess."

"There's not much to tell. I imagine Mother already told most of it. They camped here for over a month, until Forrest arrived in the area. When they left, they burned the house, then the bridge over the creek."

"And our cousin was with them?"

Startled, Jessamy's head jerked up. "No! I mean, yes, he was, but not like you think."

Nick started walking again, pulling his horse behind him, saying nothing else until they were inside the stable. Most of the stalls were empty; they had once held expensive, beautiful horses. Only a cow and a few goats occupied the stables now, and Nick stalked down the wide corridor between the stalls.

James and Charles began rubbing down their animals, and Jessamy busied herself with William's horse. There wasn't much grain, but there was plenty of hay. The bales had been too bulky for the Yankees to carry with them, and in the chaos of discovering Forrest was near they'd forgotten to burn it.

She kept her head down, feeling Nick's intent gaze but afraid to look up. She knew her brother, knew that he didn't forgive and forget easily. If he already knew that Alex had been there as one of the enemy, he would never forgive him for the destruction of Clover Hill. Nick had the fiery blood of their mother's family, and it had not been tempered with the calmer Windsor strain as the twins' had. Jessamy—who once was just as quick to denounce Alex—hoped her brother would not press the issue.

Her hopes were in vain.

"Tell me about Alex, Jess," Nick said when the horses had been fed, watered, and rubbed down. He rested one arm on the top of the stall door and looked down at her.

"Oh, not now, Nick. It's cold out here, and . . . and I want to go inside where it's warm."

"And you don't want to answer my question." His eyes narrowed. "Mother wrote he was here, but she didn't say much else about him. I want to know from you. And I want the truth, which I see you are about to hide."

Her head jerked up. "I am not! You can be so mean, Nick Windsor!"

"And you can be so foolish, Jessamy Windsor."

James and Charles hung back, not wanting to get involved but not wanting to miss anything, either. Jessamy slid them a contemptuous glance before lifting her chin and glaring boldly at her brother.

"Yes, Alex was here, and yes, he is a captain in the Union army, and yes, he was involved in the burning of the house. But that last part was indirect, and I believe him when he said he had nothing to do with it—"

"I believe you have more than a cousinly affection for Alex, don't you?"

The question hung in the air for a long moment, said as soft as velvet but sheathing steel. "And if I do?" Jessamy countered.

It was a direct challenge, said in the same tone she had used as a child when she dared her brothers to do something.

"And if you do," Nick said after a tense pause that stretched interminably, "you are doomed to grief. If I meet him in battle or on the road, I intend to kill him. There will be no mercy for the man who burned down our home, Jess, and I'm surprised that you don't feel the same way." He stepped close, grabbing her shoulders, his fingers digging painfully into the soft flesh beneath the blanket. "What happened after you disappeared, Jess? Mother wrote that Alex was found missing about the same time, and it's odd that it happened that way. Did you help him escape? Have you betrayed not only your family but your country?"

Wrenching away, she stared up at her brother with a tight-lipped frown. "No! I would not have helped him escape and you know it, but I did . . . did see him later. I was looking for Bryce, and I didn't even know Alex was gone until we found each other in the woods down by Piney Creek. Oh Nick, I felt the same way you do at first! But he isn't like that, and he's only doing what he thinks is right, the same as you are. Can't you see that—"

But Nick was turning away and stalking from the stable so that she had to run to catch up with him, putting out her hand to grab his arm. "Nick!"

He shook off her hand, and his eyes were flint-hard and cold. "I never thought my own sister would be a traitor. I never did."

"I'm not!"

"You have to choose, Jess. You can't have both worlds."

Stomping her foot, Jessamy cried, "It's not my fault that this stupid war made everything such a mess! I hate it! I hate for everything to be so mixed up, and now I don't know how I'm supposed to feel or what I'm supposed to do!"

Nick shrugged. "You need to figure it out before somebody gets killed over it."

Jessamy watched him leave the stable, and when she turned to look at James and Charles they couldn't meet her eyes. There was a cold, sinking feeling in her stomach. If Nick chanced to meet Alex on the battlefield or elsewhere, there would be bloodshed, and Alex would not be expecting it. Did she warn her lover or risk her brother? Blood was supposed to be thicker than water, but she loved Alex as a woman loved a man.

It was a long time before Jessamy could sleep that night.

Chapter 15

WILLIAM AND HIS SONS went back to the Ninth Tennessee, joining their regiment at nearby Corinth, Mississippi. They left early, when sunlight glittered on fields of frosty furrows and in the tears of their family.

Abigail clung to her husband briefly, then stepped back and tried to smile through her tears. Pretense was openly sobbing, and Celine stood with a grave expression on her angular face. Infected by the others' tears, Carrie Sue and Sarah Jean wept loudly, and Maribelle attempted to comfort them. The stay had been all too brief, and now they had to go.

A little apart from the others, Jessamy stood with her arms folded over her chest. Nick looked up and saw her, and his expression subtly altered. He had barely spoken to her since their argument, but now he came and put an arm around his sister.

"You're still family, and no matter what else

happens, you'll always be my sister," he said gruffly.

It was what she needed to hear, and though she wanted to ask him not to judge Alex too harshly, Jessamy only nodded. "I know, Nick. And you'll always be my brother."

Grinning, Nick chucked her under the chin. "There's to be a battle in the next few weeks, Jess. Do you think you can manage to say a few prayers for your bullying brother?"

"A . . . a battle?" She stared up at him with wide, frightened eyes.

"Yeah," James put in before Nick could shush him, "we've got the Yankees almost where we want them, up near Pittsburg Landing by the old Shiloh Meeting House. Grant's back in command, and the Yanks don't seem to be expecting anything. If things go right, we—"

"Shut up!" Nick said so fiercely that James paused with his mouth still open. "He doesn't need to be telling you any of this. Jess . . ." Nick put out a hand to grab her arm.

"Yes?"

"Guard your tongue. There's a lot of Rebel lives in the balance if the wrong word is said."

She swallowed hard. "I . . . I will, Nick. God-speed . . ."

In the days that followed their departure, Jessamy frequently found herself wondering what it would be like when the war was over. If it was ever over. Could all their differences be reconciled? Or would there be bitterness and hatred between countrymen forever? No matter which side won there would always be that between them, she thought with a pang of regret. And she couldn't forget that she had killed a man, one of her own countrymen. It haunted her dreams and sometimes her waking hours, and she prayed no one would ever find out. What would Abigail say if she knew that her daughter had murdered a human being? But only Alex knew. . . .

Several nights after the Windsor men had gone to rejoin their regiment, another visitor arrived at Clover Hill. It was Alex, and he was tired, wet, and hungry. It had stormed and the rain had drenched everything for miles, causing the creeks to rise and rivulets of water to form in the newly plowed fields. Alex came just at dusk when purple shadows lay on the soggy fields and a mist hid the trees.

The knock sounded softly, and it was Jessamy who went to the door. A fire burned brightly, and dinner was on the plank table in the center of the room. She had the weary thought that it was probably another deserter from the army who had smelled their meal cooking and come to beg. That thought evaporated when she swung open the door.

A tall man in a blue uniform blocked the fading light from outside, and her heart grew wings.

"Alex!" Jessamy flew into his arms, forgetting about her family. Her arms went around his neck, disregarding the damp clothes he wore or those watching. There was a shocked silence behind her, and Alex gently put her from him. Stubbornly, Jessamy clung to his arm, turning to face her family with a defiant tilt to her chin.

Celine was frowning, and Aunt Pretense was fanning herself with her handkerchief, moaning. Maribelle stared at her curiously. Only Abigail reacted normally.

"Captain Steele. Do come in," she said, stepping forward with a smile. "We are about to sit down to eat. Would you care to join us?"

Flicking a glance at the table, Alex was tempted to refuse, seeing that there was little enough, but Jessamy would not allow it.

"Of course he'll eat. He's bound to be hungry," she said, pulling him forward and shutting the door behind him.

Dinner was a silent, awkward affair, with stilted conversation and sidelong glances. Dried peas with fatback, fried corn, sweet potatoes, and cornbread had replaced the sumptuous meals of prewar days. Tea and coffee were also things of the past, and the most frequent beverage was sassafras tea made from roots dug up and stored.

Alex took a sip of the scalding brew, then set his cup down and looked directly at Abigail.

"I found Bryce."

Abigail's face grew even paler, and one hand rose to her throat. "Is he . . . is he . . . ?"

"He's fine," Alex hastily assured her. "If there had been time I would have tried to bring him with me, but as he is now in Forrest's command, that would have been rather awkward."

"Indeed!" Pretense said with a nervous flutter of her handkerchief. "*Dangerous* would be a more appropriate word, I would think, Captain Steele."

"Ah, and I must agree with you," Alex returned with a smile. "But negotiations could have been carried out had I had enough time."

Abigail leaned forward, fixing Alex with a steady eye. "Where is he?"

"As I have said, Mrs. Windsor, he is safely with Colonel Forrest. They are camped at Corinth right now. My troops are not far away, at Pittsburg Landing. When I get back to my regiment I will try to secure his removal."

At the words *Pittsburg Landing*, Jessamy's heart sank. Wasn't that where Nick had said there was to be a decisive battle? Did Mother know? *Did Alex?*

A glance at her mother assured her that Abigail knew nothing of it, and a quick glance at Alex caught him looking at her with a cocked brow. Did he sense what she was thinking? She smiled brightly.

"Well then! Bryce should be home soon, Mother, isn't that wonderful?"

"Yes, dear, it is." Abigail turned back to Alex. "We have a small bottle of brandy put back if you would care for some, Captain. I'll have one of the men take care of your horse for you. You must stay the night, of course. I apologize that I cannot offer you better accommodations, but I am told the stable is warm and dry and the hay provides a most comfortable bed."

Rising, Alex pushed back his chair and inclined his head slightly. "Thank you, Mrs. Windsor. I am indebted to you for your hospitality."

"Not at all. It is I who am in your debt for news of my adventurous son. Jessamy, if you will come with me, please, I will give you some blankets for Captain Steele."

Obediently, Jessamy rose and followed Abigail to the small wooden cabinet where the linens were stored, while Celine saw to the clearing of the table and Pretense went to fetch the brandy. It wasn't until Abigail clutched her arm that Jessamy realized her mother knew full well the danger her youngest child might incur.

"Don't dare tell the captain of your father's visit!" Abigail warned softly. "And do not mention anything else you might have heard."

Staring at Abigail's face in the dim light, Jessamy saw that she knew everything. So much for shielding her mother from the unpleasant truth.

She slid a surreptitious glance toward Alex, who was seated in a straight-backed chair before the fire with a glass of brandy in one hand and Pretense chattering at him about the lack of silk thread for embroidery. Alex looked bored, but polite, and Jessamy stifled a nervous giggle as she turned back to her mother.

"But if Bryce is at Corinth with Forrest, and there is a concentration of troops there," Jessamy began before she thought, "then—"

"Then Bryce is in danger and we have no way of getting word to your father in time," Abigail finished for her. Her mouth was set in a thin slash, stitched with fine lines that made her look suddenly old.

"We could ask Alex."

"No! That would be like telling Grant personally that the Confederates are planning to battle." Abigail took a deep breath. "No, we must not say anything, Jessamy. It would endanger your father and brothers if we did, and give warning to the enemy."

What it came down to, Jessamy realized, was choosing between Bryce's safety and the safety of several thousand soldiers. There was no choice to make, of course, but it had to be twice as hard on Abigail as it was on Jessamy.

It was hard enough for Jessamy to converse politely with Alex, to refrain from blurting out that he might be riding back into danger, to refrain from touching him when her mother was near. Celine watched over them like a hen with its only egg, her dark eyes narrowed with suspicion. When Jessamy mentioned that she would walk Alex to the stable, Celine gave a shake of her head.

"Maybe I am old-fashioned, but I don't think I approve of your going out there," she said. "It's late, and I have this little feeling, me, that it does not matter that he is your cousin."

"Oh Celine, how you do run on," Jessamy said quickly, too quickly. "I only intend to show Al— Captain Steele—the path, then I'll be right back in."

A delicate brow arched. *"N'est-ce pas?* Then wait the little moment while I fetch my cloak to go with you," Celine began, but Abigail intervened.

She recognized the faintly desperate gleam in Jessamy's eyes and took pity. "Now, Celine, Jessamy will only walk with the captain to the end of the path. Isn't that right, Jessamy?"

Left with no choice but to agree, Jessamy gave a nod of her head. "Yes, ma'am, that's right. I won't go far."

Abigail bent back over her sewing. "Of course you won't, dear. Good night, Captain."

"Good night, Mrs. Windsor."

Though it was early April, the nights were still crisp and cool, and the recent rain had left everything wet and lush. There was a stillness to the air as they walked toward the long stables.

Before they reached the end of the path she turned and shoved something into Alex's hand. "Here. It's for you."

He seemed surprised. "What is it?"

"It's a Christmas present. I . . . I saved it for you."

"Aw Jess, I didn't bring you anything—"

"That doesn't matter! Open it."

When he unwrapped the thin tissue paper, he held the gift up so that the moonlight would shine on it. It was a leatherbound Bible, and Alex opened the cover with one finger. His name was inscribed inside, *James Alexander Steele*, and the sentiment, *To keep you safe from harm—Love, Jessamy Ann Windsor*.

Clearing his throat, Alex said, "It's beautiful, Jess. I don't know what to say."

"Didn't your mother ever teach you to say thank you?"

Grinning, he leaned forward to press a light kiss on the tip of her nose. "Thank you, love!"

She smiled. "I just want you to be safe, Alex. That's kind of like a lucky charm. Keep it with you."

"I will. And I'll think of you every time I feel it in my pocket or bring it out to read."

"Good." A comfortable silence stretched as they began walking again.

"Come with me?" Alex inquired softly when they reached the end of the path and stood beneath a towering oak, but Jessamy gave a regretful shake of her head.

"I can't. Mother has my word."

Alex grinned. "She's a very intelligent lady. Maybe she saw the way I was looking at you. . . ."

"Or the way I was looking at you!" Jessamy gave a brief sigh, then forced a smile. "Oh, Alex, I . . . I . . . I'm going to miss you," she ended lamely, not quite certain what she had been about to say. There was so much she wanted to say, so much she needed to say, yet somehow she was afraid to say anything for fear of blurting out the truth, her fears for him and Bryce and the rest of her family. How could she keep such knowledge to herself when it might endanger the man she loved? Yet, how could she endanger not only her father, but her country?

"Jess?" Alex was looking at her curiously, a faint frown between his brows. "Are you all right?"

When he drew her into his arms, holding her tightly against his broad chest, she nodded, glad he could not see the guilt that she was sure was in her eyes. "Yes," she mumbled against his blue coat, "I'm fine. Just wanting you, is all."

At that he drew back slightly, his head coming down to press a hot, fierce kiss on her willing lips. Jessamy shut her eyes and yielded gladly, clutching at him and holding on as he tracked hot kisses from her mouth to her ear, then down the side of her neck to the pulse beating in her throat.

"God, Jess," he muttered hoarsely against her skin, "God, I've missed you so!"

"I've missed you, Alex. . . . Alex, no, not here!"

"Why not? What's so bad about right here?" he murmured as he pressed her back against the tree. She couldn't reply to that, not coherently, anyway. Everything was so mixed up, and she wanted Alex to hold and caress her, make her forget reality for a little while. Nothing else seemed to matter when she was in his arms, when he was kissing her or caressing her.

His lean, hard body was molded to hers as he pinned her against the oak, and she could feel the imprint of his desire against her. Alex's breath was warm, smelling faintly of the brandy her mother had given him as he kissed her again, kissed her until she felt as lightheaded as if she were brandy-drunk. His fingers fumbled with the buttons of her blouse, and Jessamy gave a helpless little moan that went unnoticed in the passion haze.

Boldly, he pushed aside the opened edges of her blouse and the night air whispered across Jessamy's bare skin. She caught his hands between hers, holding them against her heart.

"No, Alex . . ."

"I know, I know," he said with a groan. "It's just that I want you so badly, Jess."

"I want you, too."

Night shadows danced across the ground and the two lovers beneath the tree, flitting capriciously around them. They were partially hidden, but she felt as if they were highlighted by a thousand lanterns as Alex dragged his fingertips over the shivering bare expanse of her stomach. Tiny flames erupted wherever his hands grazed, igniting her quivering nerve ends in a raging inferno. When his hands closed over her breasts, Jessamy's eyes closed and she gave a long, slow shudder that ran all the way down to her toes. His lips followed the path his fingers traced, and Jessamy gasped, arching her back, wanting him to stop yet wanting him to ease the coiling fires that burned deep inside.

Alex curved her slender frame into him, his tongue tasting, teasing, curling around the tight bud of her breast and making her moan with longing. Neither of them noticed the night wind, the sharp chill in the air or their surroundings. Nothing mattered but each other and the wild, fierce sweetness of their passion.

Sliding her hands up under his shirt, Jessamy felt his muscles flex with his movements, rippling beneath her fingertips as she slid her arms around him. She wanted to hold him so closely nothing could ever come between them again, not miles or war or even family.

It wasn't until a door slammed in the distance that they broke apart, disheveled and breathless, looking guilty and defiant at the same time.

"It's probably Celine," Jessamy murmured after a moment in which she tried to rebutton her blouse with shaking fingers. Her hands were trembling so that Alex had to help her, a rueful smile curving his mouth as he reached out and fastened them.

"Does that mean she'll be after me with a buggy whip?"

"More than likely."

"It would be worth it."

Jessamy looked up with a smile. "I'd advise you not to tell her that. It's too tempting."

"Are you suggesting a strategic retreat?"

"Strongly!" When Alex turned toward the stable Jessamy put out a hand to catch his arm. "I —I'll try to see you before you go," she said, and he knew what she meant.

"I'm leaving at first light in the morning."

"I know."

He smiled, and when they heard heavy foot-steps scrunching on the graveled path, he gave her a quick kiss and beat a hasty retreat to the stable. Celine arrived in a whirlwind of indig-nation and righteous wrath, a voluminous cloak floating behind her slender body like great wings. Sighing, Jessamy turned to face her.

"*Sacrebleu!* I did not think even you—who have flown in the face of every convention con-ceived—would go so far! Do you expect my ap-proval? I will not give it!"

Jessamy met the flashing eyes stoically. "I know you won't, Celine, and I'm sorry."

"Hah! Sorry? You haven't learned the mean-ing of sorry until your poor *maman* discovers what you have done! What are you going to do when your handsome Yankee gentleman runs off again?"

"I'll wait for him."

"Wait for him! For what? For him to marry you? Don't be so foolish, Miss Jessamy Windsor! Why should a man, even a wretched Yankee gentleman, marry you if you are so free?"

Jessamy gazed at Celine's angry face for a long moment, finally feeling the bite of the wind through her thin blouse and light cloak. She shivered, wondering for a brief instant if her old nurse could be right. Alex had never mentioned marriage, and she had just as-sumed—

"Because he loves me," Jessamy finally re-plied, and winced at Celine's sudden burst of laughter.

"So? Your precious love would not be the first

man to say that in the heat of the moment, *chère.* Think about it. Think about what was really said, not what you wanted to hear."

The small chin came up, and her eyes glittered. "He does love me, and I love him. He may be a Yankee, but he's a good man."

Celine looked at her sharply. "You certainly have changed your tune in the past few months. Once, I remember you telling your *maman* how bad he was, and that you would never forgive him. You said, 'Never in a blue never,' *n'est-ce pas?* And you must think of your family, *chère!* What of your papa, out fighting men just like your Yankee?"

"Papa is a fair man. He will want my happiness!"

Celine shook her head, and taking pity on the girl she'd helped bring into the world, she put a slender arm around Jessamy's shoulders and turned her toward the cabin.

"*Ma petite,* do you not know that your papa—while he is a fine and fair man—will be saddened? And think of your brothers, who are fighting every day. Will Nicholas be glad to see you with Alex? Somehow, I think the answer is *non!* Ah, *chère,* listen to old Celine. I know what trouble can be when family does not care for the man who is your love." She smiled softly. "I was once in love, you see, but my *maman* and papa did not approve. I was strong like you, and I said I would have him anyway." She gave an eloquent shrug. "But in a while, he did not want me anymore, and I could not go back to my *maman* and papa."

"That is when you came to us?"

Nodding, Celine gazed at Jessamy with brimming eyes. "*Oui*, that is when your *maman* and papa gave me a home, and their children became the children I would never have. I feel about you as if you were my own, and I want only your happiness."

"Then you will understand when I follow my heart," Jessamy said quietly.

Shaking her head, the older woman slowly climbed up the short, shallow steps of the cabin. "*Oui*, I will understand, but do not ask me to approve. I hope that I am wrong, and that your love does not leave you, but it scares me at times."

"Me, too."

Celine wrapped her in a brief, fierce hug, then turned and went into the cabin.

Lying on her narrow cot a few hours later, Jessamy was forced to see the common sense in Celine's words. Part of her was yearning for Alex, who was only a few hundred yards away in the stable, and part of her—the common sense part—was warning her not to go to him. The battle raged between heart and head.

Heart won.

A hazy moon was sliding toward the western sky when Jessamy slipped from her bed and out the door of the cabin. She hadn't been able to sleep for thinking of Alex, and had to talk to him privately before he left. There were burning questions that only he could answer.

The door to the stable creaked slightly as she pushed it open, and Jessamy paused. Her eyes had not yet adjusted to the hazy light from the sliver of moon, and she stumbled as she took a step forward. A soft cry escaped, and before she could catch herself she was grabbed and thrown roughly to a pile of hay on the stable floor.

Coughing at the chaff stirred up by her fall, Jessamy heard Alex say, "Oh, it's you! You should have warned me."

Irritably, she snapped, "Next time I'll sound the bugle so I don't get slammed to the ground!" He stood over her, legs apart, his thumbs tucked into the waistband of his trousers. He wore no shirt or boots, and his bare chest gleamed softly in the dim light of the stable. Tilting his head to one side, Alex grinned and she added crossly, "Are you going to help me up, or do I just lie here the rest of the war?"

"I think I prefer you on your back—"

"Sadistic monster . . ."

"—but in a better mood."

Glaring up at him, Jessamy felt her irritation fade when he cocked a dark brow at her. He stood with one foot firmly planted on each side of her body and his gaze roamed from her flushed face to where her skirts had flown up around her knees.

"In fact," Alex said slowly, "I think you *should* lie there the rest of the war. Or at least, the night."

She smiled at the sudden spark in his eyes. "Alone?"

"Definitely not."

Jackknifing his long legs, Alex lowered his body to slant atop hers. Jessamy swallowed the sudden lump in her throat, and the steady pop-pop of her heart accelerated to a mad beat that sounded like thunder in her ears. It was warm and cozy in the stable, and the high mound of hay that cushioned her body smelled faintly comforting. It reminded her of the abandoned barn so far away, when Alex had taken her in his arms and made love to her for the first time.

Jessamy forgot the reason she had come to the stable. The questions that had burned so hotly they couldn't wait began to fade as he put his arms around her and tucked her body into his. All she could think of was the moment, of Alex, and his hard male body and searing kisses.

Feverishly, Alex began to unfasten the blouse she wore, his fingers tugging roughly at the small wooden buttons. She wore nothing beneath her blouse and skirt, not even her pantalettes or a slip. It had been dark, and with everyone sleeping she had not dared search for her garments and risk waking Celine.

"Alex . . . the hay . . . it's so prickly," she murmured when he tossed aside the blouse and her bare skin pressed into the dry stalks. Pulling her to her feet, Alex swung her into his arms and carried her to the stall where he had spread his blankets. It was warm and cozy and intimate, shrouded in shadows and the sweet fragrance of hay.

"This better?" he breathed against her ear, slowly lowering her to the blankets.

Jessamy nuzzled his neck, her lips teasing his ear lobe for a moment before she replied, "Much."

Bending his head, Alex kissed her gently on the mouth, kissing her until she began to arch into him. Then his lips moved lower, trailing damp kisses along the delicate arch of her collarbone and back to the small flutter of pulse in the hollow of her throat. His hands slipped beneath the waistband of her skirt, and somehow it was loosened, sliding down over her slender thighs in a swift movement. Jessamy lay in his arms quivering as he sat back and gazed at her for a long moment, his eyes slowly moving from her flushed face to the firm thrust of her small breasts, the tight, tiny waist and womanly swell of her hips.

"God, you're beautiful," he said huskily, "more beautiful than I dreamed of at night. I used to long for sleep just so I could remember, and now I know that my dreams could never compare with the real you."

"Alex . . ."

"Shush, love. Just lie there for a moment."

Quivering, Jessamy felt a surge of love and tenderness and the desire to always be beautiful for Alex. The thick, straight sweep of her lashes lowered to hide the glitter of sudden tears in her eyes, but he saw.

"What's the matter, love?" he asked, lifting her chin with a forefinger, frowning at her. "Are you all right?"

She nodded. "Yes, it's just that . . . that I'm afraid I won't always be beautiful to you."

Alex laughed and bent forward to kiss her on the tip of her small, straight nose. "Don't you know that doesn't matter? Oh, don't get me wrong! I love to look at you, love, to watch the way you walk, and the dainty sway of your hips and the way your hair reflects the sun and your eyes shine when you laugh, but that's not what love is all about, Jess. Love has to do with trust, and loyalty, and the way a person feels on the inside. The outside is just a pretty container. The real person is inside, like you. Don't you know how much I admire your spirit, your heart, your fire?"

She shook her head in mute denial, and he grinned at her.

"Well, I do! Even when you were a little girl, and you would get angry at me for not getting angry at you, I had to admire your dedication to a single purpose—that of pricking a reaction from me."

She gasped. "You knew?"

"Of course I knew! Even at ten I wasn't an idiot. But it was a harmless game most of the time, and I enjoyed beating you at it."

"Wretch," she muttered with a smile. "You must think I'm pretty terrible."

He smiled back. "Look, Jess, I admire the way you do things you don't like to do or don't want to do just because you're supposed to do them. And you love your family, not because you're supposed to, but because in spite of various idiosyncrasies, they are your family. That is loyalty, sweet Jess." He took her hand and uncurled the fingers from where they were digging quarter-moons into her palm. Caressing the sensitive skin, brushed now with faint calluses from uncustomary chores, he lifted her hand and pressed a tender kiss on the work-roughened palm. "And I love how you love me even though you think I'm dead wrong, even though I'm fighting for the 'wrong' side."

A faint smile touched her mouth, and she looked up at him almost shyly. "Maybe I'm hoping you'll see the light and give up your mistaken beliefs."

"And will you leave me if I don't?"

Her arms closed convulsively around him. "Never in a blue never!"

"That's why I love you."

Sliding her hands up over his broad chest, letting her fingertips graze the tiny curling hairs, Jessamy rose up to cling to his mouth, closing her eyes, losing herself in Alex. When he began kissing her again, his tongue slipping gently between her lips in light touches, she kissed him back. Alex's hands moved to caress her, sliding across her body in lingering motions, pausing to tease the hardened peaks of her breasts until she writhed beneath him.

It was sweet torment, delicious agony, and her breath came in short, hard gasps for air. Sitting back on his heels, Alex let his hands roam the hollows and curves of her body, exploring, taking his time, relishing her every moan. She watched him through narrowed eyes, through thick straight lashes that shuttered what she was thinking from him, but could not hide her desire.

Somewhere deep in the recesses of her brain, Jessamy recalled that she was supposed to have asked him some questions, but she could not at the moment think what they might have been, only that they had seemed important at the time. Nothing seemed as important now as Alex, and what he was doing, and how she felt about him. He hovered over her with soft words and caressing hands, his dark tanned face creased into the blurry lines of passion.

Reaching out, Jessamy began to caress him again, her hands sliding over the hard, muscled ridges of his chest and belly, exploring, marveling at the taut flesh. Even though she had many brothers, she had never seen them completely unclothed, and she was still shy when Alex removed his trousers with a quick twist and flung them away. Her cheeks flamed, and she wasn't certain where she was supposed to look, or if she was supposed to look. This was so new, and she didn't want to appear too naïve or too experienced. How was she supposed to act? The first time had been different, because then she had been too wrapped up in the moment to wonder if she was saying or doing the right thing. But now, now she was no longer a virgin, and now she was supposed to know what to say or do. Wasn't she?

"Let me hold you, love," Alex was saying, sliding his body down over hers, pressing intimately close as if he sensed her indecision. "Don't talk, not now. Just kiss me."

Obeying instinctively, Jessamy put her lips up to his, trying not to appear as insecure as she suddenly felt. Alex kissed her gently, his mouth moving softly on hers instead of with the familiar urgency. His kisses strayed from her parted lips to her throat, then became lavish, hot, moist caresses on her breasts, then moved along the fragile curve of her ribs to her stomach. Jessamy gasped with surprise, and Alex smiled against the gentle round of her belly.

"It's all right, love." He kissed her quivering flesh, then lifted to kiss her mouth again. Slowly, he built the fires within her, until she pressed against him with the urgency he wanted her to feel.

"Alex . . . please," she muttered when he continued to kiss her slowly, lingeringly. "Please!"

Shifting his body, Alex moved forward. She arched against him with a soft cry, and his arms curved around her in a tender embrace. There was only love between them, only the sweet pleasure that comes with giving to one another, and Jessamy knew that she would never want it any other way. Surging upward, Jessamy held tightly to him as Alex swept her to the heights of love.

It was only later, when they lay in a mist of satiation and love haze, that she recalled the burning questions she had come to ask. Celine's scornful words still rankled, and she had to know. They lay curled together, Alex lying half across her with his left arm thrown over her body, a light blanket pulled over them. Jessamy twisted to face him.

"Alex?"

His eyelashes briefly flickered. "Ummm?"

"Alex—listen to me."

Groaning, he rolled over on one side. "Wha—?"

"I have to ask you something."

"Now?"

"Now," she confirmed, giving him a light push with the heel of her palm.

Sighing, he forced his eyes open again. "What, love?"

"Is this forever?"

Alex's eyes opened wide, and a frown etched his brow. "Is this forever?" he repeated.

"This—us. Being together, I mean."

"As forever as anything can be, I guess. There *is* a war going on, and—"

"Oh, you know what I mean!" she said in exasperation. "I'm talking about . . . I'm talking about *us*."

Not quite certain what she meant, Alex pulled back a little bit. "You are talking about marriage, right?" he asked carefully, and Jessamy abruptly sat up to glare at him.

"No, I mean dancing in fairy rings in the moonlight! Of course, I mean marriage!"

"Oh. Well, what is it you need to discuss about getting married?"

A trace of impatience threaded her voice as she replied carefully, "Just small details, such as—do we intend to?"

"Now?"

"Oh, Alex! I mean ever! The future, a month, a year, ten years from now!" Her eyes narrowed slightly. "Don't you want to?" she couldn't help asking, wondering if his hesitation meant just that.

"I guess I hadn't thought about it."

"I see!" Scrambling to her feet and snatching at her clothes, she avoided looking at him as he reached out for her. Hot tears burned her eyes, and she choked back a sob as she tried to climb into her skirt. She couldn't see it for the blinding tears, and stumbled.

"Let me finish!" Alex growled, rising to grab her around the waist. "I hadn't thought about it because I naturally assumed that we would get married when the war is over. God only knows when that will be, Jess."

"You don't have to marry me just be—"

"I know that!" He gave her a gentle shake. "I wouldn't marry you for any reason but one, Jess. I love you. It's as simple as that."

Sagging into him, Jessamy dropped her skirt

back onto the hay-strewn floor. "I love you, too," she said with a teary sniff.

Alex wiped her tears away with his thumb, then folded her into his arms. "I knew that."

Rubbing her nose against his bare chest, Jessamy smiled into the dark pelt furring his skin. He held her close as they sank back to the stable floor.

Somewhere a cock crowed, and the morning sun was just brightening the eastern sky when Jessamy slipped into the cabin door to lie back down in her narrow cot. She would hold the memory of the night with her in the long hours to follow, and prayed that soon she would be with Alex again.

Chapter 16

"I SUPPOSE that you have said your farewells to the captain this morning, *n'est-ce pas?*" Celine asked with a suspicious glance in Jessamy's direction.

Jessamy didn't look at her. "Yes, as a matter of fact, I did, Celine. Would you please pass the sorghum?"

Shoving the crock of thick black syrup toward Jessamy, Celine watched silently as it was spooned over biscuits and grits. "Then you know where the enemy is going to be, I suppose," she said just as Jessamy lifted a forkful to her mouth. The fork tilted and spilled sticky sorghum onto the table beside Jessamy's plate.

Laying her empty fork carefully on her plate, Jessamy finally met Celine's watchful gaze. "Why would you ask me that?"

"Mon Dieu! It is because I think that you know these things, that is why!"

"And if I do?"

Slowly, "If you do, you may endanger the lives

of your papa and your brothers. You must know they will be in the thick of any fighting."

"Captain Steele is under the impression that there is to be no fighting," Jessamy said quietly. "At least not soon."

"And did you tell him differently? Is there to be any fighting?"

Wincing, Jessamy shook her head. "No, I didn't say anything."

Her heart ached, for she hadn't corrected Alex when he'd told her he had orders to join Sherman at Shiloh Church, that though there had been sniping between the two armies, no battle was expected. In fact, the Federals were so unaware, Grant was away from camp attending a strategy meeting with Admiral Foote. There was only one Union commander, who was as nervous as an old maid, Alex told her, and that was Brigadier General Benjamin M. Prentiss, who had placed pickets in a perimeter stretching a mile and a half from camp. Yet Jessamy had not spoken up. How could she have endangered her family? But how could she live with knowing that Alex might be killed if she didn't warn him?

Common sense told her that even if she'd warned him—if Forrest himself informed him of Confederate plans—Alex would still have gone to join Sherman. He wouldn't hang back just because there was going to be a battle, he would be in the thick of it and she knew it. It was foolish to suppose that he would behave otherwise.

"If you did not then I am wrong, *ma petite*," Celine was saying. "I know what is planned. And I want you to know that I am aware of how hard it must be for you, having to choose between the men that you love, family and . . . and friends."

Nodding, Jessamy whispered, "Yes, I suppose it was, but I don't know what else I could have done."

They were alone in the cabin, and Celine came to her and put a trembling arm around Jessamy's shoulders. "That is right, *chère*, and I'm proud of you for doing what you had to do. It was a terrible decision to have to make, and I must admit, I'm not sure what I would have done had it been me. I should have known that you would do the right thing."

"Was it right, Celine?" Jessamy turned to look at her steadily. "Was it right when I killed a man in November, a Confederate? You didn't know about that, did you? But I did it, I killed him and I'm not really sorry!" Her voice was fierce and low, and Celine just stared at her with wide, red-rimmed eyes. "No one knows but me and Alex, and God. He would have . . . have killed me, and I hit him and hit him and hit him again, until he was dead! I dreamed about it at first, but now . . . now I don't. I don't think much about it, not when men are killing each other like flies. What's right anymore, Celine? Was it right not to warn the man I love that he might be riding back into a hornet's nest? Whom do I owe my allegiance to, my family or my love? And why must I choose between them? At least Bryce was able to make a free choice, even though it may be one that hurts us all. Alex said that he admired my family loyalty, but I wonder how much he'd admire my decision if he dies because of it. . . ."

Celine swallowed hard and put out a hand. "*Chère*, you have had to make some hard choices, that is certain. I don't know exactly what I should tell you, except that you know the only way to do things is to go out and just do them. That is what Bryce did, and that is what your Alex has done and what you expected him to do. He will understand when he knows."

Rising abruptly, Jessamy tore out of the cabin and raced across the barren yard toward the grove of hickory trees. Harsh sobs ripped at her, and she let the hot tears flow freely. Everything was so confusing! How much easier it must be for the men who simply chose a side and fought. For one fierce moment, she wished she could do the same.

And that's what she told her mother an hour later, when Abigail asked her why she was wearing her brother's clothes again.

"Simple," Jessamy replied curtly as she continued to fold away her skirt and blouse. "I'm going to Shiloh after Bryce."

Gasping, Abigail snatched at Jessamy's arm. "You can't do that!"

"Of course I can. Alex and I were there just a few months ago, and it's not that far. I can steal a horse—"

"Jessamy!"

"—and find Bryce and insist that he come home before he gets his stupid self killed." Jessamy flashed her mother a glance devoid of pity for her fine-tuned sensibilities. "It was suggested to me that the only way to get things done is to do them yourself, Mother, and that's exactly what I intend to do."

Wringing her hands, Abigail bit her lower lip

and stared at her daughter as if she had never seen her before. And she hadn't. This was a Jessamy she didn't know, a Jessamy who was filled with new determination.

"But what horse will you steal?" she asked at last. "And what if you get caught?"

"I'll worry about that if it happens," was Jessamy's terse reply. She was busily stuffing bread and johnnycakes into a large square of cloth, and when Abigail recognized that nothing would dissuade her, she began to help.

"Tell Bryce he must come with you," she said briskly as she cut off a chunk of hard cheese to put with the bread and corn cakes. "He's been gone from home long enough."

"Do you really think he'll listen to me?" Jessamy asked quietly.

"If you tell him how worried I am."

Jessamy tied the square cloth into a knot and set it on the floor, then turned to face her mother. "I hope you're right."

"Take the mule," Abigail said as Jessamy reached for a battered felt hat hanging on a wooden peg by the door. "I won't have to worry about your being hanged for stealing a horse."

Swallowing the sudden urge to weep, Jessamy just nodded and said, "Thank you."

"And Jessamy, if you should happen to catch up with Captain Steele, tell him I said thank you."

"Ma'am?"

"Obadiah Johnston passed this way yesterday, and he told me that Captain Steele did, indeed, try to stop the Yankees from burning our house. In fact, Alex was so vehement about it, the Yan-

kee general threatened to court-martial him
and throw him into prison."

Jessamy was quiet for a moment. "I'm glad,"
she said at last. "Now we know that Alex really
did try, like he said."

Abigail smiled. "Yes, we do. Now go. And
please bring Bryce back with you."

It was only later, when she was trotting down
the road atop the broad-backed mule that Old
Billy had managed to "requisition" somehow,
that she had second thoughts about her ability
to convince Bryce of anything. He was as hard-
headed as any thirteen-year-old boy, and if he
encountered opposition, he rarely yielded. It
had been almost five months since he'd gone,
five months without a single word from him.
Bryce would not give in easily.

Clucking to the mule, Jessamy spurred him
into a faster gait. Maybe she could catch up
with Alex. Alex would know what to say to
Bryce. And maybe she could convince Alex not
to go to Shiloh Church. . . .

"What in the hell are you doing here?" Alex demanded angrily. He fought his horse to a standing position, barely able to keep him down after
Jessamy had burst through the thickly wooded
copse where he was camped.

"I came to find you. And Bryce," she replied as
she swung down from the mule. She moved
stiffly. She had spent almost an entire day in the
saddle, and her muscles cried out for relief.

"It wasn't easy to find you, you know," she
grumbled. "If I hadn't remembered that we

camped here before, when . . . when Bryce first ran away, I might not have come this way. And then I had to hide and make sure you were alone, and I waited so long my muscles hurt from being still—hey!"

A startled gasp erupted when Alex grabbed her arm and jerked her close, his jaw muscles clenching in fury. "This is ridiculous! Don't you trust me to find Bryce? Do you have to endanger your life and the lives of others just to find him yourself?"

"You're hurting my arm—"

"Dammit, Jess, now I'm saddled with a female when I should be worrying about more important things!"

"More important!"

"And Sherman is definitely going to want to know just why in the hell I brought a woman with me!"

Jerking away, Jessamy glared at Alex. "I thought you might be glad to see me!"

"Didn't you listen this morning? War is no place for a woman, Jess, especially you."

"And why 'especially' me?"

"Because you're young and pretty and as hard-headed as that damned mule you're riding, that's why 'especially' you!"

"And I suppose you're perfect?"

"I'm expendable, Jess. You're not."

At that she felt a wave of weariness and fear wash over her, and Jessamy sank abruptly to the ground, sitting cross-legged in a pile of dead leaves.

"You're not expendable, either," she said miserably. She looked up at him with a worried frown. "I had to find you, Alex, really I did. I've been following you almost since you left this morning, and—"

His dark eyes narrowed. "Why? It can't be just because of Bryce."

She plucked idly at new grass sprouting between fallen leaves. "No, it isn't," she said so softly he had to kneel down beside her to hear.

One finger hooked under her chin to tilt her face up. "You know a lot more than you're telling, don't you?" She gave an unhappy nod. "And you don't want to tell me because you'll be a traitor, right?" Another nod. "Ah, Jess, I can't help you now. This is a decision you have to make on your own."

"I know."

Nothing was said for a moment as the afternoon shadows deepened and birds sang in the tree branches overhead. A soft April breeze blew, stirring tendrils of her hair as she sat and pondered just what she should say. Dare she trust him with the lives of her family? Dare she risk his life? Life could be so complicated at times, she reflected wearily, and looked up at him. He was watching her closely, waiting, his lips compressed into a hard line.

"Well?"

Jessamy cleared her throat. "Well, I guess I'll have to trust you. . . ."

"But you don't want to."

"I'm scared, Alex."

"Of me?"

"*For* you. For me, for Bryce, for my father and my other brothers. . . . I'm scared that nothing is ever going to be the same and I'll live the rest of my life wondering why."

"The only thing that ever remains the same is

change, Jess. Everything changes, every day, from the moment we're born until we die." His hand moved to rest on her shoulder, and he smiled. "Even my love for you will change. It will grow stronger and stronger."

Squaring her shoulders, she muttered, "I hope you're right," and took a deep breath before continuing. "There's going to be a battle, Alex, a big battle."

He stiffened, his gaze searching her face for signs of contradiction. When he saw none he asked carefully, "Are you certain?"

"Yes. Nick told me. He said the Yankees weren't expecting it."

"At Pittsburg Landing?"

She nodded.

"Do you have any details?"

"No—why?"

"Why? I have to warn Sherman—"

Leaping to her feet, Jessamy shrieked, "No! You can't do that! I only told you because I want you to be safe, and because I want to find Bryce before the battle starts."

Alex rose, too. "Jess, you knew that I would have to do what I could."

"I never thought you would betray me when I trusted you like . . . when I trusted you," she ended brokenly. Snatching her arm away when he reached out for her, she turned her back on him and stalked toward her grazing mule. "I should have known better," she said bitterly over one shoulder.

Alex reached her before she could mount, and dragged her from the mule. His strong grip was like steel, and even when she kicked viciously at his shins, he did not release her.

"Be still, Jess!" he commanded quietly, but she would not listen.

"Let me go, you traitor."

"Ah, are we back to that again? It sounds all too familiar," Alex muttered, flinching away from Jessamy's flailing fists and kicking feet. "Give it up, Jess! I can hold on to you a lot longer than you can . . . ouch!"

The heel of her shoe had caught him on his kneecap, and his leg buckled beneath him. However, Jessamy did not gain her release, as Alex kept his grip on her when he sagged to the ground.

"Little hellcat," he muttered into the wild mane of her hair. He was only a little out of breath from his efforts, while Jessamy was panting for air. Her hair hung in her eyes and his arm around her rib cage was constricting her lungs.

Disappointment clogged her throat as much as the lack of air, and Jessamy finally sagged into Alex's hard frame. Tears streaked her face and her expression was so woebegone that Alex felt a pang of regret. He brushed her hair back from her face, keeping a wary eye on her feet and a tight grip on her wrists.

"Sorry, love. I guess I thought you'd know what I'd have to do."

"And I guess I thought you'd be more honorable."

"I am honorable. I owe allegiance not just to the Union but to those men like your father and brothers who are fighting for their beliefs. Don't you see?" he asked in a pleading tone when she turned her face away from him. "If we are a nation divided, we cannot stand against foreign powers! There are countries just waiting to rip us apart, who are watching this war with a great deal of interest. If we're split, with the South and the North both holding fast in opposite factions, then we're just easy pickings for any dictator with enough men and ships to sail over here. Ah, Jess, listen to me!"

The blunt fingers of one hand gripped her chin and turned her to face him. "You can't ask me to compromise my beliefs, not when it's this important."

"Yet you're betraying me by doing so," she said. "Does that not matter to you at all?"

"Not matter? It's tearing me apart. I know what you think, and I know there's a possibility that you will never forgive me, but I have to do this. There has to be a future for us, and if the South should win the right to be a separate nation, then the United States is doomed to fall as easy prey."

"Let me go, Alex."

Her voice was soft and quiet, but there was a steely glint in her blue-gray eyes that left him doubtful. "Will you promise not to run off?"

"Let me go, Alex."

"Not until you promise me."

She shook the hair from her eyes and gazed at him steadily. "I promise."

Reluctantly, he released his tight grip on her wrists. She sat for a moment, rubbing sullenly at the bruised flesh of her arms and wrists. Slowly Alex rose to stand over her, not quite trusting her, yet wanting to.

"Take a hand up?" he asked finally, holding out one hand to help her rise. She hesitated briefly, then reached out to take it.

Gripping his fingers, Jessamy uncoiled in a smooth, swift motion, bringing up one knee as she did. It struck Alex squarely in the groin and he doubled over. Coughing, he dropped to one knee while Jessamy scrambled through the underbrush to her mule. She fumbled frantically for the trailing reins, then flung them over the mule's neck and vaulted into the saddle. The beast balked at first, and she drummed her heels into his ribs as she saw Alex stumble to his feet.

"Go, you damned jackass, go!" she screamed at the mule, finally succeeding in turning him through the underbrush. His eyes rolled wildly, and his nostrils blew out with fear as Jessamy urged him faster. She could hear Alex behind her and knew what he would do if he caught her.

Trailing vines and low branches slashed at her face as she pushed the mule blindly through the woods. She hoped to reach the road before she was cut to pieces. When the mule staggered out onto the road, Jessamy gave a sigh of relief. Her heels beat against the mule and it leaped forward. Dust rose in a thick haze behind her, and she leaned over the animal's neck as they galloped down the road toward a sharp curve. Now she could warn her father before Alex was able to give the alarm to his officers.

Twisting in the saddle, Jessamy gave a last glance behind her just before she rounded the curve, and did not see Alex. He must be tangled in the vines, she thought, and turned back around. At that moment the mule screamed and reared into the air, its forelegs thrashing wildly.

Taken off guard, Jessamy fell from the saddle

to the road. She landed with a hard thud, and it knocked the breath from her lungs. Gasping, she looked up through a haze of pain and saw Alex's grim face looking down at her.

"Don't even think about it," he warned when she made a move to rise. "I'm afraid I'm not in a very good mood right now, and I might do something I'll regret later."

Jessamy heeded his advice, and lay still and quiet while Alex unlooped the coil of rope from her saddle. She didn't utter a sound when he approached her and knelt down. He tied her wrists silently, then jerked her to her feet none too gently, pulling Jessamy and the mule behind him.

Alex tied the mule to a tree, and gave Jessamy a rough push that seated her on a fallen log. She glared at him through the tangles of hair in her eyes, but did not dare offer a protest. His face was hard, his eyes as cold as stone.

Heaving his saddle up from the ground, Alex began saddling his horse while Jessamy watched sullenly. It wasn't until he'd broken camp and stamped out his fire that he spoke, and then it was with a thick edge of venom.

"So much for your code of honor! I suppose your promise not to run was meant to be broken?"

"I never promised not to run," Jessamy said defiantly, shaking the hair from her eyes and glaring at him. "I did just as you did when the officers asked for your oath."

"But I never gave my promise—"

"Neither did I! I just said 'I promise' without saying *what* I promised."

"A technicality, Jess, and you know it!"

"And yours wasn't?"

His mouth tightened angrily, and he stood glaring at her with his legs spread and his thumbs tucked into his belt. Jessamy glared back at him, refusing to back down an inch, feeling as righteous as a martyr. Finally Alex shook his dark head and tugged on his hat.

"Someone is going to have to teach you another method of battle, Miss Windsor. One day you're going to use that knee on some man who won't take it as kindly as others."

Jessamy didn't answer. There didn't seem to be anything to say to that, and so she remained quiet. She didn't even speak when Alex threw her atop her mule with more force than was necessary, or when he stuffed a wad of cloth in her mouth.

"So you can't warn any soldiers we happen to come near on the way," he said in answer to her inquiring look. "You are now officially a Union prisoner, and as such, will be treated accordingly."

Her spine straightened, and Jessamy lifted her chin and stared straight ahead, refusing to even glance at him again. How could this be happening to her? How could things go so wrong in such a short time? Only a few hours ago she had been worried about Alex, and now she was his prisoner. His prisoner! It was humiliating, devastating. And worse—it was heartbreaking.

She must have dozed, reeling in the saddle and then jerking herself awake, because when she

272

heard the first shot Jessamy's eyes snapped open.

"What was that?"

"It wasn't the dinner bell," Alex muttered, "and be quiet or I'll stuff that rag back in your mouth!"

Knowing that he would do just as he'd threatened, she subsided, cringing down close to the mule's neck and wishing Alex would let her take her own reins. What if a stray shot hit her? And why did they keep on firing like that? She could hear men screaming, hear the high-pitched whine of cannonballs streaking through the air before landing with a thundering explosion. Who was screaming—the blue or the gray?

They had ridden through the long night and Jessamy was numb with exhaustion. Her mind was dull with fatigue and now fright, and she could only cling to the terrified mule and pray Alex wasn't so mad at her that he'd risk her life just to teach her a lesson.

He wasn't. He was mad, all right, but not at Jessamy. Alex was angry because he was too late, because the battle had already begun and caught the Federals by surprise. Men were scrambling for their lives, leaping into trenches and behind bunkers, firing, reloading, firing again.

It was Sunday, April 6, and the Confederates were drawn up in four massive lines. In spite of the constant sniping of the past night, the Union army was taken completely by surprise as the Confederate troops poured from the trees toward Prentiss's pickets. Prentiss's and Sherman's troops bore the weight of the first assault, and though Sherman's men wove a stubborn ring around Shiloh Church, they were slowly forced to give ground under a combined flank and frontal assault.

By nine o'clock, Sherman's and Prentiss's troops had been taken by the Confederates' initial charge. Union troops gave way and fell back to secondary lines along the Purdy and Hamburg River roads. Even after the remaining three divisions that were camped five miles downstream at Crump's Landing were advised of the battle, Grant could not be persuaded that it was, in fact, a true battle. He was certain that Johnston would not risk a full-scale attack on the Union encampment.

A frustrated Alex saw that within an hour of his arrival, both forces were totally committed to battle.

"Come with me!" he snarled at Jessamy, yanking her from her mule and tugging her along with him.

She stumbled, panting. "Where?"

"To the church! I'm going to leave you there."

Jessamy caught a glimpse of the small stone church that rested in a clearing. "Here? But . . . but there are Yankees in there!"

Giving her arm another tug, Alex shot back, "Since when have you been scared of Yankees?"

"Since I met you!"

"I'm sorry to hear that, Jess, 'cause this is where I'm leaving you."

Alex swung her up the steps and inside the door, ignoring her furious attempts to evade him. They burst into the church with a loud noise, capturing the attention of all within hearing distance. Blue-coated officers glanced up, then looked back down at maps spread on long tables. Outside erratic cannon boomed, and the ground shook ominously. When a shell hit one of the windows, shattering glass and splintering wood, Jessamy swallowed the sudden surge of fear that rose in her throat and gave Alex a pleading stare. He ignored that too, and gave her a push forward.

"Adjutant Jackson, take charge of this young lady. She is a Rebel spy, and should be watched closely."

A beardless youth gulped and stepped forward to take Jessamy's arm. Speechless, she looked from him to Alex, then took a quick step backward.

"No! I won't stay here!"

"Take her to the field hospital. Maybe she can be of use there," Alex said to the bewildered, obviously nonplussed young soldier. "And you better do it quick. It looks as if this church is about to be filled with Rebels."

Alex's prediction proved to be true. Within the space of an hour the church had been taken over by Confederate forces. It was the most exposed position, about three miles west of Pittsburg Landing, and held by the rawest of Union troops commanded by Sherman. It fell quickly.

Jessamy was escorted away by the adjutant just before a swarm of Confederate soldiers stormed the building.

"Better not, miss," the young adjutant advised when he saw the glimmer of hope in her eyes. "In the heat of battle a man don't often know just what he's shootin' at."

It seemed like sound advice, but in the hours to follow Jessamy was often to wonder what might have happened had she not heeded his advice.

Her stomach heaved when Adjutant Jackson showed her into the tiny log cabin that was being used as part of a field hospital. Canvas tents sprouted at intervals, and busy surgeons occupied them with emergency medical care for the wounded. Just outside the cabin door was a pile of amputated arms and legs, and flies had begun to swarm in droves. The stench was overpowering. Surgical conditions were appalling, and the one room was filthy.

"Excellent!" a weary surgeon exclaimed when he saw Jessamy staring at him. "I need a nurse. Here, take hold of this man's arm."

Jessamy recoiled. "I will not! I refuse to do so much as lift a finger for a Yankee!"

When the surgeon glanced at the adjutant he apologized. "She's said to be a Rebel spy, Dr. Yandell. Captain Steele brought her in, and thought she might be of some good here."

"Well, it's obvious she's not! Bring me help, and bring it quickly!" the surgeon commanded in a brusque tone. "I don't need a petulant child to hinder me."

Jessamy ceased listening. Her gaze shifted among the crude tables that served as operating tables. Men lay on them in bloody tatters, and more men were stacked at the sides of the cabin waiting their turn. The din was terrible. Outside, shells whined and loud explosions sounded at regular intervals. Occasionally the ground would tremble with the force of an explosion.

Sensing her terror, the adjutant hesitated in taking her back outside. "Miss, if you would just be kind to these men and think of them as fellow Americans, perhaps it would help," he said softly, and Jessamy's head jerked around. She stared at him with wide eyes, then finally gave a nod of her head.

"All right."

"Miss?"

"I said all right! I'll do what I can to help, but I'm no surgeon."

There wasn't time to regret her decision. Dr. Yandell put her to work, having her clean wounds and wrap bandages, hold basins and hand him instruments, then take them to be cleaned. Conditions were bad, but he insisted upon having reasonably clean surgical implements to cut down on the risk of infection.

"I believe there's a strong connection between the two," he muttered once, wiping sweat from his brow with the back of his arm. He wielded a small saw across an arm bone that a bullet had splintered. It cracked loudly, and Jessamy felt suddenly sick as blood spurted in a crimson fountain, spattering the surgeon and herself. Yandell looked at her sharply. "You're not going to faint, are you?"

She shook her head. "No . . ."

"Good. There's no time for that. Bring me another basin. And take this arm with you."

A wave of nausea washed over her, but Jessamy fought it successfully as she took the arm and threw it out the door onto a growing pile. Men shrieked, and the incessant din of battle raged like a hellish nightmare.

Hours passed in a blur of time and motion, of jogging from one bed to another, wiping foreheads, bandaging wounds, and holding the hands of dying men. Jessamy discovered that it didn't really matter if the man was young or old or an enlisted man or an officer. They all died with the same puzzled expression on their faces, as if just discovering their mortality. The young ones were the worst, though, for some cried out for absent mothers and reminded Jessamy of Bryce. Some of them were just boys, beardless youths who had come to fight for their beliefs and died for it.

Hot tears often streaked her face as she went about her work, pressing cups of water to thirsty mouths, soothing fevered brows, offering a word or two to men who spoke with the hard, flat accents of the North. That was what caught her sometimes, that she had hated them so badly and now she was tending them.

Hands reached out for her, catching at the baggy pants she wore, admiring the long tangles of tawny hair that she had caught back with a strip of cloth.

"Yore voice is as soft as yer hands," one blood-grimed soldier said with a ghost of a smile. "I like to lissen to yew Rebel gals talk."

"Does that mean you don't like to listen to our boys talk?" Jessamy asked briskly as she removed his makeshift bandage and put on a clean one. She wrapped it tightly as Dr. Yandell had shown her, trying to stem the spurt of blood from a severed artery in his arm.

The soldier grinned in spite of his pain. "No, I shore don't like to talk to them Johnny Rebs! It was a hot conversation that got me this ball in my arm!"

"Well, I have a feeling that you are an excellent conversationalist yourself," Jessamy replied as she tied the last knot and stood up.

"Now drink this before the orderly carries you out."

Laughing weakly, the soldier obeyed, and Jessamy signaled for the orderly to carry him outside. There just wasn't enough room for the wounded to remain inside. Tents had been set up to house some of them. The rest lay under trees or tarpaulins or the gray sky.

Storm clouds swept over the battleground and a pounding rain slashed down, making conditions even more miserable. The humidity made the stench even worse, and as her stomach revolted, Jessamy damned Alex Steele again. It was his fault she was here, his fault she had to endure this living death! She'd wanted to find Bryce, but now—now there was very little hope that he was even alive. She'd seen too much in these past few hours to think otherwise.

Snatches of talk made her heart sink.

"We're holding them damned Rebs along the Sunken Road. . . ."

"It's a hornet's nest out there—bullets as thick as a whole hive of hornets. . . ."

"The dead are everywhere. . . ."

"Cain't walk fer th' dead an' dyin'. . . ."

"Them gawdamned Rebs captured Prentiss's entire division with most near a hunnerd cannon. . . ."

"Colonel Peabody was killed right beside me, tryin' to rally us. . . ."

"Saw the Reb General Johnston go down under a tree. Damn fool didn't even know he was kilt 'til all his blood run down into his boot. . . ."

"Looks bad fer th' Rebs. . . ."

"Looks bad fer us. . . ."

The gossip was right. The Southern army had swept across one Union position after another until noon. Along the Sunken Road the Federals had finally been able to establish a line that halted the rolling Southern advance. It was, indeed, a "Hornet's Nest," and the Rebs called it just that as they charged it repeatedly. It wasn't until General Daniel Ruggles called up sixty-two cannon that one of the attacks finally succeeded. It was the largest concentration of artillery yet seen on a North American battlefield. Under the cover of those hammering guns, the Confederate infantry surged forward with their high-pitched Rebel yells and managed to surround and capture the Union defenders under General Benjamin Prentiss. But that Union sacrifice only bought more time for Grant to establish a solid line of defense near Pittsburg Landing.

The Federal forces fell back to the right and the left of the Hornet's Nest, slowly giving way to the Rebel forces. The fighting degenerated into little more than a slugging match, with confusion and disorganization on both sides.

A little more than a mile away from the Hornet's Nest, Captain Alexander Steele was fighting at Tilghman's Hollow with General Wallace. Alex tried to rally his men, most of them terrified country boys who had never seen war before.

"Come on, Collins!" he yelled to a lanky country boy who stared with trembling lips and his hands glued to his rifle. "Get out there and shoot! Aim and fire!"

Collins threw down his rifle and whirled, running in circles like a scared chicken, and Alex swore softly under his breath. He didn't have time to go after him. There was too much at stake, and those Rebels were swarming like angry hornets all around him.

"Strothers, Lawson, flank that line!" he yelled then, "and don't waste ammunition on the trees!"

They were in a thick-vined ravine, with towering trees and dense underbrush hindering their movements. Bullets flew overhead and men screamed as some found their mark. Smoke burned his eyes and his nose, and Alex shook his head to clear it. He'd never seen so many waves of enemy soldiers, and it was as awesome as it was frightening. It didn't seem as though the Federals could carry the day, not with the Rebs coming in wave after wave of assault.

General W.H.L. Wallace gave the order to abandon position in an effort to join the main part of the army. They were to escape via Tilghman's Creek, and Alex led the first line of men. The Rebs discovered what they were doing and advanced, shooting and firing and bayoneting any soldier who managed to crawl out of the deep ravine.

Alex's foot snagged on a vine, and he bent to untangle himself, cursing as he slid down in the ravine. To his left were Strothers and Lawson, and he could glimpse Collins just a few feet away. The terrified soldier had lost his rifle and his cap and was attempting to claw his way up the sides of the ravine with his bare hands, stepping on fellow soldiers along the way. Alex's mouth tightened. If Collins made it out alive, he'd personally see to it that the coward was hung.

He didn't have to worry about that.

As Collins reached the lip of the ravine a Rebel appeared above him with bayonet fixed. Instead of wasting ammunition, the gray-clad soldier lunged forward with the end of his rifle, the bayonet piercing Collins square in his middle and lifting him up. Collins squealed and tugged at the bayonet, his eyes bulging and his mouth gaping. The Reb took his boot and pushed Collins from his bayonet, and watched him fall back into the ravine. Alex shot the Reb, though he had the brief thought that the man had saved the United States the cost of a trial and hanging.

Then there was little time to think of anything but survival. That one incident had attracted the rest of what seemed like the entire Confederate army, and they appeared on the lip of the ravine and began shooting Union soldiers as if they were shooting fish in a barrel. General Wallace went down, and too many others to count as Alex snaked over the bodies of fallen comrades. There was an opening at the end of the ravine, his only chance, and he took it.

He clambered out, and was immediately charged by a Reb. Acting instinctively, Alex swung around and fired from the hip, hoping he would at least give his adversary momentary pause. The Reb stumbled slightly, and wavered. There wasn't time to reload. Alex yanked his pistol from the holster and brought it up, but it wasn't necessary. A slow stain spread over the gray coat of the soldier, and his jaw drooped in surprise as he pitched forward. Not taking the time to see if he was still alive, Alex began to sprint through the trees. He splashed through a shallow stand of water beneath some oaks and crouched down behind a huge rock to catch his breath. All around him were belching cannon and screaming men and horses.

In the confusion and smoke, he lost his bearings. Rebel troops almost surrounded him, and Alex swore softly. Not far away was Stuart's camp, but he'd have to go through dense Confederate lines to get there. The outcome seemed doubtful. Dropping to his knees, Alex crawled through the brush for a while, while around him shells burst and rifle fire shattered tree limbs and men with equal anonymity.

Several times he had to hack his way through a group of soldiers who seemed just as disoriented as he was, and Alex had the disturbing thought that none of them would be missed. The heavy artillery was far behind him now, but he could hear the staccato bursts of sharpshooters just ahead. Stuart's camp, maybe?

It wasn't. Between Alex and Federal troops there was a thick swarm of Rebs. He crouched in the underbrush, fully aware that this hour might be his last. His shirt was wet with sweat, and somewhere in his crawlings he'd managed to lose his canteen and extra ammunition pouch. The canteen was the loss most regretted at the moment. Insects buzzed around him, finding the tiny scratches and cuts and stinging them with maddening bites. The sky was gray, and Alex wondered briefly what time of day it was.

A winding road cut just ahead of him, and he peered through the budding spring foliage to watch. He figured it was the east Corinth Road that ran to the Tennessee River. Due south of the road should be Stuart's camp, set up at the edge of a small farm and orchard. He pondered his chances of making it, wondering how far the Rebs had advanced. Did he have a chance, or was he still behind Confederate lines? Alex shook the sweat from his eyes and reloaded his rifle before he began another march through the fighting.

It took him nearly two hours to push his way to the farm where Stuart should be, and he discovered that he was too late. Heavy fighting had decimated Federal and Rebel troops alike, and now the battle had progressed toward the Tennessee River, where two Confederate brigades had just attacked the Union guns supporting Pittsburg Landing.

A blue-coated horseman galloped close, and Alex leaped out to grab his bridle. "Hey! Where's Stuart's command?"

Yanking away, the soldier started to swear before he recognized the bars on Alex's sleeve. "They're headed that way, sir. Toward the river. The Rebs attacked our guns and Buell's coming up the river and our gunboats are firing back. Webster's put fifty-three guns on the bluffs."

Alex stared blankly at the Union cavalryman. "Are you sure?"

"Hell yes, I'm sure! I'm headed that way now with a dispatch for Grant. . . ."

With that the mounted soldier pivoted his horse and rode off at a gallop, leaving Alex staring after him. Weary and drained by his exhausting struggle to reach his own troops, Alex sagged against an outcropping of gray rock to consider his next action.

To his right stretched a line of fencing, and he could see the neat rows of a peach orchard. Entire batteries were hammering away at one another, and fragile white peach blossoms littered the ground like snow. Alex could just make out the defensive Union line in the woods as the Confederates charged again and again. A small cabin stood in the midst of the barrage, and behind it stretched more woods and thickets filled with Union soldiers.

Alex was separated from his men. It was impossible to get to them. He'd have had to get past the withering fire of the Confederates. Panicked horses, some of them riderless, pounded past him, and sucking in a deep breath of smoke-filled air, Alex surged up from his crouch and ran across the narrow road. Bullets chewed up the ground at his feet, but miraculously, none hit him.

Diving for cover, he landed in a shallow depression that was already occupied. As Alex rolled to a halt a gray-clad soldier looked up at him and grinned weakly. His rifle lay across his lap, and the Rebel made a vague motion with one hand.

"You got me, Cap'n. I'm plumb tuckered out, an' 'sides that, I got a ball in my side near as big as a goose aig."

Alex just lay there and stared at him for a moment. The soldier's face was as gray as his coat, and there was the look of death to him.

"Now what would I want with a Johnny Reb?" Alex asked after a few moments. "There's plenty of you Rebs out there if I decide to get me one."

"Mebbe. But th' best is right chere. An' 'sides, Cap'n, I'm too tired to do enny more fightin' today."

Alex rested on his heels and flipped back the edge of the Reb's bloody coat. The entire right side of his rib cage looked as if it had been blasted away. He let the coat fall back over the gaping wound and wondered how the man was still alive. A huge puddle of blood lay beneath him. The Reb shifted position.

"Got enny water, Billy Yank?"

"No. I lost my canteen somewhere."

"There's a pond 'crost th' road a mite. Reckon since I'm yore pris'nor an' all, you could get me over there? I got a powerful thirst, Cap'n."

Alex hesitated. The Rebel didn't seem like he'd make it. "I don't know. . . ." The Reb didn't say anything, just looked at Alex, and he gave a brief nod. "We can try, Johnny Reb, we can try," he ended up saying as he slipped one arm under the man's legs and the other around his back.

This was crazy. He was bound to be shot by one or both sides, and if he wasn't, he'd still end up in a Rebel prison somewhere. Those were hellholes, he'd heard, and he had a feeling that the Union prisons weren't much better.

But Alex carried the soldier with him, making it across the road to the pond. The sight that met his eyes stunned him, and the wounded man began to weep softly.

Dozens—no hundreds—of bodies lay in and around the pond. Horse carcasses, mules, and men littered the area so densely it was impossible to walk between them. The dead and the dying had colored the shallow pond water a bright crimson, and Alex felt suddenly sick. Unearthly moans filled the air, and bluecoats and butternuts alike lay side by side in the rigors of death. Shredded trees cast faint shadows, and the backdrop of red and orange fire from rifles, cannon, and burning underbrush shed a hellish glow on the scene.

"Dear God, it's Armageddon," the Reb moaned softly, and Alex nodded.

Gently lowering the wounded Reb to the ground beneath a shattered tree, Alex took off his cap and made his way to the pond to fetch some water. Dying men clutched at him, and shrieks and cries filled the air as he pushed past.

"Help me, Yank!"

"Get a message to my wife . . ."

"My leg, my leg . . ."

Alex tried to shut out the cries for the moment. There was nothing he could do now but tend to the man he had brought to the pond. He stepped around broken, torn bodies and to the edge of the pond, doing his best to avoid the piles of men who lay there. Entire horse carcasses were lying half submerged where the poor creatures had come to slake their thirst, and stayed to die. Man and beast had not gotten up again. It was a sight he would never forget.

"Thanks," the Reb said when Alex had taken him the small bit of water that he'd been able to dip.

"I waded out toward the middle to get the cleanest," Alex said after a moment. His stomach churned, and as thirsty as he was he knew he could not swallow a single gulp of the water after what he'd just seen.

Leaning back against the tree beside the Rebel, Alex kept his rifle in his hand, though none of those there seemed inclined to fight.

"Hornet's Nest," the Rebel soldier observed, waving a weak hand toward the men scattered across the ground.

"What do you mean?"

"Them soldiers come outta th' Hornet's Nest just beyond that line of trees. That's whar I was until I caught this ball that's killed me."

Alex flicked him a glance. "You're not dead yet."

"Naw, but I will be soon, same as most of those poor souls. Death don' pay no 'tention to th' color of yer uniform, I noticed while I was in th' thick of th' fightin'. It jus' kinda happens an' you ain' even expectin' it much. An' here I am without even a Christian word to be said over me. I'll jus' be thrown into a hole along with th' rest of th' boys, but I reckon I didn' expect no more'n that. A Bible verse would be nice, though."

Several moments passed while they rested, then Alex asked softly, "Don't you have a Bible, Reb?"

"I did have. It got lost somewhere."

Reaching into his coat pocket, Alex withdrew the Bible that Jessamy had given him. His fingers traced the smooth leather for a moment, then he handed it to the soldier. She would understand and approve, he thought.

"You take it, Johnny Reb. It'll give you comfort while you wait for the orderlies to come take you to get some care."

Grinning, the Reb reached out for it. "Thanks, Billy Yank. God willin', I'll give it back to you one day."

Alex doubted that, but he gave a short nod. "I'll look for you. My name's in the front."

"You goin' to join your regiment?" the Reb asked as Alex rose.

"If I can find them."

"God be with you, Yank."

"And with you, Reb."

As Alex walked away, headed back toward the east Corinth Road that would lead to the River Road, he could hear the soldier reading aloud, " 'The heavens are thine, the earth also is thine: as for the world and the fulness thereof, thou hast founded them. The north and the south thou hast created them. . . . Justice and judgment are the habitation of thy throne: mercy and truth shall go before thy face. . . .' "

Mercy and truth. Where was the mercy shown to those men in the bloody pond, Alex wondered bitterly.

Chapter 17

RAIN SLASHED DOWN in blinding sheets, and thunder rumbled almost as loud as the thunder of the Union cannon. Blue thunder, Jessamy thought when she saw the bellowing guns of the Union soldiers. The blue thunder of the Yankee cannons was slowly wearing down the boys in gray. She fought back a tear and turned from the window as the front door to the cabin crashed open.

An imposing bearded figure stepped into the room shaking rain from his visor and slapping his hat against one leg.

"Stop that!" Jessamy commanded sharply. "You're dousing these men with rain and they don't need that on top of everything else!"

There was a short, appalled silence in which she could have heard a pin drop to the floor, then Adjutant Jackson ran up beside her.

"Miss . . . uh, miss, you shouldn't . . . maybe you should say you're sorry—"

"Don't be ridiculous! That man doesn't appear

to be wounded, yet he's in here wetting down men who are!"

"But . . . but that's General Grant," Jackson said with a miserable groan. "Please!"

"I don't care if he's Godalmighty, he can't come in here endangering wounded men!" Jessamy returned with more spirit than she felt at the moment. Grant? Dear God! Now she would be hung for sure, and all because Alex had brought her here to tend men she shouldn't be tending!

"No, the young lady is right," Grant said when one of his aides stepped up to grab Jessamy. "Leave her be. I admire a woman who says her mind, especially when she is right. These men are wounded, and I have just come in to get out of the rain."

"But your wound, General . . ."

"It's only a bad knee from a fall from my horse, Lieutenant. These boys have earned their wounds bravely."

Jessamy bent to tend to a soldier with a head wound, and had the brief thought that at least the Yankee general was honest about the severity of his wounds. Swiftly and efficiently, she went about her work, ignoring the general as best she could. It was faintly galling that she should have to endure his presence, knowing that he was responsible for so many Rebel deaths.

Several times, Jessamy had to pause in her duties to sidestep the general, who leaned back in a chair in the corner, talking quietly with an aide. Resentment began to smolder in her, so that when Grant made an innocent remark commending her dedication to Union wounded, she rounded on him in a fury.

"If I could snap my fingers and see every damned Yankee in Tennessee back up North I'd do it! I wish you all to hell and I wish you there now! You started this war, with all your meddling, you and the rest of those narrow-minded men in Washington who think they are God! Now look what you've done! I hope you're proud!"

Pivoting on her heel, she stalked back to the bedside of a boy of no more than eighteen and began applying a fresh tourniquet to his leg wound. Grant watched in stunned silence, while Adjutant Jackson whimpered pitifully that he had not brought her there willingly.

"Do you mean this girl is a Rebel?" Grant thundered at last, his face purpling with rage. "By all the minions of hell, did you stop to think that the girl may be murdering good soldiers right in front of you?"

Dr. Yandell looked up from his surgery and said in a calm voice, "Don't be fooled. I would not allow her within fifty feet of this hospital if I thought such a thing for a single instant. She's already saved more lives than I can count this day, and has a good pair of hands. She may be a Rebel, General, but she's also a nurse."

Not quite appeased, Grant glowered in the corner for quite a while, keeping a sharp eye on Jessamy. Though the fighting had ceased before dark, the Union gunboats were shelling the Confederate positions at fifteen-minute intervals so that the remainder of Don Carlos Buell's army could cross the Tennessee River. The ground vibrated and hollow echoes sounded in the night. The Confederate attempt to cross the rugged Dill Creek terrain had been aborted, and finally the fighting had sputtered out for the night.

"More wounded," an orderly said as he burst through the cabin door carrying a litter of screaming men.

Jessamy never even noticed when Grant rose from his corner and departed the cabin. His aide reported that the general went back into the rain rather than remain in the cabin with the chaos of wounded men. Thunder rolled, and Jessamy didn't know if it was man-made or heaven-made as she worked into the wee hours.

When her vision blurred and she was half weeping with exhaustion, Dr. Yandell finally noticed.

"Make her a pallet and give her something to eat," he ordered Jackson. "She'll be of no use if she's a patient."

"His compassion is heartwarming," Jessamy muttered as she allowed Jackson to take her to a pallet on the tiny porch out back. It was separated from the rest of the cabin and contained four narrow cots, with just enough room for a slender girl to squeeze through. Jessamy sank wearily onto the nearest cot.

"Don't be hard on Yandell," Jackson said hesitantly. "He recommended you for a citation to the general."

Her heavy lids briefly lifted, and she stared at Jackson in the gloom. "Citation? What are you talking about now? What citation?"

"A special citation for bravery to the enemy wounded."

"You don't make any sense, Jackson! I think

being a Yankee has addled your brains," Jessamy snapped sleepily.

Stiffening, Jackson shot back, "No, it hasn't! I heard it myself. Grant said you were to be commended for your actions today in caring for Union wounded, and that when this battle is over you shall be escorted to safety."

Jessamy sat back up. "Just tell the general that I want to look for my family when this is over. My father and my brothers, and . . . and the man I love are out there somewhere, and I want to find them!"

"I—I don't know if—"

"Well, you find out!"

After a brief hesitation, Jackson asked, "Is Captain Steele of interest to you?"

Fear clawed at Jessamy's throat, but she managed to nod. "Yes, he is. Why?"

" 'Cause one of the orderlies found a dead Reb holding a Bible that belonged to the captain. He wouldn't have stopped to look, but the Reb was wearing a blue captain's hat and died with his finger resting on the open page of a book. That stirred his curiosity, and he . . . well, he stopped."

"And Captain Steele?" Jessamy forced through suddenly stiff lips.

"Nowhere to be found, miss."

"The Bible—could I see it?"

When the small leather Bible was placed in her hands, Jessamy's heart sank. It was the one she had given Alex, the Christmas present she had saved for him, so that he would be protected.

"Thank you, Jackson," she said tonelessly as the adjutant shifted uneasily from one foot to another. "Wake me when Dr. Yandell needs me."

But in the long hours that followed, Jessamy found that sleep evaded her. She could only lie and wonder where Alex was, and if he was still alive. Why would a Confederate soldier have his Bible unless . . . it was more than she could think about without crying into the rough army blanket spread over the cot.

The rest of Buell's army had made it across the river, and the Federal forces numbered over fifty-five thousand men. Beauregard had taken over Johnston's command and, unaware of the reinforcements, planned to continue his attack and drive the Federals into the river.

At six in the morning of April 7, the battle began again when the Confederates went on the offensive. At first they were successful. It wasn't long before the Union armies began to push them back, however, and the Rebels fought desperately to hold their ground. Finally realizing that he had lost the initiative, Beauregard attempted to break the Union push by counterattacking at Water Oaks Pond. The Federal advance was halted, but their strong line did not break. It was a minor triumph.

By early afternoon Beauregard realized his dilemma. With fifteen thousand of his men killed, wounded, or missing, and low on food and ammunition, he knew his options were few. Frustrated, he drew back beyond Shiloh Church and headed his army toward Corinth. The heartsick Rebels were not pursued by the weary Federals. The battle was over.

For Jessamy, the waiting had been intolerable. Though Yandell kept her busy enough, she could not stop thinking of her family, of her father and brothers and Alex. A cold weight had settled in her chest, and she performed her duties by rote, not really paying attention to anything she was doing. She bandaged, bathed, and listened, but could offer little hope to those poor men who beseeched her to write letters to their families, to tell the surgeon not to cut off their arm or their leg, to pray for them. It was all too much.

Maybe that was why she didn't respond at first when Alex came through the door, when he approached her with long, firm strides. Staring at him as if he were a ghost, Jessamy only reacted when he pulled her into his arms.

Sobbing, she dropped the bandages she held and leaned into his comforting embrace. "Alex! Oh Alex, I didn't know what had happened . . . and the Bible and your hat . . . I thought that . . . that you might be—"

"Hush, I'm here now, not even wounded, unless you count the blisters on my feet from these damned boots."

"But the Rebel who had your Bible?" She tilted back her head and he gently wiped away the tears streaking her cheek.

"That's a long story I'll tell you another time, love. Right now I have to worry about getting you home. I managed to get leave—though damned if I know how. It was denied, of course, and when I was trying to explain why I wanted it, Grant himself came up and approved it." He shook his head in amazement. "I guess war does strange things to a man."

Jessamy exchanged an amused glance with Adjutant Jackson. "That's a long story too, Alex," she said. "I'll explain it to you sometime."

"Here! You're not going to take away my nurse, are you?" Yandell protested when Alex pulled Jessamy toward the door. "What will I do?"

"Draft Jackson there. He looks capable," Alex shot at the doctor, ignoring Jackson's startled yelp.

Outside in the fresh air that should have been scrubbed clean by the torrents of rain, Jessamy could still smell the pressing, sickly-sweet odor of death. It clung to everything. Smoke drifted on wind currents, and the stench of decay hung in the air.

"Don't look," Alex advised when they passed a stack of dead bodies. "They're digging trenches for them." She nodded and turned her head into Alex's coat sleeve, trying not to think of those brave young men who had died.

"Wait a minute!" Jessamy exclaimed when Alex paused in front of a wagon and mule. "What . . . what are you doing?"

He stared at her. "I'm going to take you home, love."

"No!"

"What . . . ?"

"I came here to find Bryce, and now . . . now I have to find my father and brothers, too. I won't leave without knowing where they are, or if they survived."

Staring at her in amazement, Alex shook his

head. "Do you have any idea how massive an area we're talking about, Jess? This isn't just a few hundred yards, this is an area three miles across and three miles long! These battles were hot and devastating, and it may be years before the dead are all accounted for."

"I'll look for my family," she repeated stubbornly.

Gesturing toward the mule, Alex grated, "You're as hard-headed as that damned mule!"

Her chin lifted. "If it was your family, wouldn't you look?"

Silence fell, then Alex said, "I only have a few days' leave."

"That should be enough."

It wasn't.

They walked among the dead for the rest of the day, and several times Jessamy had to pause to retch weakly against a tree or into a bush. At the Hornet's Nest where the fighting had been most vicious, bodies lay so tightly packed that she could have walked across the entire battlefield and not set a foot on the ground.

It wasn't far from the Hornet's Nest that Jessamy made a heartrending discovery. William Windsor lay dead on the field, his body propped against a tree, his hands folded in his lap as if he just napped.

Dropping to her knees, Jessamy slowly reached out as if to touch him, but could not. She buried her face in her hands and sobbed; harsh, racking sobs that threatened to tear her apart. Alex tried to comfort her, but she jerked away.

"No! Leave me alone!"

"Jess . . ."

"He's my father, and he . . . he's dead!"

Alex put his hands on her shoulders and lifted her in spite of her efforts to pull away, slowly pulling her up against his chest. "He was a soldier first, Jess, and he did his duty. You can be proud of him. Look at him . . . *look* at him, Jess!"

He turned her around and forced her chin up. "Does he look like he died needlessly? He died as he would have wanted to die, with his head up and his uniform on. He died with dignity, and if there's any comfort in dying at all, it's dying with dignity. Remember the men in the hospital? Would you want that for him?"

Shuddering, she turned back into Alex and let him hold her. After a few minutes she pulled away. "I have to look for my brothers now."

Not far away, just over the next rise, lay James and Charles. They were only a few feet apart, dying as closely as they had lived, inseparable to the end. Alex gently removed their insignia and swords and gave them to the orderly he had summoned for Jessamy's father. The grim task of burial had begun, and soldiers moved through the field with planks and carts for unclaimed, unidentified bodies. Alex quietly made arrangements for the Windsors to be taken home by train, while Jessamy sat in stunned silence.

"Nick? Bryce?" she inquired when he returned to her. "What about them? I don't see . . . see their bodies."

"It's possible that Nick is still alive. Just because they were in the same regiment doesn't mean he died, Jess."

"And Bryce?"

Grabbing her hands he said, "Anything could have happened to him, love. He's a boy, and boys are resilient. I bet he's off somewhere making the best of it."

But when they finally found Bryce, he wasn't exactly "making the best of it." They spent another day searching for him, a long day that almost convinced Jessamy her youngest brother must be dead. She'd seen so much death, so many bodies and wounded men, that she had steeled herself for the worst.

It was on the word of a wounded Confederate that they searched in the field close to the Tennessee River. It was a ground deeply cut with trenches and natural ravines, an area where Indian mounds humped skyward from the ground. A tangle of underbrush rose several feet from the earth, covering the ground so thickly it was almost impossible to walk. It also hid the ravines and trenches, and deep shadows shrouded the area.

"Here?" Jessamy asked doubtfully, gazing down a steep slope. "I can't imagine how any man could begin to fight in this tangle, much less an entire regiment!"

"Men fight wherever they can," Alex replied, coming to stand beside her. He realized how tenuously Jessamy held to the hope that her brother was alive, and he hoped for her sake that he was. Another death could push her over the brink.

They started to move on, deciding that the ravine was too deep and thickly grown to permit soldiers, when Jessamy heard a faint thump. She paused and looked at Alex.

"What was that?"

"It sounded like something falling. A pine cone, maybe."

"Do you see any pine trees here?"

He shook his head, then reached out to grab Jessamy when she would have slid down the ravine without waiting. "Stop! If there is someone down there, it doesn't mean it's your brother. It could be a soldier who wouldn't recognize the fact that you're a woman." He'd seen the broken limbs, and had the thought that if her brother was there, he might very well be dead. He wanted to get her away from there before he sent someone down to look.

Then the sound came again, a distinctly deliberate tap of a drum. *Rat-a-tat-tat*, it rolled, and Jessamy screamed.

"It's Bryce! I know it is!"

"Jessamy, control yourself. It could be anyone," Alex said firmly, jerking her back from the edge. "Orderly! Over here," he called over his shoulder.

Surging away from him, Jessamy gave a leap and half slid, half fell down the ravine. Rocks skittered from beneath her feet, and vines and bushes tore at her face and hands. When she landed at the bottom she found Bryce. He was lying beneath his broken drum, and a dead Union soldier lay beside him.

"Jessamy! I thought it would be Nick! Oh Jess, if it wasn't for this Yank I'd be dead by now . . . I saw Dempsey, and I saw Nick, and now you're here. . . ."

"Hush," she whispered hoarsely. "You're delirious. Let me help you up."

"No!" His face was creased in white lines, and the look he gave his sister was agonized. "It's my leg. It's broke, I think. Guess it kinda got twisted when I skidded down that ravine, there."

By this time Alex had arrived at the bottom, and though he was glad to see Jessamy he was furiously angry with her.

"You little fool! What if it had been a soldier with a loaded rifle! You could have been shot!"

"But it wasn't," she pointed out reasonably, "and we don't have time to think about 'what-ifs' right now, Alex. Bryce is hurt."

Though angry, he saw the sense in her comment, and said he would go back up for the orderly and a litter to carry Bryce out. "Can you move that drum, Bryce?"

The boy shook his head. Dirt and sweat had plastered his fair hair to his head, and he slid a sorrowful glance toward the dead Union soldier at his side. "No, that Yank already tried it. He was wounded bad enough to die, but he came down here to try and save me. He was a good man, Alex, even if he was a Yankee. He gave me the last of his water."

"There are a lot of good men on both sides," Jessamy said as she knelt down and tried to shift the heavy drum. It was lodged between a tree and a rock, with Bryce's leg caught in the middle. It didn't look good. She'd seen men in the hospital with wounds like that, and they'd all lost their leg or arm. Maybe Dr. Yandell could save it.

Alex had begun climbing back up the ravine, hand over hand on a vine as thick as a man's arm. When a shot rang out, Jessamy screamed and stood up, not knowing what to expect. Then her heart stood still.

At the edge of the ravine stood a man with a loaded rifle pointed down at them. It was Nick, and he slowly lifted his Sharps rifle to take aim at Alex.

"Nick! No!" Jessamy screamed. "Don't do it!"

Pausing, Nick slid his sister a cold glance. "Dempsey found me. He told me about Bryce. I'm here to help him and get rid of this damned Yankee. Move out of the way, Jess."

"No!" She clutched at Alex's leg to pull him back down so she could shield him, but he kicked free.

"Move out of the way like he said, Jess," Alex ordered coldly. "I'm not about to start hiding behind a woman. Not now, not ever."

Pushed over the brink, Jessamy lunged forward and yanked Alex's pistol from its holster. It was heavy, but she managed to thumb back the hammer and hold it steadily pointed at her brother.

"Enough! Enough killing! Have you gone mad? Can't you see that we're trying to help Bryce? Are you so blinded by hate that you can't let us save our brother? Look at his leg, Nick! He'll lose it if we don't get him to a surgeon as quickly as possible, and we don't have time to stand here and argue like children." When Nick did not move, but still stood glaring down at them, Jessamy took careful aim. The pistol leaped in her hands and a branch fell from over Nick's head. "The next ball goes into you, Nick," she said. "I've already killed one man. If I have to, I'll make you the second. Make your choice. There's not much time."

Nick hadn't moved when the pistol exploded and the branch fell, but finally he let the stock of his rifle slide slowly to rest on the ground, the muzzle pointing skyward. Behind him, William's faithful companion Dempsey muttered a "Praise God!"

"He's a very lucky young man," Dr. Yandell said solemnly. He indicated Bryce with a jerk of his head. "All odds say he should have lost that leg."

"But you saved it," Jessamy pointed out with a smile.

"With God's help." The doctor ran a hand across his unshaven jaw and managed a bleary smile. "It's too bad not all of my patients were this fortunate."

"I'm just grateful Bryce was." Jessamy gazed past the doctor to where Bryce lay on a narrow cot, his face thin and pinched but showing a healthy pallor.

Nick leaned back against the outside wall of the cabin, his dark face set and grim. Each time he glanced at Alex his gaze smoldered, and Jessamy hoped to avoid trouble if at all possible. Only Bryce's teary pleas had moved Nick to come into the Yankee camp at all. It had been touch and go, and she had been surprised when Nick had at last yielded, even to the point of wearing a blue coat so he would not be arrested.

Now the operation was over and he had to go. Alex had relented only as far as letting Nick linger at the hospital until the surgery was over, and had asked for Nick's word of honor that he would repeat nothing he happened to see or overhear. It wasn't unreasonable, and as the field hospital was far away from the Union encampments, Alex didn't expect any trouble.

The only trouble came from Nick's flaring hatred for Alex. It seethed inside him, evident whenever his gaze happened to meet Alex's, and Jessamy was helpless to end it. This was a Nick she did not know, an implacable soldier who would give the enemy no quarter nor ask for any. If not for Bryce, Nick would probably have killed Alex and both men knew it. Her heart wrenched, yet there was nothing she could do.

Dempsey met Nick at the River Road, nervously waiting in a small copse. They were to rejoin Forrest as soon as possible. Shrugging out of the hated blue coat, Nick tossed it to his sister and turned to take the reins of his horse. Jessamy's gaze flicked to the sorrel mare and she gasped.

"Nick! Is that . . . is that Sultana?"

The first sign of the old Nick appeared when he gave a curt nod and a half-smile touched the corners of his mouth. "Yeah. I found her wandering in the woods about a month ago. There had been a skirmish with the Yanks, and I guess her rider got himself killed. At least, no one has tried to claim her, and she was wearing Confederate tack."

Stepping forward, Jessamy ran a hand lightly over the sorrel's flanks. She shied away, rolling her eyes and dancing skittishly. Blowing gently into the mare's nostrils, Jessamy quieted her until Sultana allowed herself to be stroked.

"Take care of her, Nick. She was the best birthday gift I ever received. Papa outdid himself."

"He paid too much for her. I told him that at the time, but you couldn't tell William Windsor anything when it came to buying his daughter a birthday present." Nick reached out to lightly stroke the mare's neck. "I'll take good care of her, Jess."

Hot tears stung her eyes and she nodded. "I know you will." A long pause stretched out, then she looked up at her brother. His eyes were shuttered as if he had secrets he did not want to reveal. "Nick, will it ever be . . . right?"

"If you mean you and Alex, no. I'll never come around him, Jess. I'm sorry. There's too much that's happened, too many good men killed. Your own father and brothers . . . aw, hell, there isn't any use in talking to you. You're in love and you won't listen!"

"But he was our friend before, Nick, before the war! Why do we have to hate him now just because he's wearing a blue coat?"

Passing a hand over his eyes, Nick blew out his breath in a long sigh. His tone was hard, flat, when he looked up again. "There's no more *we*, Jess. There's *us*, and there's *them*, but there's no more *we*. That's all over with. It won't ever be right again."

She reached out to touch his arm and felt his muscles bunch beneath her fingers. There was no compromise in the long, dark look he gave her, and her hand slid away. "All right, Nick. I'm sorry for all of us."

"Save your pity for the Yankees, Jess. They're the ones who are going to need it," Nick said as he swung into the saddle and whirled Sultana around. Digging his heels into the mare's sides, he let a high, shrill Rebel yell erupt as he galloped down the road toward Corinth.

Dempsey leaned from his mule to say, "Give him time, Miss Jess. He had to watch your father and brothers die. Give him time."

She nodded through her tears and waved farewell as Dempsey followed his master's son, just as the faithful old Negro had followed his master.

Alex found her dissolved in tears, weeping silently beside the River Road.

"Jess! Are you hurt?"

She shook her head, and looked up, clawing damp strands of hair from her eyes. "No-o-o! I just can't stand it anymore, Alex! I want to go home! Everything's horrible, and I think I should go home."

Holding her in his arms, Alex rocked back and forth, ignoring the interested stares from passersby. "And so you shall go home, love, so you shall. As soon as Bryce is able to travel, I'm taking you home."

Chapter 18

THE FOLLOWING DAY, on April 8, Grant ordered Sherman to march south along the Corinth Road in an effort to catch the retreating Confederates. But Sherman was no farther than ten miles away before he smacked into the rearguard under the command of Colonel Nathan Bedford Forrest. Wisely, Sherman abandoned his pursuit and headed back to report.

On April 10, Jessamy and Bryce were rocking along the rutted roads toward Cloverport, Tennessee. They passed ruined houses and farms, still smoldering, and the vacant stares of the occupants haunted her thoughts. The people just watched sullenly as they passed in a Union wagon pulled by a Union mule. Alex wore his blue coat, and no one spoke as they passed.

Even when they were close to Clover Hill and passed friends and neighbors she'd known since she was born, no one spoke. The Leathers sisters, who had known her all her life and been the best source of gossip in Hardeman County, turned their backs on Jessamy, their verdict plain: There was to be no welcome home for a girl who had chosen the enemy. If it weren't for Bryce, no one in Hardeman County would have visited in the days following their return, even after Alex had gone back to his command.

Although Abigail grieved for her husband and her twin sons, she regarded Bryce's return as a miracle. Jessamy thought that she had never seen her mother look so old, and it frightened her. How could that be? Abigail Fontaine Windsor, who had always been the soft-voiced, iron-willed matriarch of the family, now looked to Jessamy for guidance. It was devastating.

Celine found Jessamy at the window of the tiny cabin, staring listlessly out at the rain falling softly on the green grass. Her mood was as gray as the day. Gone were the bright flowers of yesteryear, the velvet lawns and neat rail fences. Only weeds and wild roses were hardy enough to have survived.

"*Chère*," Celine said behind her, "do you know what day this is?"

Slowly shaking her head, Jessamy turned to look at her old nurse. "No, Celine, I don't think I do."

"It's your birthday, *petite*! You are twenty years old today."

Slightly taken aback, Jessamy could not say anything. Her birthday? Only a year before she had swept down the graceful staircase of Clover Hill to find a new sorrel mare waiting outside on the drive. A gift from her father, the Barbary horse she had wanted for years. There would never be any more gifts from him, never another kind word or gentle scolding for her wild ways. Her throat tightened.

Once, she had wanted to stay home forever with her parents and brothers, playing pranks on Alex or riding her horse, or dancing until dawn at barbecues and garden parties. Now all that had changed, was gone forever.

"*Oui*, it is your birthday," Celine was saying. "And Miss Abby has planned a little *soirée* for you. The neighbors are coming—those who are still able—and already the Leathers sisters have accepted, and the Kings and the Weavers, and anyone else who wants free food in this time of famine." Celine's smile was wry. "Do not let your *maman* know that I told you about it, but I did not want you to go off in the woods as you've been doing lately. She would be very disappointed if you were not here—or not surprised by her party."

"I understand. And I'll be surprised."

Peering closely at Jessamy, Celine gave a doubtful shake of her head, her dark hair now liberally sprigged with strands of gray. "You sound so drained now. This war has taken more out of you then I ever thought anything could, *chère*. Somehow, I never thought you would give up so easily."

Eyes flashing, Jessamy's head snapped up. "I haven't given up!"

"No? Then don't act as if you have! You mope around here as if you don't care about anything anymore, instead of doing something about it as you once would have done!"

"And what can I do? Will anything I do make a difference?"

Celine put out a slender, caring hand and

rested her palm gently on Jessamy's shoulder. "*Ma petite*—though I suppose you are no longer a small one—you have already made a difference. Can't you see that? It was you who had the strength and courage to go after Bryce when he ran away and did not return. Why, you brought him back when all the Yankees in Tennessee stood in your way! And it was you who kept Nick and your captain from killing each other. Those are only two of the differences you have made. No one else has done that. No one I know, anyway. You are a survivor, when other people would wither away like well-protected house ferns."

A smile flickered on Jessamy's lips. "I suppose I'm like those weeds and wild roses out there," she said, gesturing out the window toward the profusion of pink blooms and tall, scraggly Jimson weeds.

Celine smiled. "*Oui*, that is a good description! You are a weed if ever I've seen one!"

Laughing, Jessamy said, "I don't suppose you could have been kind enough to choose the wild rose for comparison, could you?"

"No, *chère*, you are definitely a weed. But the weeds will be growing and thriving long after the wild roses have lost their blooms."

"I suppose there's something to be said for that. I think I'll put on my cloak and walk down to the road. It's stuffy in here, and I get so restless at times."

"In the rain?"

"It's a gentle rain. And the fresh air might do me some good."

"Remember the party."

"I'll remember, Celine. Is Bryce resting easy?"

After a vigorous shake of her head, Celine declared, "No, he is not resting! He's as jumpy as a cricket, and twice as spry! I don't believe that the surgeon knew what he was saying when he said that child may not walk again."

"With proper care, Bryce may walk again, but he'll always have a limp according to Dr. Yandell."

"Well, the doctor has not seen him hopping all over his bed!"

Jessamy laughed. "Maybe he should. It would give him more confidence in his medical powers."

"Dieu! It would give him a stroke, in my opinion," Celine muttered as she turned away.

Rain fell softly, pattering down on leaves and grass as Jessamy strolled slowly down the curving drive toward the road. Moisture pooled on her face, sliding down and leaving her skin slick, as if morning dew had fallen, mingling with her salty tears. Birds chirped noisily in the trees, and the rhythmic melody of the falling rain played a sad refrain that made Jessamy wonder if things would ever be right again.

She hadn't heard from Alex since he'd gone soon after bringing her and Bryce to Clover Hill. There had been no word, though she'd heard rumors of the war. Beauregard's retreat to Corinth had opened the door to the entire Mississippi Basin. Not only had the Confederates suffered great land losses at Shiloh, but the Yankees had succeeded in capturing Island No. 10, an important fortification that had heretofore blocked Federal use of the Mississippi River. Union gunboat traffic now flowed freely.

Kicking at a mound of pebbles, Jessamy had

the thought that in many ways the war was already lost for the South. It was only a matter of time, just as Alex had said. A sad smile curved her mouth as she thought of the last time she had seen him, when he had held her tightly and whispered that it didn't really matter who won.

"I think I know that now," she had whispered back, and clung to him until he had pushed away with a regretful sigh.

Now she wondered where he was, and if he was thinking of her as she was thinking of him. Was it possible? Was he still in Tennessee, or was he marching toward Corinth with Major General Halleck's forces? Rumor had it that the force was comprised of nearly 128,000 men consolidated from the independent armies. Such news was depressing.

Dorothy and Ann Leathers had announced yesterday to Abigail that they were certain Beauregard would trounce those Yankees before they ever got to Corinth, and if he didn't, "Old Bedford Forrest surely will!"

Weary of the war, Abigail had smiled politely and murmured, "Do you think so?"

Virginia Leathers leaned forward, her gray eyes shining with anticipation and her teacup rattling in its chipped saucer. "Mark our words, Abigail—Forrest can whip Grant any day of the week!"

Such afternoon tea parties—sassafras tea, of course—were not Jessamy's favorite diversion, which was one reason she would rather walk in the rain than stay inside and endure another visit from the Leathers sisters. One of them would be certain to go on and on about their cousin the riverboat captain, until Jessamy would want to run screaming from the confines of the cabin. War, war, war! She didn't want to think about it, didn't want to consider the possibility that Alex was in danger.

Retreating to her favorite hickory grove down by the road, Jessamy leaned against a rain-wet tree trunk and stared out over the rolling fields. They still stretched as far as the eye could see, as far as she wanted to see. April rains had made this year's grass a bright green, and the sweet, subtle fragrance of honeysuckle scented the air.

A distant roll of thunder made her shudder, and she thought of the cannon again. Sometimes at night she would hear the cannon and men screaming, would jerk awake with sweat rolling down her face and her entire body trembling. On those nights she could almost smell the sharp scent of gunpowder.

Pushing away from the tree, Jessamy gazed up the far hill where the tiny whitewashed church stood. There were three new graves. The headstones were plain, but better than those she had seen at Shiloh, better than the rough wooden planks thrust into the raw earth with a soldier's name scratched into the surface. William Windsor and his twin sons lay side by side in the ground, and every day Abigail made the pilgrimage to the small family plot in the cemetery. There were lots of new headstones there, many more than had been there a year ago.

Stepping out onto the road, Jessamy walked up the hill toward the church. She had not been there since the day of the funerals, yet she felt compelled to go there now. So many new graves, so many.

King, Mullen, Leathers, Anderson, Weaver, Tyree . . .

Jessamy paused, letting her fingers trace the name etched into the granite. Theodore Tyree. He had been buried here, close to his mother's people instead of in Shelby County where he'd been born. Teddy Tyree. Well, she couldn't feel any sorrow for a man who had changed so much, but she did feel sad for his family. The Tyrees weren't bad people, and maybe war did change a man. *Would it change Alex?*

A gust of wind whipped at her long skirts and tore at the cloak she wore over her head, and Jessamy tilted back her head to stare up at the sky. Black clouds scudded past the white church steeple, and sheets of rain waved over the cemetery. She should run for shelter, but suddenly she wanted to defy the storm, to defy the very elements, to defy the war clouds that rumbled on the horizon. Lifting a fist, she shook it at the clouds.

"You can't win!" she shouted into the wind. "We will weather this storm!"

"Are you sure?" a deep voice asked behind her, and Jessamy whirled with a gasp, feeling slightly foolish and very melodramatic. Her embarrassment vanished when she recognized the man in the blue cape.

"Alex! Oh Alex, it's you!"

Folding her into his arms, heedless of the rain and the wind and their wet garments, Alex kissed her deeply. His mouth was warm, his arms strong, and Jessamy felt a surge of happiness.

"Do I taste salt?" he asked a few moments

later when their lips parted. His thumb gently traced the rivulets running down her face.

She smiled. "Maybe. What are you doing here?"

"Can't a man visit his intended?"

"At the cemetery?"

Alex looked faintly disconcerted. "Well, I brought a few things with me, things that we forgot when we left Shiloh."

Puzzled, she looked behind him at his horse. Dangling from the saddle was a long canvas bag. Jessamy didn't say a word as Alex unwrapped three Confederate swords and went to lay them atop the new graves. Neither of them spoke for a long time, each lost in his own thoughts. Then Alex stood and turned back to her.

"They should be kept in the house, of course, but I thought perhaps I . . . Hell, I don't know why I felt compelled to bring them here first."

"I understand," she said, moving into his embrace again. "Even though they're not really there, it's as if they're nearby."

Arm in arm, with Alex leading his horse, they began the walk back down the hill to Clover Hill. Just as they reached the long, curving drive that led up to the ruins and the overseer's cabin, the rain stopped. In the distance a shimmer of color glowed, soft at first, then brighter. It bent over the blackened ruins of Clover Hill, where ivy and vines had already begun to twine around the charred timbers and brick. The remaining chimneys glistened with the hues of the rainbow, gold and pink and blue.

"Look," Alex said softly, "a rainbow!"

"It's not a rainbow," Jessamy said, "it's a promise."

He smiled, and they both knew that in the years to come there would be many hardships, but none too great for them to face together.

Chapter
19

CAPTAIN ALEXANDER STEELE MARCHED steadily down the aisle with his bride on his arm and a broad smile on his face. Jessamy had never looked so beautiful, so radiant, and even the disapproving neighbors who had only attended the wedding for Abigail's sake could not help but notice her happiness.

Garbed in black like old crows, the women thawed the tiniest bit when they noted how tenderly Captain Steele kissed his new wife, how lovingly he turned her and put her hand in the crook of his arm. It had been a surprise to the neighbors when they'd been asked to attend the wedding on short notice, but not totally unexpected. Hadn't she just had her twentieth birthday the day before? And hadn't she stood there in front of everyone and invited them all back the following day to attend her marriage to Captain Steele? Gossip had run like wildfire among those at the party, but of course, they had returned for the wedding. There were Abigail's feelings to think of. And of course, Bryce was a joy to behold as he hobbled proudly ahead of his sister and her new husband. Bryce had had the honor of giving his sister away, and he wasn't about to let anyone forget it.

The reception was not exactly the affair that Jessamy had once dreamed of and expected, but somehow that just didn't matter. Not anymore. Not since she had Alex for the next month. He wasn't to join his regiment until the end of May, by which time Major General Halleck should have reached Corinth. Of course, Beauregard was long gone from that city. New Orleans had fallen late in April, and the river was now open to Union shipping from the Gulf of Mexico all the way to Vicksburg.

A letter had arrived from Nick the day before, and he was still riding with Bedford Forrest. It was said that Forrest didn't lose many men, and Jessamy prayed her brother would survive and come home one day. Then, perhaps, they could settle the conflict that had divided her family.

Until then she had Alex, and that was enough.

The church lawn was dotted with guests, and Celine, Aunt Pretense, and Abigail had spent the night baking more cakes and pies. Maribelle spent most of her time talking with one of the few young men in the area, a young man too sickly to have gone to war, telling him all about her brave fiancé, Stuart Armstrong, who was with Forrest now.

Everyone seemed to be having a good time, especially Bryce, who had stationed himself by the refreshment table. Laughing, Jessamy pointed him out to Alex.

"Happy?" Alex murmured, curving one arm around her shoulders.

She nodded. "Ecstatic! I just wish your mother could have been here."

"She sent her love along with that godawful silver soup tureen. What on earth does she think we're going to do with that?"

"Don't worry—it'll more than likely be melted down if more Yankees come through here," Jessamy returned with a wrinkle of her nose, and Alex stared at her.

"A Rebel as always! I don't know how I forgot that," he finally replied.

At his elbow, with a mouthful of cake, Bryce nudged Alex. "Tell her we're all alike underneath the color of our uniforms, Alex. I found that out at Shiloh."

Though she'd been teasing, Jessamy nodded. "You're right, Bryce. And you're probably a long way ahead of most people."

"Such as you?" Alex murmured in her ear, and swept her away to stand beneath a spreading oak.

Dimpling, Jessamy looked up at him through the thick fringe of her straight lashes. "Oh, I think I can tolerate a Yankee or two. . . ."

Catching her close to him, Alex growled, "Better think again, love! Tolerate only this Yankee."

Smiling, Jessamy whispered, "I suppose I must, since we have defied the blue never."

He stared down at her with a frown knitting his dark brows. "The blue never?"

"Don't you remember? 'Never say never'? You told me that, after I said I would never forgive you, never in a blue never."

"Ah, yes. And have you? Have you forgiven me for being a Yankee?"

"For being a Yankee, yes."

"What haven't you forgiven me for?"

"For taking so long to claim your husbandly rights," she said throatily, and her breath caught at the sudden sharp glitter in Alex's dark eyes. His hands moved to her waist.

Tangling her fingers in his dark hair, Jessamy pulled his face down until their lips met. Her mouth moved softly on his, then more firmly, until when they pulled apart, her blue gray eyes were smoky with desire.

Alex let his finger trail from her mouth to the soft curve of her chin. Clearing his throat, he asked huskily, "Who's in the stable?"

Jessamy's eyes danced with laughter as she replied in a whisper, "If we hurry—us!"

When the young woman awakens in the hospital, everyone recognizes her as Amanda Farraday, the selfish socialite wife of Dr. Brent Farraday—yet her clouded memory cannot recall her glamorous lifestyle, nor can she understand why her handsome, desirable husband detests her. The secret lies buried in her true past—a past she must now uncover, or lose her heart's deepest desire...

SHATTERED ILLUSIONS

A NOVEL IN THE BESTSELLING TRADITION OF SANDRA BROWN BY

LINDA RENEE DEJONG

She was a pawn in one man's quest for power.
A man who stole her legacy and ignited
a passion deep within her...

BLOOD RED ROSES

KATHERINE DEAUXVILLE

"A DAZZLING DEBUT...
A love story to make a medieval
romance reader's heart beat faster!"
—ROMANTIC TIMES

BLOOD RED ROSES
Katherine Deauxville
_____ 92571-9 $4.99 U.S./$5.99 Can.

Heading for a new life in California across
the untracked mountains of the West,
beautiful Anna Jensen is kidnapped by a
brazen and savagely handsome Indian who
calls himself "Bear." The half-breed son of a
wealthy rancher, he is a dangerous man with
a dangerous mission. Though he and Anna
are born enemies, they find that together
they will awaken a reckless desire that can
never be denied…

SECRETS OF A MIDNIGHT MOON

Jane Bonander

IN THE BESTSELLING TRADITION OF
BRENDA JOYCE